The Holy Ghost and a Shine of Coal

The Holy Ghost

and a Shine of Coal

Peggy Konert

Farmhouse Books
2025

Designed by Liz Lester

$$[\,1\,]$$

Birth of June Ellen

I WAS BORN in Paris, Arkansas, on the day my daddy quit breathing. That was the day they set the dynamite to go off in my daddy's coal mine, the Shoal Creek, to open a new vein because the one they were working on was just about petered out. The explosion sent a ton of coal dust straight into my daddy's lungs and he collapsed right there.

They took him to the Paris hospital and Dr. John, who took care of the miners, put him in the oxygen tent. Uncle Albert took the truck and went and got Mama. When Mama saw Daddy, he had a white smear around his mouth, but his face was black from the coal-dust explosion and she thought he was dead. She screamed and slid to the floor then her water broke and I slipped out. It took all of five minutes. Fright will do that to you.

I was four weeks early, but I had good lungs, the doctor said. Since I came so quick I was born right on the floor where Mama had collapsed. My head hit the floor first and I started yelling. That is when my daddy came out of shock and opened his eyes. There we were, my mama and me, both on the floor screaming.

Dr. John said, "Fred, you got yourself a baby girl."

Mama looked up, saw Daddy staring at us with a big grin on his face, and realized she had a baby. She pulled me up to her chest, stuck a nipple in my mouth, and we both stopped howling. Meantime, the doctor yelled at the nurse, "Get her a bed." Then he cut the cord.

I was fine, but I wouldn't let go of that nipple. My mama, a big round woman, still lay on the floor. It took four people to lift her up on that bed with me on top.

My brother, Freddy, wanted to name me Snapper, 'cause with my pointy head and me holding on to my mama like that, I looked like a snapping turtle that wouldn't let go till it thundered. April Leigh, my sister, just kept hollering for Mama. She had to be sent home with Aunt Annie.

The next morning Daddy was able to catch his breath, and Mama decided to go home and take care of her kids and her chickens. Her chickens were real important to her. Dr. John said Daddy was better and would be home soon. I was still holding on so she tucked me into the top of her dress where I just kept sucking. Daddy named me June Ellen, 'cause I was born in June, and Mama took me home.

That was how I spent my first day in this new world. I was determined to grab hold of whatever and not let go and I'm still that way. Some people call it stubborn and I admit it's gotten me into trouble, but I was born with it and aim to see it through.

I wanted to be a coal miner like my daddy and my big brother, Freddy, but Daddy wouldn't allow it. He told me, "Girls can't be coal miners, June Ellen. They say it's bad luck for girls to go down into a coal mine."

I didn't believe them and that set me on my course to get down into our mine and see for myself what it's like to be down under the earth where there's no light, except for what you bring, just black dark.

Paris once boasted one of the biggest beds of anthracite coal in the state, the hardest, cleanest-burning coal. World War II and the big guys with their fancy machines took most of this good coal and they leased the mines they were through with to little guys like my daddy. He leased the Shoal Creek mine from the Sullivan Company.

Then Daddy and Uncle Albert hired a crew to go in with pickaxes, shovels, a little dynamite, and sweat and pick out what was left. He and Uncle Albert had gone to the war together and were like brothers. They married sisters, my mama, Cora, and Aunt Annie, and had been working together in coal mines ever since. Daddy worked hard to make a living for us, but after the explosion he had coal dust in his lungs, which slowed him down some. You'd think seeing Daddy cough so much would have scared me about going down in that coal mine, but I wanted to see that big, dark, beautiful place. This is the story of how I saw the shine in a piece of coal and what became of our mine, the Shoal Creek.

[2]

Breakfast on a Summer Morning

AT THAT TIME our house had two bedrooms, a kitchen, a living room, and a back porch. One bedroom for the girls, one for my parents. Before my brother Freddy went off to the navy, he slept on the back porch. He used to sleep in the bed with me and April Leigh, my big sister, but one day Daddy said Freddy needed to sleep by himself. When it got really cold, he slept on the sofa bed in the living room.

Then it was just me and April Leigh in the bed. I was used to sleeping the three of us, so I had learned to take up as little space as possible and to sleep still. April Leigh had blonde hair that curled around her smooth tanned face, slim brown arms, and bright pink lips that lit up her face when she smiled. She was starting high school in the fall and it had changed her something terrible. It was summertime and I had just turned ten years old and would be in the fifth grade in September.

I remember when Mama started working for Fr. Michael at the rectory. She said she was lucky he needed help and she appreciated him asking her. I wasn't supposed to be up yet. This was Mama's and Daddy's time together to talk about us, I guess, and money. I stretched and yawned like that old yellow barn cat. I heard the murmur of voices from the kitchen and Mama's footsteps as she walked on the squeaky linoleum rubbed smooth by all our feet walking from the table to the sink to the stove over and over. The smell of coffee hit my nose and woke me up. Daddy let me have a little coffee with him every morning, mostly milk and sugar, but it made me feel all grown up.

"April Leigh, get up, it's summer vacation, no school for three months. Let's be explorers like Dale Evans. Rex can be Rin Tin Tin."

"June Ellen, I need my beauty sleep for high school. Be quiet," she said.

"Or we can solve mysteries like Nancy Drew. She's in high school, just like you."

3

"I'm too old to play with you, June Ellen."

"I don't play, April Leigh. I have adventures. I'm an explorer like Dale Evans and sometimes I have to solve mysteries like Nancy Drew. Mama told Aunt Annie you're just boy crazy. That always does something to your brain." April Leigh turned over and pretended to be asleep.

I heard Daddy tell Mama, "Coal mining has just about petered out; the big veins are pretty chunked out. We're picking up the leftovers, trying to scratch out a living. Feeding the war took all the big stuff."

Mama said, "You don't need to work so hard. Rest until your breathing gets easier."

"I'm alright and you don't need to worry. It won't be long till we get a full hopper. I've got to get some of those tickets paid off at Jeremy's Mercantile."

Mama was baking bread early while the air was still cool and the early breeze ruffled the curtains in her kitchen window. When the cool air blew in the kitchen windows, it gathered up the smells of yeasty dough, warm brown buttery crusts of bread, and rich dark coffee and sent them right under our bedroom door. I could smell the butter as she brushed the top of the loaf, and I jumped up, kicked April Leigh for good measure, and ran into the kitchen.

First, I patted Rex on the head. He always sat by Daddy and waited for his walk even though I mostly took him now. Daddy had to save his breath for the coal mine. Keeping up with Rex made his cough worse, so I took over.

Then I grabbed my china cup, the one with the chipped handle. It had a crack down the side, but I didn't care 'cause I loved the little pink roses that ran around the top of the cup, and the fat pink rose in the bottom that you could see after you drank it empty. I ran over to Daddy, who took it from me while I scrambled into the chair beside him. He put a little coffee in it from the pot on the stove; next he filled the cup with fresh milk with globs of cream floating on the top, and he let me put the sugar in, all I wanted.

"There's nothing like that first sip of coffee," Daddy always said, and now I said it. "Daddy, there's nothing like the first sip of coffee in the morning." He laughed.

Mama looked at me and sighed. "June Ellen, what are you doing up so early?"

"Mama, when I smelled your bread baking, I couldn't sleep another wink."

[3]

Interview about the Dead Man

A NEWSPAPER REPORTER was standing at our front door. "Good afternoon, Mrs. Thackeray. I'm Jim Malloy from the *Paris Eagle*. My editor called and set up an interview with your daughter, June Ellen."

Yesterday after Mama left for Fr. Michael's, Rex and I had our first adventure that summer, with a dead man. There was no one left at home to go on adventures with. Even my best friend, Gracie, was gone to spend the summer with her granny at Morrison's Bluff down by the Arkansas River. It was mostly Rex and me having adventures and he had turned into a pretty good spy dog, almost as good as Lassie.

I sat on my bed and listened. "Glad to meet you, Mr. Malloy. Come on in. That's right, he did call and I told him I'd allow it, only if I'm also here. She's highly excitable you understand, and this whole ordeal has been quite a shock to her nervous system. I can't hardly get her to settle down."

"I understand, Mrs. Thackeray. Finding a body can be hard on anyone much less a ten-year-old."

"You don't know the half of it."

Then I heard her calling my name. "June Ellen, June Ellen, come here. The newspaper man is here to see you."

I ran into the front parlor, eager for the reporter to interview me. Mama had made me wear my school clothes, a blue plaid skirt with a white blouse and a Peter Pan collar. Blue and white were our school colors at St. Joseph's. I clipped two barrettes with bluebirds on each side of my hair.

"June Ellen, why are you barefoot? Where's your shoes? We have company. Get back in your room and don't you come back out until you are fully dressed."

"I can't find them, Mama. I looked everywhere. I think April Leigh hid them from me. Will you go yell at her for me?"

Mama stood there with her hands on her hips, fixing to tear into me, but thought better of it in front of company. "Get your socks on and I'll go see about April Leigh. This is Mr. Malloy, the reporter from Fort Smith. Mr. Malloy, my daughter, June Ellen."

I ran back into my room and right back out, sat right there on the sofa in front of the reporter and pulled my socks on.

"Well, Miss June Ellen, tell me about this adventure of yours. Sounds like that was really something, finding that body and all."

"Yes, I found a dead body. It was old and dry and it stunk something awful. It smelled just like the dead raccoon that Daddy found under our house. We couldn't eat or sleep in our house; the smell made our eyes water and our stomachs heave. Daddy had to go under the house then drag it out and throw it way out in the woods."

"Oh, my, that must've been something. Tell me, how'd you come upon this dead body?"

"Well, me and Rex, my daddy's dog, who is now kind of like mine, were going for a long walk. My daddy doesn't breathe too well since he got all that coal dust in his lungs and he has to go work in his coal mine every day, 'cause we need a payload real bad. I'm the one who walks Rex. Daddy pays me a nickel every day. I always make sure it's a long walk."

Mr. Malloy was writing down everything I said.

"Our neighbor Mrs. Lahosky asked me if I wanted to go for a drive with her to the town square. She enjoys my company and she knows I like to go to Haney's Rexall Drug, 'cause they have rows and rows filled with jars of all kinds of candy. I like their jawbreakers the best 'cause they last the longest. I got two jawbreakers and four pixie sticks for a nickel."

"Miss June Ellen, you sound like a fine storyteller, but I don't have a whole lot of time. My newspaper is waiting on this story."

"I'm trying to tell you, Mr. Malloy. You see, it's all about the jawbreaker. When I got home, I got Rex and said, 'Let's go, I've got enough candy for a long walk today.' I put a red-hot cinnamon jawbreaker right in my mouth; I like the hot ones, don't you? I feel like I get my money's worth. Anyway, I like to take out walking and walk and walk till the jawbreaker's gone, that is how I measure a good walk. The red-hot cinnamon ones last the longest, and that's how we got all the way to the old Mikel's place, and I'm telling you my mouth was on fire."

"I bet it was, Miss June Ellen. Then what happened?"

"I told Rex let's go sit inside that old ramshackle barn and rest. My mouth needs a sweet cherry pixie stick to recover from that red-hot jawbreaker. I read Nancy Drew, so I know the jawbreaker and now the pixie stick are important clues to how I found that dead man."

"I see just how important they are. Go on."

"Rex signaled me to follow him. I trained him myself to be a spy dog like Lassie. I let him lead and I just followed. Rex is the one who found that old dead body, but he won't talk to just anybody about it. I told Mama, I'd do the talking. Anyway, we walked in and he smelled something and took off while I was pouring the cherry pixie dust into my mouth. About the time it started fizzing, he started barking."

I looked at the reporter. "Don't you like the way they fizz, Mr. Malloy? My tongue was already red hot and then it starts to fizzing. I wished I had some water then."

"June Ellen, can you tell me what it was like when you found the body?"

"Well, Rex barked and barked to get my attention. I was up wind at that time, getting ready to take a rest and eat the rest of my pixie sticks. I always save one jawbreaker for the walk back home."

"Miss June Ellen, tell me about this body. I have a deadline to meet here, and I'd sure like to get you in the paper on Sunday."

"Rex howled, so I knew I had to go right then and see what was up. I smelled something and thought it was another dead raccoon. When I looked down, there was a straw pallet made up pretty as you please with that old dried-up body instead. I didn't know what to do. I still had my pixie sticks to eat and my other favorite jawbreaker to get me home; it has bubble gum in the center, but I knew Mama'd kill me if I stayed there with that shriveled-up dead body."

"Just tell me what you saw."

"Okay. I knew Sheriff Riley would ask all kinds of questions and I wanted to have all the answers ready, like Nancy Drew. I went closer and saw his sunken eyeballs and his big ugly black teeth. His lips were gone, eaten by rats, I guess, though Mama said not to say that. He still had on an old ragged shirt and overalls and dirty socks full of holes. It looked to me like some rats had eaten some of his toes, but I'm not supposed to talk about that either."

"Go on, Miss June Ellen."

"He looked scared to death, like something really frightened him. Mama said it'd give me nightmares if I kept talking about it, but it doesn't. I didn't want to get any closer, but I knew the sheriff would want me to. So, I did like in the movies. I looked in his pockets. That was scary you know to touch them like that, but I did it because I am brave and, besides, I knew Jimmy Schmitz and the other boys in my class would make fun of me if I didn't."

"Yes, yes, and what did you find?"

"I found lots of letters, old letters stuffed in all his pockets and every one had hair in it, old dirty hair. It was the awfulest thing I ever saw."

"Did you read the letters?"

"Well, of course I did, just like Nancy Drew. I read all her books so I knew just what to do. The sheriff told me not to tell anyone about the letters till he finished his investigation."

"Can you give me a hint? I might have a dime here for some of that candy."

"Well, I really like it when I have a quarter and I can go to Haney's store for a Dr Pepper and a package of peanuts and sit and read Archie and Veronica comic books. They're my favorite."

Just then, Mama appeared in the doorway. "June Ellen, I swear you'd lose your head if it wasn't screwed on. Your shoes were thrown under the bed with your nightgown on top of them. April Leigh says she didn't hide them and I believe her. Now what, pray tell, have you told this reporter?"

Mr. Malloy jumped up. "I was just leaving, Mrs. Thackeray. She sure did have an amazing day. I'll talk to you both later. I've got some business on the square and a cold drink sure sounds good."

Mr. Malloy gave me a sly wink out of his left eye; Mama didn't see it.

"June Ellen, what did you tell that reporter for him to go running off like that?"

"Nothing, Mama. He's got a deadline is all and needs to get his story in. He's just hot and tired like me. Can I put on my jeans and tennis shoes and walk downtown to get me a Dr. Pepper?"

"Where did you get money for a soda pop, June Ellen?"

Mama gave me the eye so I knew she was on to me. She laughed. "I'll swan, June Ellen, you are something else."

Sometimes you just can't get anything past Mama. I walked Rex around the yard instead, her idea.

The next morning Daddy called me to the breakfast table where he was reading the newspaper.

"Look here, June Ellen," he read from the newspaper. "The sheriff discovered that body you found was a Mr. Shag Fitts, a hobo riding the rails. They found letters in his pocket from an old sweetheart. She wrote to him while he was off serving this country, like me, during World War I.

The Depression wasn't kind to him and that is all he had left. Dr. John says his heart just quit on him."

"He died from a broken heart, Daddy. Did he ever find Mary Sue, his sweetheart?"

"The paper doesn't say anything about that, June Ellen. That's just one of those mysteries. How'd you know her name?"

I crossed my fingers and told Daddy, "I must have heard the sheriff say it." Daddy just smiled.

[4]

Freddy the Milkman

BEFORE MY BIG BROTHER Freddy joined the navy, he drove a milk truck. He graduated from the eighth grade and went to work for Mrs. Bonnett at the Bonnett Creamery in Carbon City. Her husband, Dr. Bonnett, was the country doctor, and he spent his time running the back roads in his Model-T Ford delivering babies and drinking moonshine.

Daddy said, "Mrs. Bonnett delivers the best milk and Dr. Bonnett delivers the best moonshine between the Arkansas River and the Ouachitas. That moonshine's good medicine to ailing folks."

Freddy loaded the truck early in the morning then took care of the cows. One day the milk truck driver quit and Mrs. Bonnett asked Freddy, "Can you drive?"

"Yes, ma'am, I sure can." He never told her he had only driven Uncle Albert's Ford jalopy around the pasture.

"Well, then, get in and deliver this milk. Here's your list."

He told Daddy, "I was tired of mucking out that barn every day. I grabbed hold of that steering wheel, ripped that old truck into gear, and took off. I coasted downhill to the county road, where old Mrs. Bonnett couldn't see or hear me. I revved that engine till I could slam it into the next gear. By the end of the day, I knew how to double clutch, drive backward, and down-shift going uphill."

Freddy was only fourteen when he started driving that milk truck, an old 1933 Chevrolet panel van and he drove it for two years. He told Daddy, "Thank the Lord for baling wire. That Mrs. Bonnett is cheap. She'll buy a cow before she'd buy a tire."

One day after Freddy changed his third flat tire, he asked her, "What good is another gallon of milk on a flat tire?"

"Young man, just who do you think runs this place?" Then she told him.

That's when he started trying to talk Daddy into letting him work with him at the coal mine. They paid three dollars and eighty-nine cents a day. Delivering milk paid only a dollar a day plus all the milk, cream, and butter you could eat and drink.

Mama told Freddy, "Don't you quit that milking job. We need that milk and butter. Besides I don't want you down in a coal mine. Look what it's done to your daddy."

But Daddy let him quit his milkman job anyway. He told Mama, "I have a mess of tickets at Jeremy's Mercantile I need to pay on. Another pair of hands could sure help us get that hopper filled and shipped off. And, Cora, that boy has to grow up and start thinking on his own. Let him try." Mama frowned on that because of the coal dust in Daddy's lungs and he was getting short on breathing.

Freddy turned sixteen when he started in the coal mines; he thought he was big stuff. Daddy told him straight up, "Don't start strutting your stuff. You ain't a rooster yet."

Freddy often told me stories when he got home at night. "Daddy's the fire boss. He goes down into the mine first with his safety lamp. If there's any gas in the area, the flame in Daddy's lamp burns brighter. Sometimes natural gas gets trapped in these big old pockets where the big guys years ago removed the coal. When you're picking out chunks of coal and your pick hits a rock and makes a spark, it can explode on you."

"Daddy sure is fearless, Freddy."

"He either has to get a lot of air in there fast, or he sets the gas off with his carbide lamp and hits the dirt at the same time. Only then can the other miners go down.

"Before Daddy got sick he got more coal every day than anybody else. One day Uncle Albert told all the other miners that it was no wonder Daddy got more coal out than anyone. He was down there scratching and clawing like a tom cat. And the name stuck, after that everybody called him Tom Cat. The first day I started at the coal mine they called me Kitty Cat. I didn't like it till Uncle Albert told me that story."

I thought long and hard on that. "I wish I was a coal miner. My nickname could be June Cat."

Freddy laughed at me. "Ha, they'd call you Sissy Cat."

I kicked Freddy hard, because he called me Sissy Cat and said a coal mine is no place for a girl. It made me more determined than ever to get inside the Shoal Creek mine. I wanted to go all the way down to the very bottom where Daddy said the darkness just grew and grew, the deeper you went, and that it went on forever. But I wanted to see that vast dark. I thought what a grand and amazing creature that dark must be.

[5]

Freddy's First Paycheck

AT THE END of the week Freddy got his first paycheck. He jumped out of Uncle Albert's truck before it even stopped rolling. He bounded into the house hooting and hollering. We thought something had happened to Daddy.

"Look here, June Ellen, I got fifteen dollars in my pocket. I borrowed the old Ford and I'm going to the Green Frog, tonight. I'll dance with all the pretty girls and I'm going to have me a couple of beers. Daddy don't care since he knows what a coal miner's life is like, but, hell, don't tell Mama."

He picked me up and swung me around. "Tomorrow, we'll go downtown to the Paris square. I'll treat you to a picture show and to Haney's Rexall Drug for an ice-cream soda. I'm celebrating my good fortune to finally be a coal miner; I got two days off for the first time in two years."

Freddy just started laughing, his big, deep belly laughs.

Daddy came home later, and I heard him in the kitchen with Mama. "Cora, I'm right proud of Freddy and I wish you were too."

Mama didn't say much but when I walked in to get an apple, she was smiling. The next day I woke up to dark clouds and wind rattling the leaves on the old post oak outside my window. I was afraid Freddy got too drunk. Maybe he'd just want to sleep all day.

I smelled coffee boiling and bacon frying. Then I heard his growly laugh and Daddy's voice. I jumped up and ran to the kitchen, the worn-out linoleum cracks pricking my bare feet.

"Freddy, you been to sleep yet?"

"Better get dressed, June Ellen, we're going to the Strand Theatre on Main Street to see *Abbott and Costello Meet Frankenstein*."

I looked around for Mama. She forbids me to see scary movies. "Where's Mama?"

Daddy said, "Your mama's collecting her eggs in the hen house; Freddy told her he was taking you. She told him if you got nightmares, you're sleeping with him."

"I won't get nightmares; I'm not scared of anything."

They both laughed.

I did scream several times, but so did the other kids, even Jimmy and Roy Butler, the two meanest boys from Morrison's Bluff. I grabbed Freddy's hand so hard that he said I almost broke it. Abbott and Costello acted like fools and made me laugh. Freddy laughed almost the whole movie. Nerves, I guessed. He never admitted to being scared of anything till he got in the navy.

Then it was time for my ice-cream soda. Freddy and I headed over to Haney's and sat down at the counter. Mr. Haney was working the counter himself.

"June Ellen, coal miners are a special breed. They're fearless and will die for you if necessary. Coal mining pays the best money, but you have to do your part to earn it and I'm going to do mine." Freddy made sure Mr. Haney heard him.

"What can I do for you today, Freddy?" Mr. Haney asked. "Sounds like you got you a real hard job up there at Shoal Creek."

Freddy beamed and looked around to see who was listening. "Yes, sir. I'm not a chalk-eye anymore. June Ellen, order whatever you want."

"What's a chalk-eye, Freddy?"

"Chalk-eye is what they call a greenhorn, like you. A chalk-eye doesn't have any black coal dust ground into his skin around his eyes. They don't get paid as much. Starting next week, I'm on full wages."

I smiled as I climbed up on the stool. "Freddy is getting an awful big head, don't you think, Mr. Haney?"

"June Ellen, mind your tongue when I'm shelling out the money."

I grinned at Mr. Haney. "I want a chocolate ice-cream soda and an ice-cold Dr Pepper with a package of peanuts."

He grinned right back at me. "All righty, Miss June Ellen, I'll have Isaac make that ice-cream soda for you right now."

I asked, "Freddy, what's it like to go down in a coal mine?"

"Well, the first day Daddy took me to the slope that went down into the mine, he looked at me and he said, 'That is where you go in and if you cannot get it, that is where you come out.' I didn't know what he meant by 'getting it' but when I went up on that wall of rock and slate the first time, there was thirty-six feet of coal I had to break out. Then I knew what 'getting it' meant. I wasn't that little kid anymore, helping his daddy at the mine. He let me know I had to work like a real miner."

Isaac, Mr. Haney's soda jerk, brought me a chocolate ice-cream soda.

"Isaac, I want my ice-cold Dr Pepper last. It will top off my day just grand."

I set right to work on my ice-cream soda. It took all my concentration to suck up the thick chocolate ice cream through that straw. I meant to take my time and make it last.

"Freddy, what does a coal mine look like?"

"The Shoal Creek mine winds around like a maze. Where I work looks like a honeycomb of hollowed-out tunnels, with big timbers framing doorways. Entries are what they call them. Big passages called airways open up to the outside so the gas can escape and fresh air flow in. Off the tunnels are narrow doorways about four or five feet high that open up to a wall of coal, called veins. Most men work their own vein. There's hardly enough room to stand up or turn around.

"Daddy, he's the real boss, sent me to work with this guy they called Stub. He is a big guy with arms that look like hams. I think Daddy figured Stub could teach me how to break out the coal and not lose money bringing out his own. Stub and I were breaking darn near sixty feet of coal. We made a good team. We broke the coal out of the wall with a pick and a sledgehammer. Stub rolled the big chunks to the conveyor and I broke them into smaller chunks with a sledgehammer big as you and loaded them on the conveyor."

"Wow, Freddy. You're really strong."

"Thank Mrs. Bonnett for that, hauling milk cans around toughened me up. I'm not that skinny little runt anymore."

My cheeks were getting pretty tired sucking that straw, but I wouldn't give in to a spoon. Freddy sounded like a real coal miner, and I felt proud to have a Daddy who was the boss and a brother as strong as Freddy working a coal mine.

"Oh, Freddy, take me down into the Shoal Creek mine. I just have to lay my eyes on that honeycomb of tunnels and that wall of coal."

"No way, June Ellen. I'm already in hot water with Mama for going there myself. Daddy would break my neck and more if he found out I took you down."

"Oh, Freddy, please just show me the slope where you go in."

"Nope and that's it."

I sat there sucking on that straw thinking about our mine and what it'd be like if I could work there. Freddy saying no felt like a dare to me, and I wasn't one to pass up a dare.

I looked around and saw Lizziebelle Hawkins walk into Haney's Rexall Drug.

Lizziebelle lived on Shoal Creek. Her daddy raised cattle for Camp Chaffee. They had more money than most but used to be poor like the rest of us, so she wasn't stuck up like some. She was also a cheerleader at Paris High, and her daddy let her drive the car to town for cheerleading practice.

On Saturdays I would walk to the square by myself because April Leigh was too big for her britches. Lizziebelle always went to Haney's for a soda after cheerleading practice. I met her there one day over ice-cream sodas. She gave me a ride home and after that she always came looking for me to see if I wanted a ride. I always did.

I shared my adventures with her, and she shared hers with me.

"June Ellen," she had said one day, "you tell the best stories and I can tell you're not afraid of much. I like that. Girls shouldn't be afraid to try new things. Girls can do just about anything boys can do and the war has proved that."

"Lizziebelle, I think you are a lot like me, except I'm Catholic."

She agreed, and except for her being a Southern Baptist and sixteen, we became fast friends.

"Hey, Lizziebelle," I sang out. "Come sit by us. This is my brother Freddy. He's a coal miner now and he just got his first paycheck. He'll buy you a soda pop, won't you, Freddy?"

Lizziebelle just stood there looking at us. I knew I'd put Freddy in a spot and that I'd pay for it later, but I figured maybe they'd go on a date and take me with them to the drive-in, maybe.

I looked at Freddy and whispered, "Say something. Don't act stupid."

I knew it was another mistake, but what was one more?

"Excuse my sister, Miss Lizziebelle. She has no manners and I will be teaching her some later." He pinched me hard in the side.

Lizziebelle laughed then and came over and sat down beside me, which made Freddy stop pinching me.

"Call me Lizzie please. Lizziebelle was my grandmother's name and Mother insists everyone call me that. I feel I'm old enough now and I can decide what I want to be called. Don't you agree, June Ellen? You seem to know your mind and not to have any trouble speaking it."

Finally, Freddy laughed and I could breathe again.

Lizziebelle looked right at Freddy and said, "I think I will have a Coca-Cola."

Freddy called the soda jerk over. "Give Miss Lizzie a Coca-Cola, Isaac."

I knew right then that Lizziebelle and I could handle Freddy.

"What mine are you working, Freddy?"

"I work my daddy's mine with my uncle Albert, the Shoal Creek."

"Why that mine is right below our farm. My daddy says you are probably mining coal right under our feet. He likes your dad though. Says he's a real fair man, not like that Jack Sullivan, who first opened that mine and didn't care how much land he tore up or spoiled for anything else with all his slag heaps."

"Yep, that mine is pretty played out from that big machine mining. But it's a good one for us poor guys who go in and claw it out with our hands. We are just a bunch of scrappers, but mining makes a man out of you overnight."

"And did it?" Lizziebelle asked with a real pretty smile.

"Why don't you come dancing with me tonight and find out."

I felt proud of Freddy for being a miner and I told her, "Yes, it did. He's not white-eyeing it anymore."

"My daddy won't let me dance. But I could go for a walk tomorrow around Cove Lake after church."

"I want to go to Cove Lake, and I'd like to see your farm, Lizziebelle. I mean Lizzie and I'll bring Rex. He likes adventures. Maybe Lizzie wants to see where you work, Freddy."

I could feel Freddy's eyes staring a hole in my back.

Lizzie laughed. "I don't think we'll be going to look at that old mine, June Ellen. But if you come along to Cove Lake, Daddy won't say no. I'll bring the picnic lunch. That is, if you want to, Freddy. Maybe you have someone else you're going on a walk with tomorrow."

"No, Lizzie, I'll be glad to go for a walk with you and June Ellen tomorrow."

Boy was she smart, I thought. We were a lot alike. April Leigh was going to be really jealous. I couldn't wait to tell her.

"If Reverend Spicer doesn't get carried away with the sound of his own voice, Daddy should have us home by noon. Will you be back from church by then?"

"We're Catholic, so we only have to go to church for an hour," I said, proud to be a Catholic.

Freddy laughed. "Looks like I'll be seeing you tomorrow at noon."

"Well then, I'd better pack us a picnic lunch," Lizzie said.

Freddy and Lizzie getting together was the start of my grand scheme that summer to get down into our coal mine.

$$[\,6\,]$$

First Date with Lizzie

SUNDAY MORNING AFTER CHURCH, Freddy and I got ready for a picnic with Lizzie. Daddy said I could take Rex with me and that way he would get in a good, long walk. Freddy was in the kitchen slicking his hair back with Vitalis, fancy grease in a tube. Then he threw Daddy's Old Spice shaving lotion all over his face.

I was wearing my old jeans, which I always wear when I'm going on an adventure, but Mama made me wear my blue-gingham-checked blouse because I was going visiting. Mama gave Freddy her stern "I mean business look." "You be careful, Freddy, and don't let June Ellen out of your sight. June Ellen, you behave like a young lady and be on your best manners."

We jumped into Uncle Albert's car and took off. Freddy sang "Let the Good Times Roll," and I rolled the window all the way down for Rex in the back and for me in the front. We both hung our heads out, letting the wind blow our hair and feeling the sun on our face. This was Rex's favorite thing to do.

We drove up to Lizzie's house and she came running out the door followed by her daddy and mama. Freddy jumped out of the car and I followed with Rex at my heels, seeing as how I was the official chaperone, I wanted to make a good impression with how responsible I am. I got started right away.

"This is a fine house you got here, Mr. Hawkins, and you sure keep a clean porch, Mrs. Hawkins."

Mr. Hawkins got right to it also. "Well, who might this smart young lady be?"

Lizzie laughed and Freddy just stood there all stupid like. "This is my best friend, June Ellen, and her brother, Freddy, and their dog, Rex. His daddy leases the old Shoal Creek mine. June Ellen and I talked Freddy into taking us on a nice picnic, since it's such a warm, sunny day. This is my mother and father, Harold and Gladys Hawkins."

Freddy stepped up and shook Mr. Hawkins's hand, "Glad to meet you, sir, and you, too, Mrs. Hawkins."

Mr. Hawkins looked at me and smiled. "Well, June Ellen, did I just read about you discovering a dead body at the old Mikel's place, in the newspaper?"

"Yes, sir, I did. Then I helped Sheriff Riley solve the mystery of who it was and what happened to him. I'm a lot like Nancy Drew that way and the sheriff let me know he appreciated that about me."

"I bet he did and I'm sure you have it all under control here and know how to watch over everything," Mr. Hawkins said.

"Why, yes, sir, my mama already told me no shenanigans, and I aim to do what she said. And she told Freddy not to act up either."

Freddy looked purple in the face and I knew what that look meant. I wished he could understand that I was only helping him break the ice with Lizzie's daddy.

Lizzie laughed, then Mr. and Mrs. Hawkins started laughing.

"See, Freddy," I mouthed at him. He finally cracked a smile.

Mrs. Hawkins said, "Don't forget your cold sodas in the icebox, Lizziebelle, and your picnic basket is sitting in the shade on the back porch. You children have a good time and don't be late for supper, Lizziebelle."

That was the only time Mrs. Hawkins gave Lizzie a stern look.

Lizzie grabbed Freddy's arm and pulled him toward the back porch as he seemed rooted to the ground.

When they came back with the picnic basket, I jumped into the back seat with Rex and waved good-bye to Mr. and Mrs. Hawkins. Soon we were on our way to Cove Lake.

Lizzie said, "Shall we take a walk before lunch, Freddy? June Ellen, you can come with us."

Freddy gave me that look, and I knew what it meant. "Thank you, Lizzie. I think I'll take Rex for a walk up Cove Creek. Is that okay with you, Freddy?"

"Oh sure, June Ellen, great idea and go see what everybody's catching down by the dock."

Rex and I took off on our own, but that's just how it was nowadays with Daddy either at the coal mine or home resting his breath and April

Leigh thinking she was too old for an adventure with us. We were used to it. Rex and I walked up the road to where Cove Creek flowed into the lake and Rex took off up the creek chasing a rabbit. I had no choice but to follow him.

I liked jumping from rock to rock. My shoes got wet in no time, but that's why I wore my old ones. My jeans cuffs filled up with water, those rocks can be slick, but I managed to stay upright. Rex was splashing and running everywhere, he didn't worry about falling in or slipping on anything. Sometimes I wished I had four legs.

I found a frog hiding under a lichen-covered rock that looked just like tree bark. I picked the poor fellow up to show Lizzie. She just seemed to me the kind of girl that would like frogs. I stuck him in my pocket, which is why I loved to wear jeans, lots of pockets to fill with all my great finds.

The creek got narrower as we went up, and pretty soon we were scrambling up rocks and climbing over boulders, fighting briars and grapevine. The woods got thicker, and the creek got smaller. There were a bunch of skinks sunning up here on the high rocks, so I decided to share one of those with Lizzie too. The skink went in my other pocket.

It didn't take long to work our way back down, but we were a fair sight. Mud, briars, and cockleburs were stuck all over us. In my mind you could hardly tell us apart. We got to the car pretty quick and there was Freddy and Lizzie, leaning in close to each other.

I snuck around to the front window by Lizzie, which was open, and Rex and I jumped up. "Surprise, look what we found," and I showed her the frog. Well, Lizzie screamed and wasn't near as excited as I thought she would be with this little speckled frog and Freddy was just furious.

"June Ellen, I'm going to whip the tar out of you. What do you think you're doing scaring Lizzie with that frog?"

"I thought you'd like to see it, Lizzie. I thought you were an adventurer like me."

"Oh, June Ellen, I just wasn't prepared to see a frog in my face, and it startled the blue blazes out of me."

"Apologize to her right now, June Ellen."

"Oh, Freddy, it's okay. June Ellen didn't mean anything by it. We're old friends, you know, and we like to show each other our finds." Then she smiled real big at him and then she turned and winked at me.

"June Ellen, take that frog and put it back in the lake. Now."

"Okay, Freddy." I walked to the lake and put the little frog in the water.

He disappeared quick. I decided to put the skink under a rock too. I didn't think they were ready for another treasure.

Walking back, I told Lizzie, "I'm hungry and so is Rex. We didn't eat anything yet."

"Have a ham sandwich, June Ellen, and a soda pop. There's not much left."

Well, if it wasn't just like Freddy to eat everything. "Thanks, Lizzie. Freddy can be a real pig."

"You be careful what you're saying, June Ellen. You're already in hot water with me." But then he just laughed. "June Ellen's problem is she takes after me. We'd better get going. Your parents are going to start wondering about you, Lizzie, and I need to get my gear together for work tomorrow.

"Lizzie, do you think your parents might let you go out with me again, to a movie and dinner afterwards?"

Lizzie laughed. "I think it'd be fine, Freddy."

"I want to go, Freddy, and I bet Lizzie's parents would let her go if I went along."

Lizzie laughed. "Sorry, June Ellen, I think my parents'll be fine with me going alone with your brother. I'll just have to meet up with you at Haney's after cheerleading practice sometime."

Rex and I climbed in the back seat. I knew Lizzie was the way to help me get into the Shoal Creek mine.

[7]

Freddy Joins the Navy

FREDDY WENT BACK to the mine on Monday morning. But when Daddy brought Freddy home that night he was all black, covered in coal dust, and blood was running out of his nose.

Mama said, "What in heaven's name happened to you?"

"Don't worry, Mama, water'll wash it all away," Freddy told her.

Mama gave Daddy one of her dead-eye looks. "Fred, he's not going back down there." But when she looked again at Freddy, her eyes turned warm and soft, almost watery. "Oh, Fred, get the bucket and fill it with water, let's get that coal dust off him, before he starts breathing it in. I don't know what I'd do if . . ." then she stopped.

"June Ellen, help your daddy. April Leigh, get that old quilt off the rocking chair on the back porch. Freddy, get everything off but your long handles."

Mama took charge now. She heated water in the big kettle, and Daddy poured it over Freddy till he could get in the bathtub and soak without turning it coal black. After he got cleaned up Daddy gave him a mason jar with a little moonshine in it. He sat out back on the stoop with April Leigh and me.

"Freddy, tell us what happened, you look like a ghost," I said. His hands were shaking so bad, he could hardly get Dr. Bonnett's medicine to his lips without spilling it.

April Leigh grabbed one of Freddy's hands and held it tight. That helped.

"We were about done for the day. Stub rolled out the big chunks, and I broke them up with the sledgehammer. We were at the far end of the tunnel, where one big vein ran all the way down as far as we'd blasted. We just kept going and cracking off those big chunks. Out of nowhere, I hear this terrible roar. I looked up and saw a ball of fire heading right for us. Stub yelled, 'Gas! Hit the ground.'"

Freddy let go of April Leigh's hand and grabbed his hair almost pulling it out and he got real pale again.

"I'll never forget what happened next. The flames flew right over us and charged up the wall all the way to the top where we'd blasted out heavy chunks of coal. Gas filled every hole we had dug, and that fire just picked up more speed. I hit the ground and covered my head and my ears and buried my face in the grit. I could feel the heat all around me. I felt like a turkey baking in an oven. We were covered with flames. Then there was a big boom that shook the mine. When that fire hit that oxygen rich air from the shaft, it exploded and burned out what gas was left."

"Here, Freddy, drink some more of this medicine." I could see his hands shaking as he was talking. April Leigh just kept holding on tight. "Were you scared, Freddy?" I asked.

Freddy tilted that mason jar to his lips and drank till it was gone.

"After that explosion, the top caved in right around us. I was plenty scared. I made it through that gas fire, but Stub and I were trapped. The top caving in is one of the biggest dangers all us miners face every day. Daddy does everything he can to keep the walls and ceilings of the mine shored up, but when the gas explodes like that, everything gets shaken up. The top of the tunnel cracked and caved in, and Stub and I were trapped at the far end."

Freddy's knuckles were white from gripping that mason jar so tight. He kept working his hand through his hair. I tried to imagine being trapped in the mine. What would it feel like having the top come down on you? "Was it dark, Freddy? Did your light go out?"

"We had our helmets on and our lights, June Ellen. But all we could see were huge pieces of slate from the ceiling and chunks of black rock. We were surrounded. When that top gave way, we were cut off from everybody with no way out, and the guys at the other end of the tunnel were afraid to stay, so they went up top to get help. God, I was scared. I never felt so alone in my life."

Just then Daddy walked out to the back stoop with his jug of moonshine. He didn't say a word, just poured Freddy's jar almost to half. Then Daddy took a big swig himself.

"Did you think you were going to die?"

April Lee interrupted me. "Be quiet, June Ellen."

"I thought I was going to die. It was quitting time and the other miners wanted to go home, but they didn't. I just kept thinking about all of you up here and I just prayed to make it home."

Freddy let out a big sigh and sipped some more moonshine.

Daddy said, "They know the code, Freddy, that no miner leaves another miner trapped. It's what keeps us going."

"I know, Daddy. That Stub took hold of my hand like I was a baby and he told me, 'Freddy, don't you worry. If anybody can get us out of here, your daddy sure can.' I knew cave-ins killed a lot of miners and I kept listening for any cracking sound, praying that top was shored up good enough."

Daddy said, "Stub's a good one, alright. I thanked the Lord he was the one there with you."

"Oh, Freddy," April Leigh cried.

I asked, "What'd you do, Daddy, when you heard about Freddy and Stub getting trapped down there?"

Daddy said, "Well, I was up top and I heard the gas explode, I just prayed no one got hurt. When the other miners came up and told me about Freddy and Stub being trapped, I knew I had to find them. I just took off down the slope and found an old air passageway that had been abandoned. I used to work that mine for the Sullivan boys years ago, and I knew that mine like the back of my hand. That old mine tunnels off every which way."

Daddy tilted that jug to his mouth again and I could see his hand shaking. He took a big drink this time and that set him to coughing. Mama came out to the porch, her worrying frown tight across her forehead. Daddy waved her away. "I'm okay, Cora, it just went down the wrong pipe."

Freddy just kept sipping away at his medicine, and then he'd lick his lips. I could tell he needed it. "Stub and I were lucky—Daddy used to set powder in that very tunnel to open up those rooms. He had a pretty good hunch where we were."

Daddy said in his croaky, dusty voice, "I just worked my way in to where I knew our slope was, figuring at some point I'd come to where they were trapped."

"Daddy, you saved Freddy and Stub's life. You're the bravest miner. Isn't he, Freddy?"

"He's the bravest man I know, June Ellen."

"Okay, that's enough," Daddy said. "We all do what we have to. Remember that, Freddy. I'm going in now. You stay home tomorrow and when I get home, we'll talk."

"Yes, sir."

Daddy got up slow and walked into the house with Mama. "Tell us what happened next, Freddy."

"The top of the tunnel he crawled through to get to us cracked even worse, but Daddy knew another way out. That scared him, I could tell. It was cold down there, but he was sweating. We had to lie flat and inch our way out of there. That top was almost touching us. He just kept saying, 'Don't brush against that top, boys. Anything could cause it to collapse.'"

Freddy pulled his hair some more. Nerves, I guessed.

"Take another drink, Freddy. It'll warm you up and put some color back in your face," I told him.

"Daddy led us into some places that were so tight we had to lie on our bellies and pull ourselves through with our hands scratching out the dirt and sometimes we had to push all our breath out and suck in our bellies just to get through a skinny opening between the fallen slabs of rock. I don't know how he did it. We crawled through one big black hole after another. But Daddy got both of us out. I was never so happy in all my life to breathe fresh air and see that blue sky."

"Are you going back down there, Freddy? I bet Mama won't let you."

"Mama can't stop me, June Ellen. I'm a man now and I proved it today. But no, I'm not going back down there. I have something else I need to go do first." He tipped his mason jar again and drained it, licked his lips, got up, and walked toward the front yard.

The moonshine was gone, and I figured he was going out to the beer joint.

When I got up in the morning there was a note on our bed.

"Good-bye, June Ellen and April Leigh. I have gone to Ft. Smith to join the navy. I'm going to go see the world. April Leigh, watch out for June Ellen. You might need to go exploring with her. June Ellen, keep having adventures, cause when I get home we'll have plenty more. Take April Leigh with you. Take care of Mama and Daddy for me. June Ellen, I'm trusting you to get this note to Lizzie before next weekend for me. Knowing you, you'll figure out a way. Your brother, Freddy."

There was a second page addressed to Miss Lizziebelle Hawkins.

"Dear Lizzie, I hate to leave without saying good-bye, but I have run off

to join the Navy. They need guys like me real bad right now. I'm not much of a letter writer, but June Ellen will keep you updated on my whereabouts, I'm sure. If you're still around when I come home, I'll be sure and look you up. I still owe you one." Your friend, Fred Thackeray, Jr."

It was a sad day for our whole family. Freddy had traded our coal mine for a battleship.

$$[\ 8\ ]$$

Hot Water Corn Bread

FREDDY WAS GONE across the ocean, and it left a big empty hole in our house and a bigger one in my heart. All we got was a skinny little letter written on paper so thin you could see through it. Mama went off by herself to read his letters, and we all knew to let her be. Freddy was on a big ship on a big ocean somewhere he couldn't tell us. I missed him. He was the only one in our family besides me who liked to have fun and go on adventures. Even April Leigh got quiet sometimes, and I could tell she was worried about Freddy. Daddy didn't say much either. He had been to war once and he knew what Freddy was in for.

Today, our kitchen heated up like hades. I wished I was back at Haney's under those big fans sitting with Lizzie. I found her there yesterday sitting at the soda fountain drinking a root beer. Mama let me go look for her. She was in her cheerleading skirt, spinning around on the bar stool. Her hair was golden and tied up in a ponytail with a bright blue ribbon.

"Hi, Lizzie. I thought you'd be here today after practice."

"You know my schedule, June Ellen. I was hoping you'd turn up. Now, tell me what adventures have you been on? And how's Freddy getting along in your daddy's mine?" Lizzie smiled big when she said Freddy's name.

I didn't answer; I just handed her the note from Freddy. She looked surprised when she read it. And then she turned kind of pale. I wondered was she sick. She wasn't smiling anymore.

"I have to go, June Ellen. Mother's waiting on me."

I didn't even get to say good-bye. She ran out so quick, she didn't even finish her root beer.

The sweat poured off me and we only had one old fan that Uncle Albert and Aunt Annie gave us 'cause they felt sorry for Daddy. It reminded me of just how poor we were. It sat in his room mostly at night since he coughed when he got too hot. I took my old ratty quilt and went to sleep on the floor beside his bed last night. At least that way I got a cool breeze. I'd rather listen to his old hacky cough than lay in bed with April Leigh sweating all over me.

They finished early at the mine today and Daddy ran off to the beer joint with Uncle Albert. And with Daddy out of the way, Mama could put the oscillating fan in the kitchen, where we were working. I knew Daddy was missing Freddy. I could hear him at night talking to Rex. Rex was the best listener. At the beer joint Daddy sat next to the beer cooler full of ice under the big ceiling fan. He said that was the only way he could relax and stay cool and not cough so much.

"That cold beer sure soothes my throat, better than that cough syrup Doctor John gives me."

Mama didn't say a word 'cause I think she knew being at the beer joint was helping Daddy and helped him not think about Freddy. Mama prayed the Rosary every night. That was her way to keep him safe.

I'd just come in from picking purple hull peas with Mama in our garden, and I was hot and sticky and I itched all over. When I get this hot, I liked to rest with a wet rag on my face in front of the fan on our kitchen table and turned all the way around to that old hot cookstove then back all the way to the icebox, which won't hardly hold a block of ice twenty-four hours. Mama wouldn't let me chip any ice off when it was this hot 'cause we had to save it to keep the milk from spoiling. Mama'll let me have a tiny shave if she knew the iceman was coming that day.

I went out to the well behind the house to get some fresh cool water. I found that if I put a big rock in the bucket, it would go down deeper into the well where the really cold water was. I hauled the bucket of cold water into the kitchen and put it in the sink. I wanted to put my whole head in the bucket, but Mama won't let me because we all drank from the dipper that sat in that bucket.

April Leigh said, "It's not sanitary and I'll throw up if I have to drink water that had June Ellen's head in it."

I dipped my rag in the cold water and plastered it to my forehead and let it drip down my face and arms onto my shirt and shorts while I sat in front of the fan so it'd blow right on that cool wet cloth.

Mama laughed and said, "Lordy, June Ellen, it's too hot for a body to move much less get any work done. I think I could even go hang out at that beer joint today."

I laughed because Mama never went to the beer joint.

"I know, Mama, I can't move, I'm stuck to the chair, it's like my skin melted into it. Can I take my shirt off? Nobody's here but me and you."

"Go ahead, but if anybody comes, you get that shirt back on. I sure don't want you sitting around half naked."

"Who's gonna come out in this heat?"

Mama shook her head and went outside to sit under her favorite shade tree and shell the peas that I helped pick. That's what made me so hot and scratchy all over.

I unbuttoned my shirt, which stuck to me like a fly on that flypaper hanging in the barn. I took it off and let the fan blow on my sweaty belly and chest. It felt really cool with all that sweat. I looked down at my chest and my pink nipples. They were wet too. They felt really good with that fan blowing right on them. They had little chill bumps and got real perky. Standing at attention was what April Leigh said, which hers really did. Mine just started doing it and I didn't tell anybody. But today I noticed that my bosoms were starting to swell too.

April Leigh said girls didn't have chests, they had breasts, only boys had chests. But Mama and Daddy always told me when I had a chest cold, "Here, June Ellen, put this on your chest, it'll help you feel better."

I told April Leigh, "I'm going to have a chest, not breasts, and I'm never going to wear a brassiere."

April Leigh laughed. "Just you wait."

It seemed like everything was changing and I just wanted it all to stop. I didn't want to wear a brassiere, ever. I wished Freddy hadn't run off to the navy, and I didn't want Daddy to get sick and lose our mine. April Leigh didn't want to be my best friend anymore. My heart just hurt sometimes.

"June Ellen," Mama yelled. "Put your shirt on, now, then come out here and help me shell these peas. I need to get them on for supper. Your daddy's bringing home a piece of ham to put in the pot."

Some things don't change, and Mama was one of them. She never stopped working, and ham with fresh purple hull peas sounded good to me. Mama wouldn't cook a big meal in this heat so we'd been eating hot water corn bread with buttermilk every meal. Mama poured boiling water into her cornmeal, added some lard and sugar then fried it up in bacon grease. In between I got me a glass of cold milk and dipped crackers in it.

"June Ellen, hurry and bring me that other basket of peas."

I prayed out loud. "Oh, Lord, it's going to be a long hot summer."

[9]

J. C. Higgins Fish Bait Oil

I WOKE UP to a beautiful day. The sun was just starting to come up over the top of Mount Magazine. I was ready for a day of fishing at Cove Lake and the crappie and bream were sure to be biting and even if they weren't, it didn't matter. Daddy's cousins were taking me. Buddy would row the boat and Benny would stock the cooler. Benny would even bait my hook if I wanted, but I didn't. I liked to bait my own hook, not like other girls.

I had my own special bottle of J. C. Higgins Fish Bait Oil I ordered from the Sears & Roebuck catalog for twenty-nine cents. Just a drop on your bait added that certain something that entices fish. That's what the label said, and I convinced Mama I needed to order a present just for Daddy.

Daddy told me, "June Ellen, I'd really appreciate it if you'd hold on to this for me. I might just lose it. Put this in your tackle box and that way I'll always know where it is." Daddy used to go fishing with me but now he was either at the coal mine or at home on his cot trying to get his breath back, or at the beer joint cooling off. Daddy wouldn't have to work so hard if Freddy hadn't joined the navy. Then he could rest his lungs and get well, and we wouldn't have to worry about Freddy either. I sure wished I could go down in our coal mine.

My tackle box was an old Honey Dew Brand lard can. The lid fit real tight so water won't get in. I couldn't wait to try out the fish bait oil on my stash of worms. They also fit nicely in my lard can, wrapped in a damp copy of the *Paris Eagle*.

My cane pole was all rigged up and waiting on the front porch. Freddy cut it himself. We went down to the Arkansas River to a cane patch and cut our own. Mine was about six feet tall. Freddy cut it and I stripped all the leaves and husks off the cane branch. Then Freddy wrapped fishing line around the end of the pole and tied a hook on the end. I stuck the hook into one of the joints and that made it safe to carry anywhere.

Mama said, "Finish your breakfast, June Ellen, I've got to get to Fr. Michael's."

"Mama, do you think Freddy is fishing on that big ship on the ocean?"

"If he gets half a chance, I'm sure he is, June Ellen. Catch some fish then you can write to him all about it."

I was used to going to the Arkansas River with Freddy and our cane poles. We both liked to try for catfish where the channel ran below Morrison's Bluff. "Mama, I sure hope nobody finds our fishing hole before Freddy comes home."

Buddy and Benny pulled up and honked. I grabbed my fishing can and my cane pole and ran over to the truck. Benny grabbed my cane pole and put it in back. I slid over to the middle of the bench seat and straddled the gearbox between Buddy and Benny. It was early yet with a cool breeze, so that was tolerable.

My cousins had a little rowboat that just fit the two of them and me perched on Daddy's old metal bucket lunch pail, which we also used as our cooler. The boat just fit in the back of their old Chevy pickup. My lucky cane pole slid in nice, right beside it.

Buddy said, "Well, Miss June Ellen, what newfangled fishing thing did you bring with you this time?"

I was always trying new ideas to catch more bream or crappie or even catfish and got teased a lot, but I didn't mind much 'cause they still let me tag along.

Buddy told my daddy once, "June Ellen can always come to the lake with us. She's more entertaining than the fish."

I was not telling about my new fish bait oil till I saw how well it worked, then I might share it.

"Just my lucky cane pole," I say.

Benny grunted; it was almost a laugh. He didn't talk much. But he listened good.

I had on my favorite fishing shorts. Mama wouldn't hardly let me wear them unless I was off hidden somewhere, like in a rowboat on a lake. They were dark blue faded to a soft shiny blue. They had pockets in the front and the back just like boys' jeans. Mama thought I ought to wear Freddy's old jeans, but I loved these shorts.

Now, my cousins Benny and Buddy drank a lot of beer and it had settled in their stomachs. Daddy called them beer bellies. They both had huge beer bellies and skinny little legs so their pants didn't hardly cover their behinds.

I watched Buddy and Benny both because when they bent over you could see their hiney cracks. I always sang out, "step on a crack break your mother's back," and then they knew I'd seen their cracks, white flesh like a fish's belly. They laughed. They didn't care. They had skinny butts, skinny legs, and big old bellies.

April Leigh said, "They don't make pants that fit that body shape. They're so disgusting, showing their cracks all the time and not even caring who sees it."

I never had to worry about her tagging along and that was worth it. Daddy let me go because he said I was safe with them and they were big strong boys.

Mama told me first thing this morning, "June Ellen, you can go fishing with them boys if you want to but if you ever act like them or talk like them or drink a beer, it will be your last time. Don't you listen to a word they say."

"I won't, Mama. I just watch my cork and keep my hook baited."

Now really, what kind of advice was that? They were funny and they told great stories about their adventures and they'd had plenty. I also got to wear my old tennis shoes, the ones with the holes in the front that my toes stuck through. They were really too small, but they were the only waders I had. I didn't care. I could get them as wet and muddy as I wanted to. I dangled my feet in the water and didn't even take them off.

I made my favorite fishing sandwiches—peanut butter, my own strawberry jam, and raisins on Mama's homemade bread. I took two or three and just sat and ate them all day long. I wrapped them in wax paper, and they fit nicely in my fishing can. The worms didn't seem to mind, as long as I kept them on top.

Buddy pulled into Truly Wright's Bait and Tire Shop. "June Ellen, get what you're getting. The crappie are biting."

Daddy had given me two nickels for when we stopped at the bait shop.

"Howdy, Truly," I say.

"Howdy, June Ellen, you gonna show these boys how to catch some of those crappie today?"

"Yes, sir, I truly am."

He laughed 'cause he heard jokes like that all the time.

"Well, what can I, truly, help you with?" We smiled at each other.

"I want a Grapette soda."

"Here you go, June Ellen. I know you like them ice cold. I got the one at the very bottom."

"Thanks, Truly."

Benny got his net and minnow bucket and started dipping in for minnows. He handpicked each one, which drove Buddy crazy. But I admired how particular he was about his bait.

"They got to be fresh and alive, Juney Bug. Those crappie can smell a half-dead minnow and they don't want it. They like a minnow they have to chase awhile."

Benny had his minnows and then we were back in the truck. Benny wrenched open the old glove box and handed me his naked mermaid bottle opener. I loved that bottle opener. I grabbed her green, silvery tail and fit her head over my Grapette bottle cap and popped it open. I had to drink it right away because I couldn't pass up an ice-cold Grapette. The cap landed on the floorboard and stayed there with all the others.

We topped the rise and I saw the lake in the distance. It was a contest to see who spotted it first. You had to look real hard because of the way the hills folded around it; it kept disappearing, then reappearing.

"There it is, I see it, there's Cove Lake."

"No, that's just the sky," Buddy teased me.

I was right and he knew it. We rounded the last curve and in front of us was the most beautiful lake in the whole world. Blue and green and shimmery. The sun on the water reflected light like an old-fashioned Christmas tree all sparkly with candles.

Buddy and Benny unloaded the boat while I grabbed my fishing bucket and cane pole. Finally, we shoved off. They paddled and I propped my feet on the side of the boat and leaned my back against the other side. That was what I came for. To relax and float and dream. I sure wished Daddy could be here, in this warm sunlight, instead of that cold, dark mine that just aggravated his coughing. Fishing will cure just about anything. With Freddy gone, I could help if they'd let me, but they won't. I'm working on that one, though.

Daddy's lunch pail fit under my rear end and it was cold, and that felt good. Buddy put my root beer in and an extra one 'cause I saw Cove Lake first. I always did and they always snuck in a root beer to surprise me. Benny rearranged it all to make sure his Schlitz was cold. Then he stashed his extra under the bench.

We hugged the shoreline and made our way up to where Cove Creek flowed in. That was the best place for crappie and blue gill. Everybody said so. Plus, it was shady in the morning and Buddy and Benny liked sitting in the shade. "That sun gets my beer too hot," Buddy said.

"Time to throw out the anchors," Benny said. Our anchors were old tar buckets filled with cement with ropes attached. Buddy threw one out and Benny the other. Now we just sat and cast.

I reached in my pocket and felt my bottle of fish bait oil. I picked up my cane pole, pried off the hook, and unwrapped the line. Inside my fishing bucket I got my lucky bobber and snapped it on my line about four feet from the hook. I placed my packet of worms under the bench so I could reach them easy. I slid the bottle of fish bait oil out of my pocket and laid it in the packet with the worms so only I could see it. I wanted to surprise Benny and Buddy with all the fish I caught.

"June Ellen, want me to bait your hook for you? Those worms are slimy and dirty. And they'll poop on you when you sink that hook in." Benny laughed because he knew I wouldn't let anyone bait my hook. I ignored him.

First, I picked out the fattest, juiciest worm I could find. I wove the hook in and out all the way down to the tail. Otherwise, some little bream or crappie would come along and just suck the worm off. I wanted a big old blue gill to take a big bite. Next, I took the bottle of fish bait oil and started to open it. It was hard to open and I was struggling. I finally cracked the seal and it turned.

"Why're you so slow today, Junie Bug? You're usually the first one in." Buddy grinned.

"I'm just being real careful, 'cause I'm going to catch a big one and I don't want my worm to get sucked off."

I held my breath while I took the cap off and gently shook a few drops on the worm and, boy, did he start wiggling. I didn't want to spill any and quickly put the cap back on and took a big breath. The most powerful stench rose up and my nose started to burn and my eyes were watering. I couldn't see anything. I didn't want Benny and Buddy to notice so I quick like threw out my line and bobber.

"What's that smell, Buddy? You rowed us right up next to a dead animal. Let's get out of here." Buddy was downwind and he started coughing. I tried hard not to cough, but started sputtering.

"What in tarnation is wrong with you two? How's a guy supposed to catch any fish around here? And, no, Buddy, we aren't moving. Since when does a dead possum bother you?"

About that time Benny turned around and got a whiff. "Holy God, who's sick? Buddy, I think you got a real gut problem going on here."

"It ain't me. It's June Ellen. She's done got a skunk in that bucket. What in Sam Hill's in there? Let me see that thing."

But about that time, I got a bite and my bobber went way under, bounced back and way under again. "I got a big one!" I coughed and sputtered, tipping my cane pole down to give my fish some swimming room.

"Grab the net, Buddy. Be ready. I don't want the line to break. Dang, my eyes are burning," Benny said.

Buddy was right beside me now with the net. He was still coughing and spitting but nobody cared. My bobber danced like a water bug. It skittered all around that boat.

"June Ellen, tighten up and slowly pull her in. Don't be shy. Go straight up to God with your cane pole and pray it don't break."

I hooked such a big fish, I couldn't talk. It took all I had to pull her in. I did what Benny said and slowly raised my pole and leaned way back and sure enough I saw the head of my fish start to rise, only it wasn't a fish. I hooked the biggest snapping turtle I'd ever seen.

"Holy cow, there's your namesake, Snapper." Benny pulled out his knife and cut the line and the turtle took my worm and my hook and sank back into the water.

The smell was about gone now, and nobody said anything. They went back to fishing and drinking, and I had my first root beer. Hauling in that turtle took all I had, so I got in my fishing bucket and pulled out my first sandwich. First, I licked the peanut butter and strawberry jam down the sides, then I took my first bite. There was nothing like that first bite when you were fishing, and I wished I could tell Daddy, but he was at the mine today, checking for gas pockets. "Dear Jesus, please don't let Daddy blow any more coal dust in his lungs, 'cause I really want him to go fishing with me again." I didn't always like to pray but today it felt good.

I thought about my fish bait oil and how I could use it without raising suspicion. It sure worked on that turtle.

"Well, let's head out by the island with all those down trees in the lake and see if we can get some big crappie, Buddy. Not so many turtles either, June Ellen."

The sun was overhead now, and I was ready to try again. The trick I figured is to get it in the water fast. They'd had their beer for lunch now and probably wouldn't smell anything.

I picked up my cane pole and saw that a new hook had already been tied on. I didn't say anything. I was not very good at knots and secretly I was glad Benny tied another one for me.

I opened my packet of worms and found another great big juicy one. I wove this one on and laid him on my fishing bucket. I took hold of the fish bait oil and slowly turned the cap; I only had a few seconds to get it on the worm and shut it back tight. Buddy got a bite on his rod and it zinged as the line took off.

This was a good time to put the fish oil on. I held my breath again and shook a few drops, just as Buddy pulled in a big old bass; it flew through the air and flopped in the boat. That bass was so big, it raised itself up and jumped again and knocked the fish oil right out of my hand into the bottom of the boat. I looked down and saw a tiny stream of oil leaking out of the bottle. Thick and gooey like motor oil, I watched it seep under my fishing bucket.

And that fish was jumping all get out. We were all coughing, and our eyes were watering. Nobody could see a thing. Benny had the net in his hand trying to get the jumping bass to jump in it, and Buddy was trying to hang on to his rod and the bass while he reeled in the slack as fast as he could. I stood up in the boat to try and get some air to breathe and clear my eyes and saw that we were surrounded by turkey buzzards. They circled us like we were dead.

"H-E-double toothpicks and tarnation," I managed to croak out.

Buddy took one look at me and saw what was up there and yelled, "Hell fire and damnation. Sit down, June Ellen, it smells like we're dead in here."

Just as the bass jumped up in the air again, a turkey buzzard swooped down for a closer look and just barely missed Benny's head. Buddy netted the bass and Benny started paddling, which didn't work so well. We spun around in circles.

"Grab a paddle, Buddy. We gotta get out of here, before those buzzards rip out our gizzards."

Buddy grabbed a paddle, and he and Benny both paddled faster than I'd ever seen them move. Buddy hollered, "I never seen buzzards go for a live man before. They're crazy, Benny. I can hardly see what I'm doing for them skunk fumes. My nose is burning, my eyes are burning. Hold that bass in that net, June Ellen."

I grabbed onto the net. He was quiet now, with an occasional leap for freedom. I felt kind of sorry for him, but would rather eat him than set him free. I leaned over the side of the boat where the air was fresher. Benny was in front so he seemed okay. Buddy paddled like a mad man and he looked like one too. His nose and eyes were so red and runny, he looked like he was weeping. My bottle of fish bait oil was lying open right there in front of him. I laid the bass on the floor beside me and that bass jumped up again, and about that time that buzzard dove down and took a big bite of that bass.

Buddy started yelling, "He bit my bass, he bit my bass, that damn buzzard bit my bass."

Benny was in front and couldn't see anything. "How the hell did a buzzard bite you in the ass? You're sitting on it, ain't you?"

"My bass, I said, my bass, you moron, not my ass, you ass. He's after my big fish I just caught."

That buzzard started circling again, and Buddy couldn't stand the thought of losing that bass and threw himself on top of it, and sure enough that big old buzzard zoomed in and bit Buddy right on the ass, where that pale flesh showed like a fish's belly. Now Buddy's really yelling, "He bit my ass, he bit my ass. That buzzard took a chunk right out of my ass."

I grabbed the fish bait oil, put the cap on, and swished it in the lake to get all the residue off and stuffed it deep in my pocket. I grabbed the net with the bass, pulled the net all the way up, and held it like a pig in a poke.

"Paddle, Buddy, paddle. I don't care if he bit your bass or your ass, I just want to get off this lake," Benny yelled. Their eyes were still watering so bad they couldn't see the oil.

Buddy started paddling again—I sat still as I leaned out over the water and breathed the fresh air. We weren't far from the shore and as soon as we hit ground, Buddy and Benny were out of the boat faster than you could shake a stick. Buddy hooted and hollered, holding the seat of his pants. The buzzards had scattered by this time.

I got out of the boat and ran over to Buddy.

"Here you go, Buddy, here's your ass, I mean your bass." I was rolling on the ground laughing and pretty soon Buddy was bent double laughing.

"I need a beer, Benny. Bring that cooler up here," Buddy yelled.

"Yep, I could use a root beer myself. I'll get the cooler." I ran down to the boat and found the baling can and sloshed water all over the bottom. I wanted to wipe out the smell of that fish bait oil. I dunked my fishing can in and out of the water till I was sure the fish bait oil was washed off. I hauled up the cooler and my fishing can and handed out the Schlitz.

Buddy said, "I think I need a six pack. I ain't never heard of a buzzard attacking a live man's ass before. What was that smell, June Ellen? You bring a skunk in your old lard can?"

I didn't say anything. I just concentrated on my root beer. Benny and Buddy were happy to be sitting on the ground with a cold beer, except Buddy was standing, leaning on a tree. There was just nothing like a summer day of fishing at Cove Lake.

I stood by the shore and stared at the shallow blue water, full of minnows. What did fish think about? I wondered. I liked to watch the way they jumped out of the water to catch a bug. They glided so smooth with a flick of their tail, hardly moving a fin. I looked at the beautiful small-mouth bass lying at my feet. "Look, Benny. She's so beautiful with her scales and fins glistening in the sunlight. Every scale makes its own little rainbow."

Buddy laughed and tipped up his Schlitz can to drain the last drop.

"What's it like to be a fish and get hooked? Then to get swallowed and lie in someone's stomach?"

Benny and Buddy ignored me, intent on their beers and chewing tobacco.

"What do you think it was like for Jonah in the belly of the whale? You know Jonah prayed to God to get him out of that whale, and he did.

"Did that big bass pray to God to take him back to the water when he was flipping around in the bottom of the boat?"

They laughed.

I waded along the shore among the minnows. It was moments like this that I never wanted to catch one again, but then something happened when I put a worm on a hook and I knew I really wanted to catch a big one. I thought about the taste of fresh fish dipped in buttermilk, then rolled in cornmeal and laid to rest in hot sizzling Honey Dew lard.

I wondered what the whale thought of Jonah in his belly. Did he thank God for answering his prayer for something to eat? Then I thought about Daddy in the belly of the coal mine. Today was his day to light up the gas pockets so the miners could dig out the coal. Did he pray to God to not let the mine explode and bury him under tons of rock?

Did the mine want to swallow Daddy like the whale swallowed Jonah? Did the coal mine have a God to pray to, about the miners in his belly? How did God know which prayer to answer?

April Leigh—The Bone

DADDY AND I were sitting on the front porch swing cooling off in the evening air. "Daddy, what do you think Freddy's doing right now?"

"Well, let's see, it's about six o'clock here and the time difference is about fourteen hours, so it's eight o'clock in the morning. I'd guess he's swabbing the deck about now."

"Is it hard to swab?"

"It might be. Swab is navy for mop. That ship's almost as big as Paris, so I reckon it takes a while to mop all that."

I started laughing. "Daddy, I'd like to see Freddy mopping a ship. Do you think he'll mop the kitchen for Mama when he comes back?"

"No, June Ellen, I don't see that happening." Then Daddy just stared at the sun settling over the mountain. I knew Daddy was worried about the enemy blowing up Freddy's ship because we saw a picture on the front page of the *Paris Eagle* of a ship like Freddy's that got bombed real bad and a lot of soldiers got killed.

Daddy said, "June Ellen, there sure are a lot of cars on this old road tonight."

I understood it was time to stop talking about Freddy, and I found I did better if I found something to occupy my mind. We were watching the dirt road in front of our house that ran to nowhere and back again. If you followed it the other way, it ran right into Main Street and circled the courthouse, the center of the square. Around it was every kind of store you could want.

Not many automobiles or trucks or horses, for that matter, came out our way, but since April Leigh was getting ready to go to high school, Daddy and I were seeing more of them creep by. Cars full of boys would slow down and look to see if April Leigh was on the porch. She sat there more and more, so they could get a good look at her.

Just about dark, Dewey Ladd drove by with me and Daddy sitting there. Dewey worked at his granddaddy's grocery store. He yelled loud out the window, "Hey, April Leigh, want to take a ride?" Dewey wore big round glasses with thick lenses.

Daddy said, "That boy don't see too well." Daddy stood up tall and scowled at him and he took off, stirring up enough gravel and road dust to coat the house for days.

Daddy laughed as Dewey tore off and I felt kind of good. I had on my blue jeans and a clean blouse, a hand-me-down from April with a frill around the collar trimmed in red, which matched the red snaps on my jeans. I imagined I did look a little like April Leigh.

I said, "Daddy, why do those boys keep coming by here to look at April Leigh?"

"They're just a bunch of hound dogs sniffing for a bone."

"Is April Leigh a bone?"

Daddy laughed out loud, which started him to coughing. I ran into the house, grabbed a jelly glass out of the cupboard, and filled the glass from the dipper and bucket on the back porch. I ran back to the front porch, where Daddy was hacking into his handkerchief by this time.

"Here, Daddy," I said, "Mama said for you to drink this." She didn't, but she would have if she'd been there.

I didn't understand about April Leigh being a bone, and those boys being hound dogs, but decided I'd think on it.

That night I crawled into bed with April Leigh. She had white cream all over her face and looked like a ghost. She lay there, totally still on her back, not saying a word to me.

"What are you doing, you old bone?"

"What did you call me?" She tried to jump up to kick me, I'm sure, but thought better of it with all that white stuff on her face.

"Daddy said you were just an old bone."

"He did not. June Ellen, just for once I wish you would just go to sleep. You're like a mosquito that just keeps buzzing around my ears and won't go away till it bites. Then there's an awful itch left that just can't be gotten rid of."

"Daddy said those boys driving around here all the time are like hound dogs looking for a bone, and you're the bone they're looking for."

April Leigh said nothing at first. She just lay there real still. "Daddy said that?"

"Yes, April Leigh, he did."

She looked over at me and smiled. "That's good, let's go to sleep."

April Leigh sure was strange sometimes. She liked being called an old bone. That really bewildered me.

"April Leigh, I just can't figure you out no more."

"Anymore. Good night."

[11]

Thelma Hazelwood

IN AUGUST, the dog days came on hot and dry. They're called the dog days because you can see the Dog Star, Sirius, in the night sky. Not because it's so hot that the dogs won't move. Sr. Agatha, the librarian at my school, made sure we knew that.

Daddy had coughed all night. "It's too hot to breathe," he told Mama when she went to check on him. She sat with him and wiped him down with a cold rag.

The next morning Daddy got ready to go to work. Mama said, "Fred, don't go down in that mine today. Give your lungs time to breathe some fresh air."

"Cora, it's a lot cooler down in that mine than up here. I'd probably sleep better down there, too."

"I'll sleep down there with you, Daddy," I said. "It's too hot for me to sleep up here also."

Daddy laughed till he started coughing again. Mama looked worn out today. She didn't say anything, just shook her head.

Daddy said, "I need to go, Cora. We need the money. Albert's no good by himself and without Freddy . . ." Daddy sighed, trying hard not to look all done in. "I can't hire anyone till we get another load. I'll stay away from the dust. It's the heat causing this cough, anyway."

Uncle Albert honked and Daddy walked out, slow and draggy. He waited till he got to the front porch to start coughing again. Mama heard him anyway. She shook her head and walked out to her chickens. I watched Daddy till he stopped coughing and got in the truck with Uncle Albert. I heard Mama talking to her chickens, or maybe she was praying.

"Rex, I need an ice-cream soda. You'll have to stay home, 'cause Mr. Haney won't let you in and it's too hot for you to wait on the sidewalk. You're likely to fry like an egg." Rex yawned and walked away. I was glad he wasn't disappointed.

Mama walked back in the house and started wiping down the table. "June Ellen, I'm real busy today. Find something to do and give me some peace."

"Okay, Mama. I think I'll just walk to the square."

I whined around begging Mama for enough money to buy an ice-cream soda. I found two pennies under the couch cushions. Then I searched through all the drawers in Mama and Daddy's room while she was busy outside watering their wilting tomato plants, and I found a nickel and a penny. I was only two cents short when Mama got tired of me moping around and gave me two pennies out of her pocketbook.

The sun bore down, piercing everything; nothing moved except the heat waves that dangled in front of your eyes if you squinted a certain way. I decided an adventure downtown to Haney's Drug Store would set my mind right. Mr. Haney put in big overhead fans along the bar of his soda fountain. I'd go sit at the soda fountain under a cool breeze.

He had told Daddy, "Fred, those fans paid for themselves this summer. It's so hot and humid in this swamp, people can't wait to sit down at the soda fountain under those fans and have a cold drink. I put a sign up first thing after they got installed. You can't sit here unless you buy something. I can hardly keep ice cream in stock. People are lining up to get in. Yes, sir, those fans paid for themselves."

I didn't have anybody to walk to town with since April Leigh got too snooty and read movie magazines all day, so I was particularly sensitive to my surroundings that day and that is why I noticed Thelma Hazelwood on her front porch. She wore a bright red hat perched on top of her head, which reminded me of the single red hollyhock that was left in the Lahoskys' barnyard. This single hollyhock was surrounded by barnyard dirt and dust just like Thelma's red hat on that dirty, dusty porch.

I didn't think much about Thelma because I hardly ever saw her. Her house sunk down back from the road across the railroad tracks. Daddy called it a shotgun house. You fired a gun in the front door and the bullet came straight out the back door.

Back there behind the railroad tracks it blended in with the brown fields and the dry woods that ran up behind it. It was August and everything was mostly dust. It hadn't rained in a month. Her house looked like an old grimy box. Even the tin roof was so rusty brown you thought you were looking at dirt.

Thelma Hazelwood looked like her house. She blended in with her surroundings like the chameleons I studied about in science class. They take on the color of what they are sitting on, so you don't notice them. I wished I could do that. I'd be a great spy.

At first I stopped to look close up to see if it was a mirage. But, no, it wasn't. Thelma Hazelwood sat up there in a black dress faded to dust practically and those black granny shoes like the nuns wear, in her big red hat perched on her head. I decided to take some time and visit. I never talked to Thelma Hazelwood by myself. Sometimes Mama said hello, but I had never walked up to her porch alone.

I felt the money in my pocket for an ice-cream soda. My throat was parched. My head sweated. My neck sweated. My shirt got wet from all this sweat. April Leigh had told me, "Girls don't sweat, they glisten." I admired my own sweat and thought how wrong she was. I decided to see if Thelma would give me a cold drink of water.

"Hi, Miss Hazelwood. Hot today, isn't it?"

Suddenly, a big old skinny hound dog rounded the corner barking, followed by a ragtag group of mutts all sizes and colors, and they began to bark too.

"Shut up, you mangy hounds, or I'll shoot you," Thelma yelled. It was hot and they shut up easy and slowly wiggled their way down under the porch, except for the big old hound dog, who slunk over to Thelma.

Thelma stared me down good with those coal-black eyes of hers and those eyebrows that went straight across her face like one long brush. I was not put off easy though. April Leigh calls me nosy, but I just have a great curiosity about people.

"I like your red hat."

"Who are you?"

"Why, I'm June Ellen, Fred and Cora Thackeray's daughter. I'm their youngest, so you probably don't remember me. I like your dog. What's his name?"

"Rufus. What do you want?"

"I just wanted to say hi is all. I'm on my way to the dime store for an ice-cream soda. Mr. Haney had fans put in and it's real cool there. You can sit at the bar right under them and you won't sweat or nothing. All you have to do is buy a drink and you can sit there for as long as you want. You look real pretty today, Miss Hazelwood, in your red hat. Where're you going?"

Thelma looked at me long and hard. "I'm on my way to Offenbacher's funeral home."

"Who died?"

"Me," she said looking me in the eye again.

"You aren't dead. I'm sitting here talking to you right now."

"There they are come to get me." And Thelma got up and laid herself down on the porch. She shut her eyes and clasped her purse in her hands over her big belly. I could see her red hat was held on with all these hatpins, and it sat right there pretty as you please. It didn't budge.

"I'm dead now, please leave and give me my privacy."

Rufus lay down next to her—he was hot and just panting away.

I looked up to see the old black hearse from Offenbacher's with two men inside cross the railroad tracks and turn down her dirt drive. I didn't know what to do, but I knew I needed to get help so I took off running for the dime store.

Sweat poured in my eyes and stung like salt water. I got a stitch in my side but was too scared to stop. I ran to the square and just stood there all bent over trying to catch my breath when the hearse went by.

I took off running beside it. "Who's in there?" I yelled. "Who's in there?"

The Offenbacher funeral home sat just a block off the square and soon the hearse pulled in the driveway. The driver jumped out and yelled back at me, "Young lady, what are you doing? Don't you have any respect for the dead?"

"Yes, sir, I do, but who's in there?"

"Why, this is Miss Thelma Hazelwood."

"She's not dead." I started yelling again and ran back and started beating on the back door.

Just then the door opened and Thelma sat up with her red hat on. I screamed and fell down in the driveway.

Thelma said, "Child, show some respect for the dead," and then she fell back down.

About that time Mr. Offenbacher himself came out the back door. "What's going on here? Young lady, what are you doing here?"

"She's not dead. Thelma Hazelwood's not dead. I was just talking to her on her front porch."

Mr. Offenbacher took a handkerchief out of his pocket and wiped the sweat from his forehead.

"Well, young lady, I think I can help out here, first tell me who you are."

"I'm June Ellen Thackeray, Fred and Cora Thackeray are my parents."

"Well, June Ellen, I'm glad to meet you. I know your dad. He delivered me some good coal one time. I hope he's doing good. I know he got a bunch of that coal dust in his lungs."

"My daddy's at our coal mine right now working, and he'd believe me that Thelma's not dead."

"Well, I believe you, too. How would you like to step into my office and have a cold Coca-Cola while I explain something to you?"

I looked him up and down giving him my own hard-eyed look I'd been working on. I was awfully thirsty and hot and the thought of an ice-cold drink won me over quick. I picked myself up and went with him into the old funeral parlor, and sure enough he had a little office off to the side with a big desk and a leather chair for him and two wooden chairs in front. I slid into one when a short woman with her hair in a bun on top walked in.

"Maudie, this is June Ellen and she'd like a Coca-Cola. She's pretty hot and tired, I think. June Ellen, this is my wife, Maudie. She helps me run this place."

"How do you do, Miss Maudie?"

Maudie brought me a coke with ice that slid around the outside of the bottle it was so cold.

"You got any peanuts, Mr. Offenbacher? They sure would go good with this Coca-Cola."

"No, June Ellen, I don't. But let's talk about Thelma Hazelwood. Can you keep a secret?"

"Yes, sir, I can. You can ask April Leigh, my sister, or Gracie, my best friend, and they will tell you that one thing you can count on with me is I can keep a secret."

"Well, I thought so. June Ellen, some people, say, like Thelma for instance, they like to shop around a little, know what they're getting. Now there's another funeral home here, Fenton's, you know where that is?"

"Yes, sir, I do. It is at the other end of town near the other cemetery."

"That's right. Well, now since the Depression and this war, a lot of people don't have very much money to spend on their burying and what not. Now look here at this card, and you see all those different things you get to pick. Look there under material. You can choose silk or satin to line your casket, in all these different colors you get to choose from pink or purple or white. Under wood you could have mahogany or pine or cherry or maple. It is kind of like a menu when you go to a restaurant. People can be as fancy as they want."

I looked at the menu and saw where you could get your hair done or get a haircut. You could even rent a suit for your laying out if you didn't have one. "Gosh, Mr. Offenbacher, that's a lot of stuff just to get buried."

"That's right, but when you lose someone you love you want to send them off right. Everyone wants to arrive in the glory land looking their best for Jesus."

"It sure costs a lot."

"Yes, it does and that's what Thelma Hazelwood is figuring out today. How she wants to be buried."

"But she said she's dead."

"Well, that was part of her plan, pretend she's dead and see what the ride is like here compared to Fenton's. And she wanted to be sure we could keep her red hat on right. Some people are just peculiar like that, and between you and me, she is one of them. That's our secret, okay?"

"I sure am glad she's not being buried alive."

Mr. Offenbacher started laughing.

"Well, young lady, how about a ride home?"

"In that hearse?"

"No. I have my Chevrolet in the back, I thought I might give you a ride home in that instead."

"Oh, that would be good. Mama wouldn't like it if I came home in a hearse. And, Mr. Offenbacher, I think you should add peanuts to your menu, it would really let people know how fancy you are."

[12]

The County Fair

BY THE END of August our town was pretty hot and dry, and my adventures had hit a dry spell. It was the last week of summer vacation before school began. It was then that the carnival rolled into town for the county fair. And Gracie, my best friend, came home from her granny's. She always came home from her granny's in time for the county fair and school starting. We were starting in the fifth grade at St. Joseph's Catholic Grade School. She thrived on adventure and admired me for my adventurous ways and volunteered right away to accompany me on my many exploits. I'm proud to say we had made a name for ourselves and we both loved softball.

I saw Gracie at the post office yesterday.

She was as excited as me. "June Ellen, I just dropped off my chickens for the poultry judging. You should see the rides and the carnies that are setting them up. They look like outlaws. They have tattoos all over their arms and shoulders. One guy had an anchor tattooed over his whole chest. And they all have hairy faces."

This morning, I leaped out of bed and got dressed. I could hardly go to sleep thinking about the rides—the Ferris wheel, which let you see the whole town, even the coal mines when you got to the top. Heights don't scare me. The Dark Pretzel, the most popular and scariest ride, took you into the haunted cavern.

I had one dollar and fifty cents saved up and I'd been planning everything I'd ride and eat and see. "April Leigh, get up. It's the opening day of the Logan County Fair. I'm too excited to lay in bed."

I arranged with Mama to meet Gracie at the county fair. It was the first time we'd be allowed to go off on our own. We both loved rides and didn't scare easy. April Leigh helped talk Mama into it because she wanted to be alone with her new best friend, Mary Alice.

Mama dipped up two bowls of oatmeal in the kitchen. She bustled around the kitchen filled with excitement like me and slopped the oatmeal all over the stove. She'd entered her famous blueberry preserves in the exhibition hall and prayed for another blue ribbon. Mama and her sister, Aunt Annie, always competed against each other and she knew Aunt Annie wanted that blue ribbon, but Mama had always won first prize. Nobody made jam like Mama's.

Mama made a lunch to take with us. I personally didn't see the need with all the great food at the fair. But her nerves sure made her fluttery.

"June Ellen, eat your oatmeal and drink a glass of milk so we can get to the fair. But first go tell April Leigh I said to get up now."

I ran back to the room and watched April Leigh comb her long blonde hair. "Hurry up, April Leigh, we have to eat and go. Mama said."

April Leigh scowled at me. "I'm fixing my hair. I'm brushing it till it shines."

"Mama'll snatch you bald headed if you don't come right now and you won't have any hair to get shiny," I retorted.

"June Ellen, what are you talking about?" Mama roared. "Get in here and eat. One more word like that and you can keep Rex company. Hurry up, both of you."

"You're such a kid, June Ellen," April Leigh said.

That made me mad, but I knew Mama wasn't fooling around, so I didn't kick April Leigh. She thought she was smarter than me but she wasn't. I truly was smarter. She was probably meeting Isaac at the fair. Wait till Mama found out. He was not Catholic and Mama frowned on that.

But I was too excited to waste my time on April Leigh. I put on my favorite dress, red dotted swiss with a white pointed collar. I loved this dress. It had buttons in front and so it was easy to button and unbutton. Mama had made it just for me. And best of all it had pockets to put all my stuff in. I didn't like to carry a purse around. It got in my way something awful.

I was wearing new brown Weatherbird school shoes. They're made special for all kinds of weather and were called Rockettes after the dancers, I reckoned. That was what Daddy said when I showed them to him. I wanted the red ones, but I only got one pair so they had to match everything. I had new white anklets too with red flowers around the top to match my dress.

I heard a horn and it was Uncle Albert and Aunt Annie come to take us to the fair. We all ran out together; everyone was excited, even Daddy. He and Uncle Albert weren't mining today. The heat had lifted and Daddy said he could breathe easier. Daddy and Uncle Albert always hung out in the cattle and hog barn. They also played some of the games. They both carried a silver flask inside their jacket pockets. Daddy liked to drink, which made Mama mad, so he made sure he hid his flask inside his jacket.

We drove over to the county fair and saw a long line of cars, trucks, and even a couple of horses with buggies. Dust was swirling everywhere as people young and old, horses, and vehicles made their way around the dry pasture turned into a carnival.

Uncle Albert parked close to the cattle barn so Daddy didn't have so far to walk. Daddy slipped me another quarter, then he and Uncle Albert took off. April Leigh found her new best friend, Mary Alice, and they ran off giggling. I went with Mama and Aunt Annie to the canning exhibition hall where I was to meet Gracie. She was there and we ran all excited to the carnival rides. We bought five tickets for a dollar.

First, we lined up to get on the Ferris wheel. We jumped in the red car with clown faces painted on the side. A hairy man slammed the bar down and the Ferris wheel lifted us up all the way to the very top. I felt like I could touch the sky. Everything shone brightly in the sunlight and we could see the whole carnival laid out before us. We went round and round in a giant circle watching all the people and smelling cotton candy, caramel apples, and popcorn. It was the best view ever, and I liked to get a good overall picture of everything right off.

Next, we went to the Dark Pretzel, the most popular ride. It's named the Pretzel because it made you feel like you were turned and twisted like one. We climbed into a metal car painted bright orange with blue lightning bolts that spun around on little wheels that ran on a track. There was room for two people on a leather bench with a metal bar across the front to hold on to. A greasy old man pushed a lever and the car moved through a dark maroon red curtain. Then we entered a dark cavern with no lights. We both squealed, as it was so black we couldn't see each other. We screamed loud as it turned one way and a devil head jumped in front of our faces. Later we both admitted we thought he was going to get in the car with us. Then it jerked around a curve and an alligator in a barrel charged Gracie. She screamed and covered her eyes. I wasn't scared of the alligator, and I just jumped a little.

We did another loop and a quick turn around a corner and a mule raised its leg like it was going to kick our heads; I ducked and screamed and tried to jump on Gracie's side because he was aiming for me. It wasn't real, but it sure looked it when they shined a light as it kicked at us. Then it was over.

"They shortened our ride, Gracie. That was only two minutes long."

"That alligator scared me to death," Gracie said.

I was disappointed but didn't say anything.

"Let's go get some cotton candy. The county fair is the only time I ever get any." Gracie followed me to the cotton candy machine.

"Gracie, I feel like I'm eating a pink cloud that melts on my tongue."

"It feels to me, June Ellen, like I'm eating pink sugar snowflakes. The minute you taste it, it's gone, till the next bite. You want to go in the house of mirrors, next?"

"No," I say. "That's boring."

I didn't tell her it scared me so bad once, I thought I'd never get out and couldn't catch my breath. Last year April Leigh had to drag me out—I panicked and my legs wouldn't move—but I didn't tell Gracie that.

"Let's go look at the freak show."

"June Ellen, I'm not allowed to go to any sideshows or to gamble."

"I'm not allowed to go to any sideshows either, but Daddy always lets me toss rings to get a goldfish. I don't think that counts as gambling. People sure get touchy around here about bingo and gambling and what's a sin."

Gracie said, "Mama says if the money goes to the church it's not a sin and none of this money is going to church, so that makes it a sin."

"Oh, Gracie, let's just go look at the signs. They're just as good as going and that's no sin."

We walked by the shooting tent where grown men shot at little plastic yellow ducks with a cork gun. A big sign hung next to it with big red capital letters, *SEE THE BEARDED LADY.* On the sign she wore a black bathing suit with red stripes and red pom-poms on the shoulder straps. A dark, black beard hung all the way down below her breasts and ended in a scraggly point.

"Why's the bearded lady in that bathing suit?" Gracie asked.

"So you won't think she's a man, you can see everything," Jimmy Schmitz said, leering at us as he ran by. He was in our class at St. Joseph's and he liked to annoy me. April Leigh said boys do that because they liked you. I didn't believe her. Being boy crazy had just ruined her.

"Yuck," we both said at the same time.

"Gosh, Gracie, I wonder why she doesn't shave like Daddy. You can't even tell he has whiskers if he shaves."

Next, we saw a sign for the world's fattest man. He wore a bathing suit too. Only you could hardly see it. He held a whole baked chicken in one hand and a big pink ham in the other.

Gracie said, "He's so ugly he scares me, and he weighs five hundred and seventy-five pounds."

"Gracie, look at the rolls and rolls of fat. They stack like rings on a peg, each ring bigger than the last."

A little guy in a black hat with a gold-topped cane scurried out of the tent and yelled at us, "Come on in, little girlies, watch him eat ten chickens and half a cow." We took off running and he just laughed at us.

"Look at that sign, Gracie. Alligator woman, half alligator and half woman. She has a long tail and two back feet. Why is that a sin to say hello to one of God's creatures?"

"I'm not going, June Ellen."

Then we heard someone yelling, "Gracie, Gracie, come here." We thought we were caught but it was her big brother, Maynard, yelling. "They're judging your chickens right now."

"Come with me, June Ellen, you can't stay here by yourself."

"Yes, I can."

"Gracie," he yelled.

She looked at me and took off.

Wow, I thought, rubbing the quarter Daddy gave me. The freak shows took a whole quarter; they cost the most. I walked around to see what else, when I heard a woman call out to me in a high commanding voice.

"Hey, pretty girl, want to know your future, your love life, your fortune in the world?"

I looked inside a small canvas tent with shiny beads on a dirty fringe that hung like a curtain across the door. A beautiful woman, more beautiful than Elizabeth Taylor in *National Velvet*, sat there. Her long black hair shined like the dark magic of Cove Lake in moonlight. A silver turban wound around her head, covered with every color of jewel I'd ever seen.

"Come in," she directed me and opened the beaded curtain. Her jewels flickered and danced in the candlelight. It was dark except for the candles and the light that snuck in around the curtain. I spied a round, clear, glass ball sitting on a little table in front of her.

I stared at it and colors started to swirl inside; she clasped it around her palm and it darkened.

"What's your name?" she asked. "You want me to tell you what the crystal ball shows?" Her eyebrows lifted up on her forehead and formed two perfect upside-down V's.

"I'm June Ellen and I'm Catholic," I said, my heart beating so fast, it jumped in my throat.

"Catholic?" she said.

I nodded. "And I like the Blessed Virgin the Mother of Jesus most of all."

Her eyes sparkled with kindness and glowed with a violet light to them. They pulled me in. She wore a long blue dress that swirled around her and colors started to dance among the folds. She was not so scary now. Her painted red fingernails were long and clicked on the table. She was all rouged up, as Mama liked to say, with black around her eyes like Cleopatra.

"I admire the Blessed Virgin, too," she said. "Call me Lady Diana." She pulled a locket out from under her gown just like the sisters at St. Joseph's wore, only they reached down and pulled out a crucifix. She opened her locket; inside was a picture of Mary in a long blue dress that opened into a white gown. A crown of stars surrounded her golden hair radiating light. She stood on a cloud with pink light rays surrounding her. It was the prettiest picture I had ever seen of the Blessed Virgin.

I looked at the carnival lady and asked, "Do you pray?"

"Yes, always," she replied. "When people come to me for help, to ask questions, it's like a prayer."

"What's the crystal ball for?" I asked, watching carefully, not sure what she was.

"Ah, the crystal ball. Not everyone understands the power of the Mother," she said.

"June Ellen, June Ellen."

"Uh oh, that's my sister, April Leigh. I have to go."

"Go, child, but come back and I will look into the crystal ball and see what the Mother has for you."

"Oh boy, June Ellen, are you in trouble. Gracie went to the exhibition hall looking for you and Mama's about to have a fit. You went to a fortune-teller," she said, and her eyes got as big as saucers when I came out of the tent and she saw the big sign with the crystal ball on it.

"April Leigh, it's not like that. She prays to the Blessed Virgin, the Mother of God, for people and she has a crystal ball full of lights and color."

"What are you talking about, June Ellen? You're crazy and you are so in trouble."

"April Leigh, we have to go back and see her. You can ask her about Isaac. She can tell you who you're going to marry and everything. Really, you should see what she has in there. Come back with me later."

April Leigh looked at me and hesitated. "Well, maybe I'll go with you. It's just for fun."

Wow, I thought, that sounded like the old April Leigh, when we were a team.

Just then Mama showed up. "June Ellen, where have you been?"

"Oh, Mama," April Leigh said, "June Ellen has been all over looking for Gracie."

"Gracie's mother said she never saw her."

"June Ellen was probably looking at the ducks and geese and all those fancy chickens, you know, the ones with the black plumes on their head and the rest of them are white? She probably wants some of her own to raise. Oh, Mama, you know how Gracie's mother, Mrs. Bagley, is. When Gracie's showing her chickens, she's like one herself with her head cut off."

I had just heard Mama say that herself to Daddy about Gracie's mother. April Leigh must have heard her too. April Leigh never told a lie, but she said things in a way that made you think she said it another way. "Can I, Mama, can I have some of those fancy chickens? I want to raise them and make money." I decided it was best to keep the story going. April Leigh and I were like a team again.

Mama looked confused for a moment and said, "June Ellen, next time you go looking at ducks and geese tell someone."

"Okay, Mama, I will. I promise."

Mama was happy and no one had told a lie. Just then Aunt Annie came running across the midway shouting at Mama, "Cora, they're handing out the blue ribbons."

"Almighty God, Blessed Jesus," Mama whispered.

I looked at her and asked, "Mama, do you ever pray to the Blessed Virgin?"

"Honey, when it comes to blue ribbons I pray to everybody."

I was going to ask her about looking into a crystal ball, but April

Leigh kicked me. "Honey, you go with April Leigh and, April Leigh, don't you let her out of your sight. Do you hear me?"

"Okay, Mama," I said.

Mama looked at me not quite believing what she just heard but she had to get to the judging so she looked me in the eye and said, "Don't you dare wander off again. And stay away from those side shows."

Aunt Annie yelled again, "Cora, Cora, come on quick."

"All right, I'm coming."

"Whew," I sighed. When Mama gave me the eye, it took everything I had to not tell her everything. I was getting better though, being on my own so much without April Leigh.

April Leigh went with me to see Lady Diana. She stood in front of the beaded curtain, waiting for us, I guessed. April Leigh hesitated when she saw her and hung back. It was up to me.

"This is my sister, April Leigh, she wants to know if Isaac likes her 'cause she likes him."

"June Ellen, shut up. I don't like Isaac, I mean I do, but, not like that." She was really stuttering now.

The fortune-teller smiled and I watched April Leigh fall under her spell. "I understand, let's see what the Blessed Mother has for you today."

April Leigh sat down in the chair in front of the round table with the crystal ball sitting on it. Lady Diana sat on a chair like a throne with thick golden material with little mirrors all over it and red fringe across the bottom.

"Well, young lady, it looks like you have very good fortune ahead of you. Are you in a new school?"

"Yes, I just started public school, Paris High. I'm a freshman. I've grown up a lot this summer and I love high school."

The crystal ball lit up and colors danced around the walls and ceiling, which was different colored fabrics with mirrors, and jewels that shot the light from the crystal ball back at us, and the light danced on our skin and clothes.

"Wow, look, April Leigh, I've never seen anything like this before. Is it magic, Lady Diana?"

"It's energy, the energy that comes in light waves from my crystal ball reflecting off of emeralds and diamonds and other precious jewels surrounding you. It helps me see the future."

April Leigh asked, "What's the future say about me in high school?"

"You are a very popular young woman, and your beauty will get you many gifts. You, my dear, will never have a problem with boyfriends."

April Leigh got all puffed up and her eyes got real big and shiny. "Oh, thank you, Lady Diana. Do you think I will get to be a cheerleader?"

Lady Diana studied the crystal ball and it got pure white inside. She put her hands above it, like she was holding it, only her hands just floated there.

"My hands are getting very warm, so there is definitely something in the future for you like cheerleading. Also you must be very careful who you associate with. You are a good girl, and it is very important the spirits are telling me that you stay good and don't get mixed up with bad company. High school is very different from your grade school and you must be careful. Not everyone is good. There is some darkness, I am seeing."

And the crystal ball started to dim and got all cloudy.

April Leigh gasped. "Oh, no, what's going to happen to me? Is something bad coming for me?"

"No, dear, that's just the crystal ball's way or the Blessed Mother telling you to be careful who you associate with. Not all will be kind or helpful to you in your life. But remember, you have lots of good fortune coming to you if you stay on the right path."

April Leigh got up slowly and watched the crystal ball. The light returned and the jewels and diamonds started sparkling again. She smiled and took a deep breath. "Thank you, I think. It's kind of scary hearing so much about my future."

Lady Diana held out a beautiful vase with money in it. "Just put your quarter in here, honey, and don't worry, your future looks bright, if you remember what the Mother told you."

"Yes, ma'am, I will. Let's go, June Ellen. Mary Alice is waiting on me, and you have to go back with Mama."

"What about me? I want to sit in front of the crystal ball. I want to know what's going to happen to Daddy and our coal mine, and what about Freddy, April Leigh?"

The crystal ball grew dark, almost as black as coal. I stared at it and sat down. "What's gonna happen to Daddy, he can't hardly catch his breath because of the coal dust in his lungs and we have to keep our coal mine, we just have to, and Freddy left and went to the navy so he can't help Daddy and Uncle Albert. And I want to go down there, I have to see our coal mine."

Lady Diana sat down across from me. She took my hand and looked at my palm. "You have a long lifeline, June Ellen, you will live a long time. You have many good adventures ahead of you."

When she said these words, the crystal ball started to shine again, and the lights danced around the beaded curtains and all the jewels. My own breath returned and my stomach didn't hurt so much. "Does that mean Daddy gets to keep mining? Do I get to help him, like Freddy?" The light dimmed but Lady Diana put her hands over the crystal ball and let them float above it till the light returned.

"Ah," Lady Diana said. "The crystal ball grows dark like your coal mine. I see how much you love your coal mine and how proud you are. But the mine is a dark place and the energy of the crystal ball won't reach that far into the ground. The black coal and rock absorbs all the energy and light of the crystal ball just like it takes your daddy's energy. Your daddy tries hard, maybe too hard, to take care of you, June Ellen, and the mine."

I sat real still, in front of the dark crystal ball, imagining the coal and the dark stealing Daddy's energy. April Leigh kicked my foot. "June Ellen, we have to go, before we get caught in here. Mary Alice is looking for me and she'll go right to Mama and tell her she can't find me and you know what will happen if Mama comes looking for us."

"She's right, it is time for you to go. Remember, pray to the Blessed Mother, June Ellen. She will help your daddy figure out what to do."

"Is Freddy okay? Is he coming home soon? Can you tell me where he is? He's not allowed to and it's real hard on Mama not knowing. And now you see, Daddy needs him real bad."

The light wavered and grew dim in the crystal ball. Lady Diana covered it with a white cloth.

"The light dims when there's no energy, which is an electrical current that flows through the air. The crystal ball doesn't always know the answer when someone's so far away. We're a long way from the ocean. Don't worry, June Ellen."

My heart sank a little. I sighed, big.

April Leigh grabbed my arm. "June Ellen, we have to go now or we are both in for it."

"Thanks, Lady Diana, here's my quarter."

"No, June Ellen, you keep your quarter. Light some candles in your church for Freddy. That will help him come home safely."

Lady Diana opened the curtain, and I could hardly see in the bright sunlight.

Then Mary Alice showed up and April Leigh wanted to go with her on the Cyclone Roller Coaster. This was her way of getting rid of me. So much for us being explorers again. She took me back to find Gracie since Mama said I couldn't leave her side. Gracie was with her mother and Mama and Aunt Annie at the exhibition hall.

Mama and Aunt Annie both sported blue ribbons and showed them to everybody. This year they had two blue ribbons for jams and jellies. Aunt Annie said, "Look, June Ellen, George Walsh, the agriculture agent, was one of the judges. We play bingo with his wife, Sarah Jane. He gave me a blue ribbon for best uniform color and texture. I beat your mama on that one."

Mama rolled her eyes but for once held her tongue. Then Gracie had to go home and Mama told me to come with her.

We met Daddy at the Knights of Columbus hot dog and hamburger stand. Mama said, "Fred, they made up a new category just to shut up Annie. Last year she raised such a fuss with the fair board, they just decided to award two ribbons if they had to, to keep her quiet. I know that's what they did. I still won the top blue ribbon, for best of the best in jams and jellies, but you'd think she did. She's sure acting like it."

Daddy and I just kept eating our favorite, hot dogs covered with sauerkraut and German mustard. Mama forgot about the lunch she made us.

The Big Day

I ROLLED OVER in my sleep. Just then outside my bedroom window, the old rooster Tom Foolery started crowing. Not your pleasant cock a doodle doo, mind you, but a series of squawks and screeches that hurt the ears. I opened my eyes, temporarily blinded by the sunlight.

"I sure wish Daddy'd ring his neck."

I jumped out of bed easy today, the day of the big softball game. School had started and the highlight was the softball game. The fifth-grade girls played the sixth-grade girls and the winners won free ice-cream sodas at Haney's Rexall Drug on the square. Both classes got out of school at 1:00 for the game.

Sr. Sarah played softball with the fifth-grade girls every day at recess. She loved to play softball as much as I did. I called myself a tomboy with great pride, and in my mind Sr. Sarah did too. I called her Sr. TomBoy to her face once and Sr. Sarah laughed. She liked it. I knew right then being a tomboy was a great thing.

I loved softball and I was the best player in my class, everyone said so, and with Sr. Sarah playing on our team, we were sure to win. Sr. Annunciata, who was old and rickety, played on the sixth-grade team, which sometimes caused a ruckus between the fifth and sixth grade.

My daddy was known for being pretty smart, since he ran his own coal mine, so I asked his opinion one day after Belinda told us we should name our team the Cheaters. "Daddy, Sr. Annunciata's older than Sr. Sarah, and she can't hardly run and she can't hardly hit. Belinda says it's not fair to her sixth-grade team; that the Sisters should just pitch. But I think it's fair. Sr. Annunciata's an okay pitcher, and they let a tag runner run for her. It's always Belinda who's really fast, and we're a year younger, so all in all it evens things out, don't you think?"

"Well, June Ellen, it seems to me from watching some of these games, Fr. Michael takes care of Sr. Annunciata pretty good."

I agreed. "Sr. Sarah runs fast, Daddy. She picks up her skirts all the way to her knees. She wears old black granny shoes with big heels and runs fast as lightning around the bases. And when the wind's at her back, wow, she looks like she's flying. Her skirts billow out on either side like wings, and the wind just pushes her faster and faster.

"Daddy, I told Mama, I wanted a skirt like that, and she said no, only nuns could wear them."

Daddy laughed and didn't cough this time. My daddy and I were crazy about the St. Louis Cardinals and listened to all their games on the radio. I wanted to name my team the Cardinals, but only Gracie voted with me. Everyone said we needed a holy name, like the Saints. I said the Cardinals were holy, plus they were named after a bird, and God made the birds and St. Francis of Assisi said all birds were holy, but the Saints won in a landslide.

The sixth-grade team named themselves the Holy Martyrs, but Sr. Annunciata suggested they shorten it to just the Martyrs. They were studying martyrs and reading Bible stories about them so they wanted to be the Martyrs.

Yesterday Belinda told me, "June Ellen, those martyrs are strong and can stand up against anything and never waiver and God loved martyrs more, so we will surely win."

I reminded Belinda, "All martyrs die first before God loved them and the fifth-grade Saints will help the sixth grade become martyrs by killing them in this game."

Mama called from the kitchen, "June Ellen, are you dressed yet?"

"Almost, Mama." I went to the closet to find my school clothes. I grabbed a plaid skirt and a white blouse. But that day, since we were having such an important softball game, the girls were allowed to wear their jeans under their skirts.

Quickly I pulled on my jeans. Wow, it was so great. I could climb trees, jump fences, and wrestle Jimmy Schmitz to the ground when he hit me with a spitball, which he did at least once a week.

I found a clean pair of white anklets and put on my old worn saddle shoes. They had belonged to April Leigh, but I didn't care. I'd been given a choice for my birthday, a new pair of Jeeper's tennis shoes for the summer or my own softball glove. This was an easy decision, the softball glove of course. Sr. Sarah agreed it was the best choice.

I kept it oiled up just like my brother Freddy taught me. He gave me an old baseball he found at the softball field to go with it. I used the baseball to keep a tight pocket. Everyone knew a tight pocket was essential to catching balls and not dropping them.

"Mama, I wish Freddy could watch me play today."

"I know, honey, I miss him too. We just have to keep praying to keep him safe. Tell April Leigh to get up now, or she's going to be late for school."

"I already did, Mama."

April Leigh yelled from the bedroom, "She kicked me."

Mama shook her head. "June Ellen, here's your oatmeal, eat up and be on your way."

I laid my softball glove beside my plate. I looked at the steaming bowl of oatmeal, grabbed the fresh churned butter with the daisy stamped on top from Mama's butter mold, and with my spoon took a big scoop of butter and sank it into my oatmeal.

Mama said oatmeal made you strong, and I wanted to be strong today for the game. I rubbed my glove beside me as I watched the butter slowly melt and fan out into a creamy yellow pool. I stuck my finger in it and licked the melted butter off.

Next I grabbed the honey jar from the Lahoskys' bees across the road. It still had the honeycomb in it. I poured the honey on the melted butter and watched its slow descent into the liquid pool. This time though I took the spoon and mixed it all together, stirred it round and round and imagined running around the bases after I hit a home run.

"June Ellen, stop playing with your food and eat. Get that dirty glove off the table."

I put the glove in my lap and started to eat my oatmeal from outside in where the butter and honey collected forming a yellow line around the bowl; it was the perfect bite with just the right amount of honey and butter.

"Mama, are you coming with Fr. Michael to our softball game today?"

"I'm going to try, June Ellen." Mama smiled real big. "I'm sure you'll do just fine."

I finished my oatmeal, grabbed my glove, and started out the door to wait for the Lahoskys to drive me to school.

"June Ellen," Mama shouted. "Come back here. What are you thinking about? Where's your books and don't you want your lunch? You're going to get mighty hungry playing that softball game with no lunch in your belly. Here, I made you a special applesauce cookie to give you all the strength you need to win."

"Thanks, Mama, we will win, and then I'm going to have a chocolate phosphate."

"June Ellen, come here and see me a minute," Daddy said, coughing from his bed. His cough was worse when he laid down. He worked late at the mine last night, repairing broken timbers so the ceiling wouldn't fall in and hurt somebody. I prayed every day to the Blessed Virgin, just like the fortune-teller told me to so Freddy'd come home safe and Daddy could keep mining coal. Dr. John told him when he worked late at night, he had to stay in bed the next morning. Mama was being more watchful and making him.

"Hey, Daddy, are you coming to my softball game today?"

"I'm gonna try, June Ellen, but I want you to take this dime for good luck."

"Thanks, Daddy, is it a special dime?"

"It might be *if*, now, I said *if*, mind you, you happen to lose. You can still have your chocolate phosphate, and that will make it special."

"Thanks, Daddy, but we're not losing. The Saints are going to kill the Martyrs so they can go straight to heaven."

Daddy liked this kind of joke and he laughed with me, Mama didn't. Sr. Sarah would like it too. Wait till she sees these blue jeans.

[14]

The Softball Game

AT LUNCHTIME I sat with Gracie and Margaret Mary, who we called Mags for short. Gracie played shortstop because she was great at fielding ground balls and ran quick as lightning. I had helped her learn how to stop throwing like a girl. I played first base and I liked to make double plays, which means you've got to throw strong and hard from first to any other base.

Mags was our catcher. She had arms like a fighter. She lived on a farm and milked a lot of cows to get those arms, she said. She liked to pick off runners at second base. No one expected her to throw like that.

My nerves jumped all over my skin just thinking about the big game. I had butterflies in my stomach. I could hardly eat my favorite, peanut butter and jam on Mama's homemade bread. The applesauce cookie helped. It tasted good with cold milk. Gracie ate away like nothing bothered her. She tried to get me to eat.

"June Ellen, you better eat if we're going to kill those Martyrs. You'll need all the strength you can get." Everybody laughed.

I told them the joke I told Daddy. We adopted it as our new motto. Belinda walked by with Madeline, the Martyrs' shortstop. I admitted to myself, but not out loud, that Belinda had turned into a really great ball player. She played first base like me, which made us archenemies.

Daddy told me once, "Belinda makes you a better first baseman. She's your competition and you're always trying to show her up, so you just keep getting better and better, then she does the same thing. You're good for each other." Belinda's dad belonged to the Knights of Columbus like Daddy; they were good friends.

Belinda smirked. "There's the sissy Saints. Ha, just wait and see what we do to you this afternoon. One hour, June Ellen, and the Martyrs will show you sissies."

"Remember what I said, Belinda. You won't be martyrs till you're dead and the Saints will take care of that. Especially you, you're dead meat." Well, that got everybody's attention.

Madeline said, "June Ellen, what an awful thing to say. You have a stain on your soul." We just laughed at them.

Sr. Sarah came walking over. "Let's go, girls. Time to warm up." We grabbed our gloves and ran out to the ball field. Sr. Annunciata came marching out with the sixth-grade team. While we did our stretches, Sr. Sarah flipped a nickel with Sr. Annunciata.

Sr. Sarah said, "All right, girls, we take the field first. Let's put our hands together and pray. Remember we're here to have fun." We prayed the Hail Mary and the Our Father. Secretly, like everyone else, I prayed to win.

Agnes Beaver, Beaver for short, was first up. She played outfield, ran fast, and hit good. Sr. Sarah windmilled the first pitch. It sailed across the plate with a whoosh. Beaver just stood there, and Fr. Michael called, "Strike one!" He was the umpire, but he let a lot of balls go by.

"I'd rather wait for you girls to hit it than call you out or let you walk." We put up with him because he was all we had. I liked the umpires at the boys' games who were trained and really knew how to call. But this was such an important game. Maybe he was going to get serious this time. Free sodas at Haney's; there was a lot on the line here.

Sr. Sarah windmilled another one. Beaver swung at it and missed. Mags yelled, "Strike two. Way to go, Sister, keep it up."

I really wanted Beaver to hit a line drive straight to me. I couldn't help it. I wanted all the balls to come to me, either off the bat or off a grounder that Gracie or Rosie or one of the others picked up and threw to me to get an out at first. That was why I played first base. A lot of action happened there. I really worked on my stretching all summer so I could really reach for the ball and keep my toe on the bag.

Sr. Sarah wound up again and did a slow underhand. The ball floated over the plate and Beaver swung too soon and caught it lower down on the bat. She hit a slow grounder back to Sr. Sarah, who hiked her skirt up, ran, grabbed the ball, and tossed it to me, right into the pocket.

"Out," yelled Fr. Michael. I just loved playing ball with Sr. Sarah.

Gracie yelled, "One out, two to go. Way to go, team." Gracie was our cheerleader.

Helga Meyers was up next. Helga played outfield and was a great ball thrower. She was not always a good hitter, but sometimes she connected. We called her Hell for short most of the time, when we could get away with it, but not today. Having nuns for pitchers could hurt you sometimes. We had to act more holy.

"Easy out," Mags yelled.

Sr. Sarah tried to throw balls the other team could hit. "That is what playing is all about, girls. Having a good time and helping each other be the best we can be."

Hell swung at the first pitch every time. And she did this time too.

"Strike one," Fr. Michael yelled.

Belinda yelled at her, "Hit it over the fence, over the fence."

Hell still spoke with a German accent. So she said ja for yes most of the time. "Ja, ja, l am doing that, you see."

Sr. Sarah threw a good one, a fast one, right in there and Hell went for it, an easy pop fly right straight to Rosie, who caught it easy.

Gracie yelled, "Two down, one to go. Hurrah Saints!"

"Way to go, Rosie, great catch," I chimed in. "One more, Sister, just one more, strike her out."

Nettie Bettie came up next. Nettie Bethune was her name, but everybody called her Nettie Bettie. Nettie played a tight third base. She was a little roly-poly and didn't always move very fast. But she knew how to protect third.

Sr. Sarah did a windmill pitch and she swung. "Strike one!" The next pitch, an easy underhand, floated over home plate. I could tell Sr. Sarah wanted to let them hit. More fun for me. Nettie Bettie hit a hard grounder down the third base line. Lottie went for it and threw hard as she could to first. It went over my head and Nettie made it to first. Thelma ran in from right field and scooped up the ball, but Nettie kept running and made it to second standing up.

Lottie yelled over to me, "Sorry about that, June Ellen. We'll get the next one."

"Heads up," Gracie shouted. "Two outs, just one more."

Belinda was up next and she was their power hitter. I yelled, "Come on, Sister Sarah, strike her out. You can do it."

Mags chimed in, "Batter, batter, she can't hit. Easy out, easy out."

Sr. Sarah did her wind up and threw right to her. Belinda never swung on the first pitch and let it go. Next, Sr. Sarah did a fast underhand that Belinda caught on the tip of the bat sending a line drive straight to me. I caught it easy and we all started jumping up and down, screaming and yelling, "Three outs!"

Sr. Sarah spoke up, "Okay, girls, calm down. This game's not over yet.

Here's the batting order: Gracie, Lottie, Me, June Ellen, Louise, Rosie, Margaret Mary, Thelma, and Hazel. Batter up."

Gracie grabbed a bat and stepped up to home plate. She tapped home plate twice for good luck. It was really nerves; I knew, 'cause we all did it. Genie, short for Imogene, caught for the Martyrs. "Easy out, easy out," she yelled. "Heads up. Three up, three down. Let's go." Those were fighting words to Gracie. Gracie's pretty sweet compared to me, but softball did something to you. I could tell she was ready to kill that ball, too ready. She hit an easy pop fly to right.

"Ah shucks. Sorry, June Ellen."

Lottie, our third baseman, was up next. Lottie knew how to hit. She wasn't our fastest runner, so she had to hit it hard.

Genie started her chatter again, "Eeeeasy out."

Lottie ignored her. She had four brothers. She was used to it and had lots of practice ignoring loudmouths. Lottie raised the bat up to shoulder level and leaned way back. She planned on laying into it, I could tell. Sr. Annunciata peered at Lottie, scrutinizing her.

Fr. Michael coached her while she pitched. He won't call balls or strikes because she'd walk us all the time. This put the odds in her favor, since sometimes we got so tired of standing there waiting for a good pitch, we swung at anything. She got a lot of strikeouts that way.

Sr. Annunciata tossed one inside and just about hit Lottie, who jumped out of the way. "Oh, Lottie, I'm sorry. I don't want to hit you. Let me try that again."

Sr. Annunciata wound up again and this time she focused on Genie's mitt and sure enough it went over the plate and Lottie slugged that ball out of the park. At St. Joseph's that meant over the fence. We all cheered and clapped her on the back as she crossed home plate. Sr. Annunciata beamed at Lottie. She loved it when someone hit a home run off of one of her pitches. She considered that a good pitch.

Sr. Sarah batted next. "Okay, Sister, just get it over, so I can hit it. Just try for the plate this time."

"Sister, you think I can't throw a strike at you. I'll show you," Sr. Annunciata yelled back. They liked to tease each other. They both laughed. Sr. Annunciata threw a few balls wide and outside, high, low, and then she got one square over home plate. Sr. Sarah didn't waste it and hit a line drive between Nettie and Madeleine. Sister Sarah picked up her skirts and ran to first, all that black fabric billowed out like a balloon. I just loved to watch Sr. Sarah run. Helga raced for it and held Sr. Sarah at first.

I was up next. I stepped up to the plate and swung the bat a few times, stepped out of the batter's box and stretched. This was to confuse things a little bit. But really you don't want to confuse Sr. Annunciata.

"Come on, June Ellen. Don't be scared. Step up," Sr. Annunciata told me. I was horrified at the thought.

Genie and Belinda and a few others started screaming, "Scaredy cat, scaredy cat. June Ellen's a scaredy cat."

I was mad now and stepped back up to home plate. I gave Belinda my hard-eyed look and she laughed. Louise came over. "June Ellen, just concentrate on the ball. You can do it. Show them how scared you are."

"I'll show them alright."

Sr. Annunciata tried her windmill pitch on me. It was way outside, and I let it go. "Do it again, Sister. Only this time aim for the mitt," Fr. Michael coached. She did her own version of the windmill pitch and aimed one straight at home plate. It almost made it but dropped before it got there. "You're getting good now, Sister. Keep them coming."

Who was Fr. Michael kidding?

"Stay focused," Sr. Sarah yelled at me. I stepped back, took a few practice swings, and held my bat high. She sent me a pretty good ball underhanded. I stepped into it and slugged it with everything I had. The bat connected. The ball hit the ground and headed straight down the third base line and jumped foul when it hit a rock, which saved me from an out.

"Foul ball, strike one. Keep up the good work, Sister."

This time Sr. Annunciata stared hard at me. I saw that look in her eyes. Sure enough, she did a true windmill pitch and sent it straight down the line. I lay into that ball and watched it sail over the shortstop's head. I took off running and watched Beaver run for it. I reached first just as she reached out and brushed the ball with the tip of her glove driving it to the ground but Beaver was fast. She snapped up that ball and threw it hard to Lucy, holding Sr. Sarah on second and me on first.

Louise was up next. Sr. Annunciata was on a roll and threw the first pitch right over the plate, and Louise hit a fly ball to center field. Helga took her eye off the ball just as it reached her glove to watch Sr. Sarah running for third and the ball popped right out of her glove. Louise was safe on first, and Helga and her fast arm held me on second and Sr. Sarah on third.

Rosie, our clean-up hitter, was up next. Sr. Annunciata was no fool. She liked for us to hit, but she still wanted her sixth graders to win. She did her wind up, threw a low ball, and Rosie let it go. Belinda yelled now, "Go for the double play, touch any base."

"Hit it out of here, Rosie! You got what it takes!"

Sr. Annunciata threw high and outside. Fr. Michael gave her one of his pep talks.

Sr. Annunciata winds up again and got one over the plate, a little high but Rosie went for it. A grounder bounced right to Lucy. All she had to do was step on second and throw to first, which she did perfectly. Double play, they did it.

Both teams were getting good hits and solid plays in the field. It was the top of the sixth and the Saints led by one point, six to five. We just had to hold the Martyrs. It was their last bat.

In girls' softball we only played six innings. I didn't like it; I wanted to play nine like the boys. I watched Sister Annunciata on the bench as she wiped the sweat off her forehead with the white-as-snow handkerchief she kept tucked somewhere in the folds of her robes. She looked pretty hot and tired, so it was probably good this was the last inning. Tempers flared on and off the field. This was the last up at bats for the Martyrs.

"Last chance to score. Let's take it all the way to Haney's!" Belinda yelled.

Sr. Sarah stood on the pitcher's mound with that hungry look in her eyes. She wanted to win. You could stay holy only so long in a softball game. Sr. Sarah was in this for the win. I knew she prayed the Rosary every evening and went to mass every morning so she had plenty of time to get saved and holy again. She could afford to go out for blood, and she looked determined. Me, I figured I needed to run around and get a few sins to make going to church worth it.

Little Lucy Fry, their second baseman, was up first. "C'mon, Lucy, just get on base, just get on," her bench chanted.

Lucy was not a power hitter. She was known for infield pop flies or little grounders. "Not a chance," I yelled back at their bench. I got a look from Belinda. "Easy out, Sister, easy out."

Sr. Sarah was getting ready to pitch the ball and she did her windup and tossed a little pitch over the plate. I swore a little kid could hit that ball, and little Lucy did. An easy pop fly that Gracie caught easy.

I realized how smart Sr. Sarah was. Better to let her hit that pop fly and get it over with. Beaver was up next and she was a hard hitter. The bench started a different chant now, "Knock one out of the park, just knock it out."

"Slam it down their throats," Helga barked. No one was being nice now and the nuns didn't care. This was it.

Sr. Sarah did a windmill and threw a fast one low and inside. "Ball one," Fr. Michael yelled.

This was a real game now. No pretending. Mags tossed the ball back to Sr. Sarah. "It's okay, Sister, just get it in there. She can't hit."

Well, Beaver backed off home plate and gave her a look. "You're dead meat now, Mags." She stepped back up and gave her bat a few swings and looked at Sr. Sarah like she was the devil and not a holy nun.

Sr. Sarah gritted her teeth now, and I was praying. She threw a pitch. It arced and slid right over home plate. Beaver smiled before she blasted it into the outfield between second and shortstop. Hazel and Rosie both ran their legs off trying to reach it. They got the ball to Louise on second base and Beaver ran back to first.

Helga was up next then Nettie followed by Belinda, their clean-up hitter. They've lined up their power hitters. Sister Sarah wiped her brow. Everybody was chattering. "Easy out, easy out. Take your time, Sister, take your time."

"Knock it out of here, Helga, slam it!" Belinda yelled from the sidelines, "Hit her in, tie run on first, it's your ball, Helga, your ball."

This was my kind of softball. I was ready to make a double play. "Double play, let's make this a double, Saints. Everybody heads up," I yelled. Louise, Lottie, Gracie, they all looked at me and nodded their heads. They were ready.

Sister Sarah threw a couple of easy balls, Helga just watched go by. She was trying to flummox her, I knew. Fr. Michael called one a ball and another one a strike. Sister Sarah was playing with her too. She threw one so inside Hell had to back up. Fr. Michael was still calling balls, but no way would he let her walk. The next one was going to be a good one, I could tell, and sure enough Sr. Sarah threw the perfect pitch and Hell hit a hard line drive that tipped off of Louise's glove. Gracie was there to back her up but had to chase the ball behind second base. She threw the ball to Louise, but Beaver beat the ball to second base. Hell was safe on first.

"One out. Double play, touch any base," I yelled. "Heads up, everybody."

I got the nod again from around the field. They were ready. This was the part I loved. The excitement, everything was on the line. This was playing real ball.

Nettie was up next. Sr. Sarah did her windup and threw the ball straight across the plate. Nettie swung. "Strike one!" Sr. Sarah wasted no time and windmilled in another one, dead center across the plate. Nettie went for it but was too slow. "Strike two," Fr. Michael yells. Sr. Sarah did a fast underhand and Nettie grabbed it with her bat and hit a fly ball to left field. Hazel caught it and held the runners.

"Two outs, let's go, Saints. One more and we win."

Belinda strutted up to the plate like a wild turkey. She swung the bat a few times, stepped back, wiped her palms on her jeans, then headed back into the batter's box. She gripped the bat and got in her power stance. She had that look in her eye, that home run look, and I prayed.

Sr. Sarah threw an easy underhand outside trying to lure her in. Belinda watched it.

Fr. Michael yells, "Ball one."

Sr. Sarah tried a fast windup and got it there across the plate. Belinda caught it with the tip of her bat and sent it back behind the catcher. Mags wasn't able to get to it.

"This is it, this is the one," her bench yelled. Sr. Sarah knew it too, we all did. She tried a windmill windup like I'd never seen and Belinda jumped out at it, grabbed it, and whammed it out of here, over the fence. Home run. Beaver and Hell ran the bases cheering. Belinda was right behind them with her arms held high. She looked like a goal post. The score was 8 to 6. Martyrs jumped ahead by two.

Sr. Annunciata batted next. It was only fair that she got to bat if we let Sr. Sarah. The Martyrs didn't like it. We did allow a substitute runner because Sr. Annunciata won't run. Belinda, her substitute runner, was not winded at all.

Sr. Sarah wanted Sr. Annunciata to hit the ball. "Look out—Killer's up," she yelled laughing.

Sr. Annunciata yelled back. "You got that right and I'll kill this one."

Sr. Sarah threw a nice and easy underhand. Sr. Annunciata swung and missed.

"Come on now, Sister," Fr. Michael coached. "Keep your eye on the ball."

Sr. Sarah threw another easy one and Sr. Annunciata connected, and it was a slow rolling grounder to third base. Lottie ran to catch it and made the throw, straight to first. I caught it easy, thwack, as it hit my glove. I love that sound. Belinda was fast but not fast enough and Fr. Michael called her out. I saw Daddy and Mama stand up and cheer on the sidelines. I waved as I ran in. All the Saints were cheering now. Three outs, and we were up for our last bat.

The score at the bottom of the sixth inning: Martyrs 8, Saints 6.

It was our last chance to score. We were at the top of our batting order. Gracie was up first.

"Play ball," Fr. Michael shouted. He was even acting like a real umpire. That was how important this game was.

Gracie choked up on the bat and swung it around. Sr. Annunciata did a slow windup. She didn't look so tired now. She let the ball go early and it dropped low.

"Ball one. Pick it up, Sister, pick it up."

Oh, bother, he was coaching her again. "Slam it, Gracie! Slam it out of here." I didn't say down her throat like the other team, though it did cross my mind.

Sr. Annunciata tried again and the pitch wobbled across the plate. Gracie swung, connected, and took off like a shot. She was fast when she wanted to be. The ball bounced behind Lucy on second and Hell ran up from center field and got it to second base, but Gracie beat the ball and was safe on second.

Lottie stepped up to the plate next. Sr. Annunciata threw the first ball right across the plate, and Lottie always swung at the first ball and she did. A loud crack was heard as the ball flew out to left field, and Hazel caught it for an easy out. Gracie was held at second.

Sr. Sarah strode up to the plate next. "You can do it; slam one over the fence," we all yelled at her. Sr. Sarah picked up the bat and took a few swings. The pitch came in high, but she went for it.

"Foul ball, strike one."

"It's okay, Sister. The next one's yours. Hit it out of here," we kept our chatter going.

Genie was slow to start any chatter with Sr. Sarah batting, but there was a lot on the line. "Batter can't hit, batter can't hit. Strike her out."

Sr. Annunciata threw again, over the plate this time. Sr. Sarah stepped up to it and hit it out to left field. It bounced and rolled into Hell's glove. Gracie ran like the dickens, got around third and headed for home. Hell did one of her mighty throws to home plate. Gracie dove for the plate, stretched her fingers, and caught the corner.

"Safe!" Fr. Michael yelled right as the ball hit Genie's glove with a loud thwack.

Gracie scored and Sr. Sarah was safe on first. Score 8 to 7.

I was next and I was determined to get on base. Sr. Annunciata was throwing a lot of balls to me and I just stood there.

"Come on, June Ellen, hit Sr. Sarah in. You can do it." The bench was behind me all the way.

Sr. Annunciata could wear you out. She threw one low and inside. I swung and missed.

"Strike one."

Sr. Annunciata pitched the next one high and it dropped low in front of the plate. Like a fool I reached for it and fouled behind first.

"Strike two." Fr. Michael was happy now. Sr. Annunciata was getting some strikes. "Keep it up, Sister," he yelled. "You're on it now."

An umpire was supposed to be fair to both sides, but you couldn't hardly blame Fr. Michael. Genie was behind home plate really chattering at me now. "Batter, batter swing batter. One more strike, scaredy cat and you're out of here. Batter, batter."

That was all I needed to hear, and I stepped up to the plate. Sr. Annunciata did her windup, let go, and it came sailing inside. I tipped the ball foul over Fr. Michael's head. He ducked and no way could Genie get behind him and catch it.

"Watch it, June Ellen, don't kill your umpire, foul ball."

"Sorry, Fr. Michael." I stepped back and choked up on the bat, then stepped back into the batter's box. "This is it," I told myself. Sr. Annunciata did one of her funny windups, swinging her arm around and around till I was practically dizzy. You never knew when she was going to let the ball go. Finally she did, a long slow ball that dropped right in front of home plate, but I went for it with everything I had and I blasted it hard right over Nettie's head. It hit the dirt right in front of Helga. Sr. Sarah rounded third base and I was on my way to second. Helga and her arm sent the ball to Genie at home plate, which sent Sr. Sarah running back to third and I made it to second easy. The score stood Martyrs 8, Saints 7.

Louise could be a good hitter and she batted next. "Just get us home, Louise, just get us home," I yelled.

Sr. Annunciata threw a few balls, stopped, took out her handkerchief, and wiped her brow. "Now, Louise," she said, "I am going to throw you a good pitch, right over the plate and you need to hit it. We need to get this game done."

And Sr. Annunciata did and Louise hit a pop fly over Lucy's head. Sr. Sarah had a big lead and made it home standing up, which was good because she never slid, though I would like to see that. Hell grabbed the ball on the ground and with her mighty arm threw Louise out at first and I was stuck on second. Two outs and the score was tied. Winning run was on base.

Rosie grabbed the bat and hunkered down over home plate. "This is it, Saints, get ready to roll," she yelled.

We were all sweating now. Sr. Annunciata threw a lazy one. Rosie let it go and Genie dropped it in the dirt. I had a big lead and made it to third.

Belinda yelled from outfield, "Hold on, Martyrs. Heads up. We got this. Easy out."

Rosie took some practice swings and hugged the plate. She always did this when she was nervous. "Hit it, Rosie, just hit us in," I yelled. Everybody on both teams was hollering for their side. We all wanted to win more than anything.

Fr. Michael wiped his brow and said, "Now, Rosie, back off the plate a little bit. We don't want Sr. Annunciata to hit you. Let's just all settle down and have some fun here. Okay, Sister, play ball."

Sr. Annunciata didn't even do a windup; she just flung that ball underhanded, up and almost over the plate. Rosie was pretty nervous and she grabbed for it sending a grounder right between second and third. Belinda snatched it up and held me at third. Rosie made it to first.

Two outs, bases loaded. This was it. Our best hitter was up. Mags and her milking arms could win this one for us.

The Martyrs were pumped. "Two outs, one more and we win," they yelled at each other.

Mags walked slowly up to home plate with a big grin on her face. When the ball left Sr. Annunciata's hand, we all took a big lead, getting ready to steal if we could. Genie raised her hand and backed me down on third, Rosie made it to second.

Sr. Annunciata leaned in to throw, stopped, straightened up, and said to Mags, "Margaret Mary, I want you to hit a good clean ball and end this game."

The Martyrs were furious. They wanted to spit fire.

Belinda yelled back at Mags, "Go ahead, hit it. We're ready to end it with you. You don't stand a chance, Saints."

Sr. Annunciata threw the pitch, slow and easy but so outside, Mags couldn't even pretend to go for it. Fr. Michael said, "Now, Sister, if you want to end the game, you have to get the ball over the plate. Take your time."

Sr. Annunciata did her by now famous "I mean business" windup. Mags stepped in and the ball crossed the plate. Mags slammed it over the heads of all the outfielders and we all took off.

"Run, June Ellen, run for home," Gracie yelled.

I ran as fast as I could and crossed home plate, the winning run.

Rosie rounded third and headed for home. Hazel threw fast and hard. Rosie slid and stuck her foot out willing her toe to touch home plate. But Genie caught the ball and Rosie slid right into her mitt with the ball in it. It didn't even matter 'cause we still won.

"Out," yelled Fr. Michael. "Saints win, 9 to 8. Game over."

"Super hit, Mags. You did it. You did it. You hit the winning run in. We beat the Martyrs. We beat the sixth graders." We were all yelling now, hugging and clapping each other on the back. I looked over at the sidelines, our classmates were cheering and yelling, even the boys were jumping up and down. Even Daddy got up out of his chair and hugged Mama.

Mama looked the proudest of all, hanging on to Daddy and squeezing the life out of him, as she yelled over and over, "We won, we won. We did it, June Ellen." Then she grabbed Gracie's mom and hugged and bounced her. It was great seeing Mama so excited.

Mags grabbed Lottie and Rosie, yelling at Gracie and me, "Saints are the best! We're the best!"

Sr. Sarah laughed and shouted with us, "Great job, girls. You played a great game. Hurrah for the Saints."

Then Thelma started the chant, "Hurrah for the Saints, hurrah for the Saints." Louise and Hazel joined in and soon we were all shouting.

"Okay, girls, that's enough, time to thank the other team. What a great game they played," Sr. Sarah reminded us.

Sr. Annunciata ran up to Mags, "That was a great hit. I knew you could do it." Sr. Annunciata felt like she won the game because she pitched the winning hit. Belinda looked like she wanted to kill the Saints and make them martyrs. She walked up to me, spitting fire. "You only won because Sr. Annunciata let you. She didn't want to pitch any more so she threw a pitch that anyone could hit out of here. You didn't win it, June Ellen, and everybody knows that."

Part of what she said rang true. Sr. Annunciata couldn't play like Sr. Sarah. But we did win fair and square. "You're just a sore loser, Belinda. We played the best and we won. Mags hit that ball, fair and square. Sr. Sarah pitched so you could hit too. It's what nuns do. They have to."

Gracie ran up just then and grabbed me. "Let's go, June Ellen. Those ice-cream sodas are waiting. Belinda's just a sore loser. Don't pay her no mind."

By the time we got to Haney's, I'd forgotten all about Belinda. We

were all screaming and laughing and hugging. We were just plain happy.
Sr. Sarah came with us and she had a chocolate soda just like us. It was a
grand day and I still had a dime in my pocket.

[15]

Halloween Pirates

THE DAY BEFORE HALLOWEEN, Gracie and I sat on the porch swing figuring out our Halloween costumes. The crisp air heightened the electric current of the autumn blue sky and made my skin tingle. The bareness of the trees, the light and shadow of late afternoon made all possibility of haints, ghosts, and witches true. School seemed pretty dull and slow ever since we beat the sixth graders at softball. But now everything around me had a glow to it and I could feel a buzz in the air.

Gracie said, "Ghosts are easy. All we need is a sheet with holes for the eyes and for our noses to breathe."

"I was a ghost last year and the year before. A ghost is too simple. They're for little kids. I'm looking to be something different this year, Gracie."

I didn't want to tell Gracie I felt a need to stay away from ghosts and spooks this year. Something creepy was crawling around my skin when I thought about it. Grown men dressed like ghosts haunted me. I saw them with Daddy at his union meeting where the United Mine Workers were trying to help the miners get their benefits. The white-sheeted guys had their own hall, the KKK hall on their own street, the Ku Klux Klan Street. It was a big white building with a big lighted cross on the front.

"Is that a church, Daddy?"

"That's no church, June Ellen. There are some men in there, good men most of the time, neighbors, people we know. But when they meet in there, they get nasty and decide who they like and don't like. Turns out they were against more than what they had said at first, including us Catholics. They wanted to come help the miners, but there was a big price we all had to pay and I wasn't gonna do it. They have a different view of life than most of us, June Ellen."

"How come they dress up like ghosts, Daddy?"

78

"They wear sheets over their head because they're scared, scared to let people see who they are. Something happens to men when they hide behind sheets or masks, they do bad things to people, even little children. Things they wouldn't do, if you knew who they were. I saw it in the war. Men can turn just plum evil."

"Do they scare you, Daddy?"

"No, I know who they are, most of them, anyway, so they let me be. Don't you worry about them ghosts, June Ellen. And don't you go spying on them, either. You leave them be. There's plenty of us watching them, Sheriff Tobe Riley, too."

Ever since then, I was being careful not to call in any ghosts.

"Hey, Gracie, let's be pirates. We can wear a patch over one eye."

"I never heard of a girl pirate, June Ellen."

"Then we'll be the first. Maurice is a boy and he dressed up like a witch last year and won the contest at the Bunny Inn. He got to eat there for free, anything he wanted. It's Halloween and you wear costumes to fool people and scare them. I'm going to be a pirate. It'll be a new adventure."

"I need a new adventure too, I guess. Nothing exciting has happened to me since my chickens got a blue ribbon. I'm tired of being an old ghost anyway."

"You're right, Gracie. First, we need some old blue jeans or overalls we can cut off and shred the bottom to look raggedy. Remember the pirates in the Peter Pan picture book in the school library?"

"My jeans are new and my mother won't let me cut them off, and anyway I don't want to."

"No, silly, we need old pairs of our dads or brothers that no one wants to wear anymore. For hats, I'll ask Uncle Albert. He keeps all his old hats in the barn 'cause Aunt Annie would throw them away. I bet he'll let us have two and we'll pin them up to look like pirate hats, and I bet Mama will let us have some of her quilting scraps to tie around them. And we need long sashes for our waists."

"I can get some red material for the sashes. Mama has long strips she cut off some curtains to make them fit the kitchen windows."

"Yes, and now we need to figure out a shirt to wear. My daddy doesn't have any old shirts he doesn't wear."

"I'll ask my daddy, June Ellen. He knows the rag man and maybe he has something."

"Great idea. Ho, ho, ho and a bottle of rum. Where can we get an

empty whiskey bottle? We can fill it with root beer and drink it like rum.
I'll ask Uncle Albert. We may have to hide it in our pants, just like pirates.
We can sell slugs to the boys."

"Yuck, June Ellen. I'm not drinking after any boy."

"Ho, ho, ho and a bottle of rum."

Just then Gracie's dad drove up and honked. "Hello, Mr. Bagley."

"Hello there, young ladies. Did you get your costumes figured out?"

"Oh, Daddy, we're going to be pirates, just like in Peter Pan. I need
some old pants and we both need an old shirt. Do you think the rag man
will help us?"

"Let's get home before your mother skins us both and see what we
can do."

I ran in the house to the kitchen where Mama was frying potatoes
and ham, and Daddy was sitting at the table breathing good while he
drank a cup of coffee.

"Mama, I need some old pants I can cut off and shred to look like
pirate's pants. Gracie and I are going to be pirates for Halloween."

"Where do you think you can find old pants around here someone
isn't wearing?"

Daddy said, "I've got just the pair for you, June Ellen. I found them
lying in the changing room at the mine. I hung them up, but it's been
a month and nobody's claimed them. When you see them, you'll know
why."

"Thanks, Daddy. I also need two of Uncle Albert's old hats for me and
Gracie."

Daddy laughed, but that started his coughing. Mama and I waited.
We were used to it, but Mama still frowned watching him. I just prayed it
didn't get any worse. Dr. John said that the coal dust won't ever leave your
lungs for good.

"He doesn't like to part with his hats, but I'll see what I can bring
home tomorrow."

"And, Mama, can we have some quilt scraps to decorate our hats like
a pirate and some black to make an eye patch? Gracie's bringing some red
material for our sashes and her dad is finding us a shirt."

"I'll look through my sewing basket and see what I can find."

I knew better than to mention the rag man. Mama would never let
me wear a shirt from the dump. I didn't care though. I liked the rag man,
and I thought he had neat stuff. I wouldn't mind being a rag man at all. It
was like always being on a treasure hunt.

That next day after school we gathered all our stuff. Uncle Albert gave me a whiskey bottle right out of his trunk and a root beer to fill it with.

Mama got out her sewing basket and pinned our hats and added a shiny gold hatband that hung over the side.

"Mama, they look just like real pirate hats." I ran and gave her a big hug.

Mama laughed and said, "I think you two are going to make good-looking pirates."

I pulled on my coal-mining pants—they were still coated with coal dust, which flew everywhere. Mama made me take them outside and shake them real good. They were big and long and ballooned out like clown pants till Mama cut them off below the knees. She did the same to Gracie's. Then Gracie and I cut and shredded the bottoms.

"Now put them on, girls, and we'll see what we can do." We put them on and we both had to hold them up or they'd fall to the floor. Mama started laughing but she was smart and went and got some rope and cut off two pieces she measured around our waists. Then she put the rope through the belt loops and tied them like a shoestring.

"Don't get them in a knot. You'll wet your pants," she said.

We laughed. We were so happy, and Mama was happy.

"Here's our sashes, Mrs. Thackeray," Gracie said. "Mama cut these off some curtains so they'd fit the kitchen windows."

"Why, that's some fine material, Gracie. What beautiful curtains your mother must have."

"Here's your shirt, June Ellen. My daddy found us each one."

I grabbed the shirt and pulled it over my head. It was big and blousy, but I tucked it in. Mama laughed at us. Then she tied the bright red sashes around our waists and let the ends hang down to our knees.

"You girls look like real pirates. Behave yourselves and stay around the square where Gracie's dad can keep his eye on you. Your daddy'll pick you up after his meeting."

Gracie told me, "June Ellen, you look like a real pirate. I can hardly recognize you."

"You too, Gracie. Now we need our eye patches and some makeup to look really scary."

Mama took up her scissors and cut two round circles out of an old black sock. "Here you go. I'm about worn out. Go get some string, make a hole with my darning needle, and tie a knot then tie it around your head. You're all set. Now I need to get some supper for your daddy."

"Gosh, Mama, I sure wish I had a hook for a hand, then I could be Captain Hook."

"You're enough of a pirate. You don't need a hook."

"Yes, Mama. I don't know where I'd find one anyway."

We fixed our eye patches like Mama said. When we put them on, I felt like a real pirate.

"Let's ask April Leigh to do our eyebrows with her eyebrow pencil."

April Leigh stared into the mirror on our dresser in the bedroom; she colored her lips in bright orange lipstick. She made herself up for a Halloween party at the high school and for Isaac, even though she wasn't supposed to have a boyfriend. Since it was Halloween, Mama figured all that makeup was her costume and let her put on as much as she wanted.

"What do you brats want?"

"April Leigh, we're pirates and we need to look mean and scary. We want dark eyebrows."

April Leigh laughed as she scratched dark bushy eyebrows over our eyes. Then she drew a mustache on each of us with sideburns. Gracie and I both looked in the mirror and could hardly believe our eyes.

"We look like real pirates, June Ellen!"

"We look better than real pirates. These are the best costumes I've ever seen. Wait till the other kids see us."

[16]

Trick-or-Treat

THAT HALLOWEEN NIGHT we walked to the square, which was all lit up with jack-o'-lanterns. Some with big evil grins and pointy teeth that shot out orange light from the candles inside, and some with big smiles all happy and warm. Gracie squealed every time some boy ran by and yelled boo. I could tell who all the haints were, the same old sheet ghosts, and hobos in their own clothes with a handkerchief on a stick, and witches in their granny's dresses. It took a lot to scare me.

No one guessed who these pirates were for a long time. We looked like real pirates. Everybody said so. Even Maynard, Gracie's brother, said, "Cool, June Ellen."

Sr. Annunciata took over the soda fountain at Haney's Rexall Drug and handed out apples. She watched to see if we behaved, I'm sure. "Oh, June Ellen, don't you look cute."

I wanted to act like a pirate and steal all her apples; make her walk the gangplank, but instead I just said, "Thank you." I didn't want to look cute, so I waited in the dark and leapt out at little Lucy Fry and Genie from the sixth-grade team. They screamed and jumped. I felt better.

In front of the courthouse, Tobe Riley hollowed out a huge pumpkin—a county fair blue-ribbon pumpkin—and filled it with candy corn. I scooped up two handfuls and put it in my pillowcase. "This'll come in real handy later in the week," I told Gracie. She did the same as me.

A whole bunch of kids from St. Joseph's ran by and Jimmy yelled at me, "Come on, you pirates. We're going to Hospital Hill where all the good stuff is."

We passed the Green Frog Cafe and Bar just then and saw Gracie's dad, Mr. Bagley, sitting there with a beer talking it up.

"June Ellen, we're not supposed to leave the square. We can't go to Hospital Hill."

"We're pirates, Gracie. We gotta act like it. We can't go around like the little kids too scared to leave our daddy on the square. Hospital Hill is right there. We'll just hit a few houses, scare those old widow women who live up there, and fill our pillowcases with some pirate booty." One thing I'll say about Gracie. She listened to me and quite often heard the wisdom in my words.

"Okay, but let's hurry and you swear on Mrs. Katzwaller's grave that we'll go to just a few houses, and then come back to the square. If you lie, June Ellen, Mrs. Katzwaller will rise up out of her grave and haunt you. I know she does 'cause I seen her do it to Maynard once when he lied to Mama about the gum in his pocket."

"Okay, I swear on her grave." She didn't scare me anyway, but I didn't tell Gracie that. I liked to cover all my bases.

We took off chasing after Jimmy and our school gang. Gracie and I stood out as the only girls, but we made up for it with our great costumes. I made sure we acted like pirates, and pirates always went after the best bounty. Dr. John lived at the first house we came to, and a big scarecrow hung from his front porch rafters with a jack-o'-lantern head with a real candle inside. Nobody had ever seen anything like that.

"Wow, that's downright spooky," I said.

"You scared, June Ellen, of a scarecrow? What kind of pirate are you?" Haney, Jr., squealed at me.

"Nah, I ain't scared one bit, but I know a good haint when I see one. I was just admiring him."

Everybody laughed, but I could tell they agreed with me. Just then Mrs. John opened the door with a big bowl of popcorn balls, all different colors. "Trick or treat," we all yelled and she handed them all around. I got a big red ball, and carefully stowed it in my pillowcase or my booty bag, as I liked to call it.

"Imagine, Gracie, April Leigh gave all this up to go dance with boys. I bet you, we never do that. I'll have to hide all my treats from her except my candy corn; that'll keep her quiet."

We yelled, "Thank you," then ran on up the hill. A big two-story house stood on the crest of Hospital Hill with porches everywhere you looked, all screened in. I dreamed about this house when I wished Daddy made more money at the mine. It'd hold everybody. It belonged to Mr. Blackstone, the bank man that Daddy always went to talk to. The house sat there quiet with one jack-o'-lantern all lit up under the tree on some hay bales and cornstalks.

We knocked and knocked yelling, "Trick or treat," but no one came. Jimmy shouted, "Let's go, nobody's home." And then a blood-curdling scream came from behind us. We all just about wet our britches and screamed as we turned around and a real live ghost flew out of the tree with a noose around its neck. Gracie took off running and so did the Haney boys, but I grabbed Gracie and let the Haney boys just keep on running.

The ghost kept flying up and down and eerie sounds floated down from the tree.

Then the porch light came on and some of us screamed again, but I didn't. I saw Mr. Blackstone up there and knew it was one of the best tricks ever played on me. Then his son Robert stuck his head out of the tree and he grinned big, almost as big as the jack-o'-lantern.

"I sure scared you, didn't I?"

Robert was in high school and I wondered why he wasn't at the dance. Then Mrs. Blackstone came to the porch laughing and handed out regular-size Baby Ruth candy bars to each of us.

"This is so worth it, Gracie. One more."

"Okay, just one more then we go back to the square."

Only a few of us held out for more. Others turned back to the square. They had their booty and they'd been plenty scared. Jimmy and his gang took off through the vacant lot headed over the top of Hospital Hill by the old Sullivan house. But I had to admit, traipsing through that black empty lot then going into the dusky woods with those cedar trees hanging all the way down to the ground didn't really suit me and I knew I'd never get Gracie up there.

"Okay, let's go across the street to the boardinghouse. They have a jack-o'-lantern all lit up and a lantern in the window."

Gracie looked. I could feel her start to hesitate, so I quickly grabbed our whiskey bottle, took a drink, then handed it to her. "This'll fortify us till we get to the square."

We ran across the street then stopped on the sidewalk. The jack-o'-lantern was eerie. Evil-looking eyebrows snaked their way across the top, squinty eyes shot light right into mine. I almost turned around back to the square, down the hill about two blocks away, but I was a pirate and pirates weren't scared of pumpkins.

"I'm going to find my daddy," Gracie whispered. "I'm not going up on that porch."

"Okay," I said, "take off. You'll have to go by yourself and look how dark that street is. Go on, if you're going. I'm going to act like a pirate and steal me some booty." Well, Gracie dared not take off by herself and I knew it.

The sidewalk presented its own haint, full of cracks all tore up from tree roots, that buckled up, then reached out, grabbed me, and tripped me going up to the door. I caught myself, didn't look back, and just kept on going. I grabbed hold of Gracie's hand and she just about squeezed the life out of mine, but I knew not to let go.

I knocked on the door, a big wooden door, all scarred up, hatchet marks, I thought, but didn't say that to Gracie. Big old-fashioned iron hinges held it on, and there was a tiny window on top with a black faded curtain hanging across it, ragged and torn. No one came. I knocked again and I heard this shuffling noise. The door creaked open and the oldest man I'd ever seen stood there.

He looked like a little gnome or elf from my fairy-tale book, which I still looked at for the pictures. He only had two teeth that I could see, stained with tobacco juice, some of it dripping into his white scanty beard. I kind of wished I'd listened to Gracie, but quick got a hold of myself and blurted out, "Trick or treat."

"Well, now what have we here, two old pirates, come to haunt me."

"Trick or treat," I yelled again.

"What's your tricks then, you old pirate? I have to see your trick afore I can treat you."

I didn't know what to do, so I started singing, "Ho, ho, ho and a bottle of rum." I pulled out the whiskey bottle and said in my best pirate voice, "You want some rum, Mister, from a real pirate's stash?"

Well, that got him, and he grinned and said, "That's a pretty good trick there. Looks like we got us some girl pirates. You pirates want to see what a real pirate looks like?"

Gracie was still stuck to me like melted rubber. I had no blood left in my hand, which she was strangling with her own, which did kind of hamper my pirate ways. Gracie squealed like a kitten. I pinched her real good and she finally let go of my hand and just stood there. I was glad she didn't run off. I whispered, "Act like a pirate, he's just a little old man."

I could hear Gracie breathing better and knew she was okay. "Sure, we want to see a real pirate."

The candle in the jack-o'-lantern went out about that time. Gracie screamed for real. I grabbed her and shook her. The little gnome flicked a light on, which made it hard to see inside. Just then I heard a thunk, thunk, thunk coming down the stairs. I got a chill down my spine and my knees shook. I tried hard to hold everything still.

I hung back, quiet and waiting. Another thunk, then heavy breathing and a loud gasp. I wanted to run but I looked at Gracie. She was white as a real ghost, and she scared even me with her pale skin and the dark eyebrows and mustache that April Leigh drew on. I wanted to say something, but nothing came out. Instead, I heard a deep, gruff voice.

"Okay, you pirates, just step into my parlor and meet my pirate."

Gracie found her voice and saved us both. "We're not allowed to enter any house or home or we'll have to walk the plank when we get home, and Mama will take all my candy." Gracie surprised me sometimes.

"Yes, sir," I chimed in. "We're not supposed to go into anybody's house. It's the biggest rule of Halloween and can't under any circumstances be broken. We'll have to see your pirate on the porch. And don't you have a treat for us?"

"My pirate is your treat maybe."

He stepped aside and I glanced up the stairs and all I saw was a real peg-leg thumping down the stairs. It looked just like a chair rung only it came out of the pirate's pant leg. I looked up and up and up. He was a tall one-legged pirate and what I saw next was a real black leather patch over one eye. I was too impressed by that great-looking patch to be scared. Then I saw the jagged scar over his other one. I took a step back. Gracie gasped, grabbed my hand again, and cut off the blood.

"Let's go, June Ellen."

"No, I want my treat. We've come this far."

The old gnome laughed out loud, more tobacco juice spilling out. "That's old Cyril, he ain't even in costume. He won't hurt you'uns none. He only got one leg left and one eye. I just bring him out for Halloween. Ain't that what you want, a good ole-timey scare?"

I was always curious and couldn't help myself. "What happened to him?"

"Well, what do you think? He ran into old Captain Hook and first the hook grabbed his eyeball and plucked it right out, next he pulled his sword out his scabbard and chopped his leg. Well, Cyril had had enough and knew to get out, but he couldn't run. He jumped overboard and his mates grabbed him into their old rowboat and they got away, just barely."

"Does he have a hook?"

"Sure, he has a hook."

The pirate held up his empty sleeve and jabbed his arm down at us. We screamed and the pirate laughed and pulled his hand out of his sleeve and flipped up the best eye patch I'd ever seen.

"World War I got my leg."

"Your costumes are the best I've ever seen," I told him.

"Well, these ain't costumes, girly. This is what we wear every day."

"Oh, my lucky stars, you get to wear that every day?"

"We sure do, it's just us and a few boarders come to see their kin at the hospital."

"Wow."

The old gnome laughed. "I'm Delmas and you ought'er see my wife, Lily Rood, but she's asleep. You want to see her. I'll show you. Now she'd really scare you. Imagine a scarecrow in a ghosty dress and a mushroom head, with red and white clown stockings on."

I really wanted to see her, but I knew we couldn't. "How about our treat?" I asked again. "We saw your one-legged, one-eyed pirate and didn't run off and we offered you our rum."

"Young lady, you're a really brave pirate, I must say."

I grinned real big 'cause I knew it was true.

He turned around and brought us each a piece of gingerbread on a napkin. It smelled good. Even Gracie smiled.

"Thank you," we both said.

Gracie took off like she was being chased, and I had to run real hard to catch up with her.

We made it back to the Green Frog just in time for the costume judging. Gracie and I won, both of us, best costume. We got to eat anything we wanted. Jimmy and his gang hooted and hollered for us and lots of other folks did too. I knew Jimmy would tell the whole school that we dressed up like real pirates and fooled everybody.

Daddy walked in with Uncle Albert looking for me. He looked real proud of me, I could tell.

"Wait till April Leigh hears about this, Daddy. She'll be so jealous with no bag of treats."

"I'm sure she's looking forward to what you share with her, June Ellen. Let's go. It's time to pick her up at the high school."

Uncle Albert grinned at me. "Did you drink all your whiskey, June Ellen?"

I showed him the empty bottle. "Ho, ho, ho and a bottle of rum, Uncle Albert."

Uncle Albert was parked on Ku Klux Klan Street. I looked around for any ghosts. Daddy saw me. "No ghosts here tonight, June Ellen. They heard about some real pirates out haunting tonight."

$$[\ 17\ ]$$

Thanksgiving Turkey

IT WAS WEDNESDAY, the day before Thanksgiving, Sr. Agatha, the librarian, gave a talk on the history of Thanksgiving. Time just seemed to drag on and on while Sr. Agatha rambled about pilgrims and Indians and how everyone gave thanks for turkey and squash.

"Class, I want each of you to stand up, speak loudly, and shout out what you are thankful for."

"I'll be thankful when this class is over," I whispered to Gracie, who just rolled her eyes at me.

"Okay, June Ellen, you go first." Sr. Agatha obviously saw me whisper.

"I'm thankful for the big tom turkey my daddy brought home for Mama to fatten up. My daddy's waiting on me right now to get home from school so he can get that tom dressed out, and he needs my help."

At 3:00 and not a minute before, the bell finally rang, and I grabbed my school bag and beat everyone to the door. April Leigh stood at the corner with that prissy look on her face.

"Oh, H-E-double toothpicks," I muttered to myself. I raced right by her daring her to catch up with me. April Leigh hated walking home from school with me, as much as I hated having to hear about high school. It turned April Leigh into a Jekyll and Hyde. She didn't even try to catch me.

I burst through our front door in a record fifteen minutes. That's my fastest time so far.

"Daddy," I yelled. "I'm here, I'm ready to help."

I heard Daddy and Mama in the kitchen. They were laughing as they gathered everything together to get our turkey ready. Daddy coughed some, but not as much as last night.

"Change your clothes, June Ellen. Where's April Leigh? Did you wait for her?"

I ignored Mama's questions. Sometimes that was the only way. I threw off my dress and pulled on my blue jeans and shirt and ran to the backyard.

Rex greeted me, jumping and barking. "I'm free, Rex, finally I'm free."

I watched Daddy sharpen his axe blade on the grinding wheel, pushing the pedal with his foot. Uncle Albert corralled Tom and waited for the final word from Daddy. I looked at that fat tom turkey and thought about all the turkey we'd get to eat. Mama didn't buy much meat, mostly bologna for Daddy's lunches and a chicken on Sunday.

"The Depression hasn't lifted for us yet," she always said.

"Daddy, does the navy have Thanksgiving? Will Freddy have turkey and dressing tomorrow?"

"I'm sure Uncle Sam will take care of those boys, June Ellen. Your mama and Aunt Annie sent him a nice care package and I bet other families did the same. They'll eat better than us probably, they'll have lots of cookies and candy."

Finally, April Leigh came busting through the back door. She wore blue jeans like mine. Even she couldn't contain her enthusiasm for a glorious Thanksgiving dinner.

"Okay, Albert, bring him here," Daddy said real quiet.

I held my breath in tight as I waited for Uncle Albert to capture Tom. This used to be Freddy's job, but since he wasn't here, Uncle Albert had to do it. Mama said Freddy was too far away to come home, but I sure missed him. I never had a Thanksgiving without Freddy. Uncle Albert walked slowly toward old Tom, grabbed him from behind, and held him close. He walked over to the chopping block, which was an old oak stump, and stretched his long neck over it.

Daddy held his sharp axe high over our turkey. Rex barked just then, a sharp piercing wail that hurt the eardrums and alerted anyone who was interested in what we were doing. About that time, a fat frisky red squirrel was maneuvering between the black gum and the post oak.

That bark must have made that squirrel feel like the hunter's prey, 'cause he took off flying through the tree branches. Tom, though already caught, was obviously not caught good enough and he went airborne, straight up right out of Daddy's big hand, since his other hand held the axe. A frightened turkey running for his life was more than Daddy could handle.

Daddy grabbed his shotgun and Mama yelled at him, "Fred, don't shoot that gobbler. That shotgun'll tear him to pieces and then what'll we have for dinner? Turkey soup if we're lucky."

The rest of us just stood there, dazed and hungry, watching our Thanksgiving dinner run through our yard and fly over the fence. Our mouths watered already for the roasted bird stuffed with Mama's famous corn bread dressing, all moist from the giblets simmered into a rich broth. Mama even splurged and bought celery for Thanksgiving.

April Leigh and I had been sitting every afternoon all week after school shelling pecans and picking out the nutmeats. Mama toasted the pecans in her black cast-iron skillet then ran her rolling pin over them and created a fine meal that she added to her corn bread. She made her own buttermilk, by separating out the cream and then churning it till it became butter. The leftover liquid became rich buttermilk. That was the secret to her stuffing, corn bread made from pecan meal and buttermilk, poured into a rich broth from the giblets seasoned with her own thyme, sage, and marjoram.

We weren't allowed to tell anyone the recipe, especially Aunt Annie, who got in a fight every year with Mama about her recipe and sometimes walked out refusing to eat if Mama didn't tell her. We knew it would be our heads on the chopping block if we dared to whisper a word of it to anyone. Mama never did tell and Aunt Annie always came back in for the blessing. Missing the Thanksgiving blessing was considered a most grievous sin.

Daddy couldn't run after Tom. The shotgun was just for show. Me and Uncle Albert had to catch that turkey for Thanksgiving dinner. Even April Leigh showed some gumption and the three of us took off. We chased him through the barnyard and he turned toward the road. He ran for his life and we sorely thought we were going to lose him.

My lungs ached and liked to have burst, but I refused to be the first to stop. Being the youngest put a lot of pressure on me to keep up.

That Tom flew across the fence and high-tailed it down the road. Uncle Albert held the fence wires up while we scrambled underneath. That slowed us down some, but I got to breathe, which made it worth it.

A big old Studebaker started up the road and honked when it saw such a sight, a big old tom turkey running full tilt, wings spread wide attempting to fly followed by one old man and two rag-tag kids hooting and hollering. The horn on that big old Studebaker screeched worse than Rex's bark. That big old tom made a sharp right turn and careened down the Lahoskys' driveway.

It lurched right by Mrs. Lahosky's kitchen window, with us close behind. That driveway was a piece of luck 'cause Tom flew right into the barn to the milking shed. Mrs. Lahosky watched Tom skitter by chased by us and figured something was up. She grabbed a feed sack full of cracked corn and raced to the barn. While we stood there just staring and wondering what to do, she walked in and shut the wooden gate behind her in the milking pen. Bossie, their milk cow, politely moved.

Mrs. Lahosky walked slowly up to Tom. She talked softly and clucked like he was some kind of chicken. "Here Tom Tom, here Tom Tom."

She held out a handful of corn. Tom stopped his strutting back and forth and watched her with his beady little eyes. Then old Tom walked right up to her open hand and started eating that cracked corn.

She must have been making piecrust or rolls. Her hands were coated with flour. She wore a blue gingham checked apron, with a ruffle around the edge. I saw floury handprints on the apron and recognized the flour sack she made it from. Mama had one just like it, only hers had rickrack around the bottom.

There, Mrs. Lahosky said softly, "Hand me that feed sack hanging on the corncrib." Being the fastest, I rushed over and grabbed it.

"Quiet, June Ellen," Uncle Albert whispered.

I walked as quiet as I could up to the milk pen, climbed up over the gate, and handed the feed sack to Mrs. Lahosky. Quick as a wink, she threw the feed sack over Tom, grabbed the bottom, and bound it up with a piece of string she must have had in the pocket of her apron. "Here's your Thanksgiving dinner," she said. "Now, you tell your mama she can give me her recipe for corn-bread dressing in return for saving your turkey dinner."

Mama never did give anyone her recipe.

[18]

Christmas Eve

I STOOD IN my bedroom and admired myself in the mirror. The woolen stockings I borrowed from April Leigh itched like hades and I tried hard not to scratch. I only wore these itchy black woolen stockings because April Leigh said they looked good with my new dress. I wanted to rip them off and go bare legged, but Mama refused to allow that.

"This is Christmas Eve, June Ellen, and you're singing at Midnight Mass in the choir. Everyone'll be watching you and you don't want them looking at your scratched and bruised bare legs."

I wore a new Christmas dress made of dark-green velvet with black cross-stitching on the front bodice. Gracie's mother gave the dress to Mama, a hand-me-down. Gracie towered over me so I got a lot of her clothes. Gracie never said a word.

Mama had taken the dress apart and pieced it back together to fit me. She sewed a white lace pinafore over the skirt that she made from an old lace tablecloth she got from Aunt Annie. She stitched tiny red bows on the sleeves and a big red bow around the collar, to make it look all Christmasy.

"Mama, this dress is like brand new. It's just like the one in the Sears & Roebuck catalog. I wished I looked like the picture in the catalog, Mama, and now I do. Thank you so much."

April Leigh dragged me into the bedroom and said, "Sit down, June Ellen, and I'll put some of my makeup on you. This is my own tin of rouge, pink coral, but don't tell Mama I bought it. It'll make your cheeks all rosy and you'll stand out so everyone will notice you." April Leigh opened the small round tin and rubbed a small powder puff over the top. Then she lightly dusted my cheeks with the powder puff and smoothed the coral pink rouge over my cheeks.

Mama walked in, glanced at me and handed her best lipstick, candy apple red, to April Leigh. She stared at my cheeks but didn't say a word.

"Mama, Sr. Joanita told us to wear a little rouge and some lipstick because our faces would show up better in the candlelight."

"Wipe some of that off, April Leigh. Don't make it so heavy." Mama was a little sharp tongued, but she let me wear the coral pink rouge. She had the Christmas spirit too, I guess.

"Hold your lips like this, June Ellen," and April Leigh poked her lips out. I started laughing.

"You look like a duck. You look just like Quacker, Aunt Annie's pet duck."

April Leigh laughed with me. "I know it looks funny, but if you don't want candy apple red lipstick all over your mouth, you'd better do it just like me."

I knew April Leigh and knew she'd give me a clown face if I didn't do what she said, so I smashed my lips together and poked them out.

"That's good, you look like Quacker yourself now. What ever happened to that old duck, anyway?" Then she painted my lips good. Back and forth and back and forth.

"Quacker got eaten by an old raccoon. Aunt Annie made Uncle Albert go find that raccoon and shoot him. Do I have any lips left, April Leigh? It feels like you rubbed them off."

"Don't lick your lips and don't pick at them and you just might get to church with some lipstick still on your lips. And don't touch your cheeks. It'll smear all that rouge." She never did wipe any off and I was glad.

Next, April Leigh fixed my hair just like the girl in the catalog. She swept it up in the back and pinned it with my new golden angel barrettes.

Daddy had polished my brown Rockette shoes with his own shoe polish and buffed them with his special buffing cloth. "June Ellen, they've got a shine on them now."

The black stockings made me feel older, more stylish, and I tried to act like it. I was quite satisfied with the overall effect. Even April Leigh told me, "June Ellen, you look just like a Christmas doll. Try not to mess it all up."

"April Leigh, I'm so happy. I don't even want to kick you."

I tried hard not to lick my lips or rub my cheeks. They itched and tingled and my face felt all prickly. I didn't understand why April Leigh and her girlfriends wanted to wear makeup. It seemed like a lot of trouble, but I did like looking at myself in the mirror.

I had to be at St. Joseph's early and Daddy took me. We stopped at the railroad crossing and watched the coal cars click past. There was soot everywhere and the streetlights showed the black soot drifting over all of Paris. "Look at all that coal dust, Daddy. It blows everywhere."

"Yes, it does, June Ellen, and it's hard on a lot of people. But don't you worry about me. Dr. John's going to get me fixed up."

"Daddy, I love the Shoal Creek mine. I just wish Freddy was here to help so you can get well."

"He'll be home before you know it. Let's get you to church before Sr. Joanita comes after both of us."

Neither of us said a word as we rode in the dark up to the front door of St. Joseph's. Daddy looked hard at me. "June Ellen, you're the most beautiful girl I've ever seen. You're all grown up tonight."

"Thank you, Daddy. I wish Freddy could see me. Sr. Joanita put me in the front row, center in the school choir."

I loved the church at Christmas. Big red poinsettias and glowing candles decorated all three altars. We collected cedar boughs and holly branches with big red berries for the doorway and the front of each altar. Sr. Roberta, the art teacher, taught us how to make garlands from all the greenery and how to fashion bows from red, green, and gold ribbons.

Maurice Lennon always helped, even though he's a boy. He loved to decorate with flowers, and he made the prettiest garlands. He got teased a lot by the other boys. They called him a sissy because he always helped decorate the classrooms. Sr. Roberta said he was artistic. I took to him because he loved horses and studied everything he could find about them, and then he told me what he'd learned. He wasn't like other boys. He didn't pull my hair or spit paper wads.

I watched the people file in for Midnight Mass. I saw Mama walk in with her black hat on. She always wore that black hat but changed the decoration on it according to the season. Tonight she had tiny gold balls arranged on green leaves with red berries and glitter, like real snow. Mama glowed tonight. She walked up to the front and went in the pew with Aunt Annie and Uncle Albert.

Oh, I squealed to myself; there's Daddy. He walked in, all dapper, with his cane and his hat. His handkerchief was folded all neat in his front suit coat pocket. Daddy sat at the end of the back row in case he had a coughing fit. I sure hoped he didn't have one before I sang "Silent Night" in front of the nativity scene with three other girls. We marched from the choir loft at the back of the church all the way to the front altar. It felt just like having a solo.

I tried out to sing the solo part in "O Holy Night," but Belinda got the part. I had to admit though that Belinda had a beautiful voice. My favorite Christmas carol was "O Come All Ye Faithful." The whole choir came in on the chorus starting real soft then getting louder and louder till they filled the church with shouts of "O come let us adore him." Daddy told me it was his favorite, too, and he sure looked forward to hearing me sing it.

I elbowed Gracie, who stood beside me. "There's April Leigh and Isaac; they're holding hands walking down the aisle. Wait till Mama sees that. We can see everything from up here." Just then April Leigh scooted into the bench behind Mama and sat down beside Isaac. Isaac put his right ankle over her left ankle.

"It's like they're holding ankles." Gracie and I got the giggles.

Isaac put his arm on the back of the bench, like a lot of men do in church. They need to stretch, I guess. "Look, Gracie, he's dropped his hand on April Leigh's shoulder."

About that time, Mama got up and moved into the pew with April Leigh, which confirmed what I already knew, Mama had eyes in the back of her head. Isaac quickly stuffed his hands in his pockets and got his own legs back under him. April Leigh just got that look on her face.

Sr. Joanita tapped her baton on her music stand to get the choir's attention. At midnight Maurice Lennon, the head altar boy, led a procession from the back of the church. He swung a bright gold metal incenser suspended from chains he held in his hands. Smoke from the burning incense spewed out over everybody. Six altar boys followed behind him. Each one carried a large white candle with a glowing flame on top.

For Christmas Eve, they wore red cassocks with white lace shirts over them that looked like dresses, but you couldn't call them dresses because only altar boys wore them. Maurice told me his favorite thing in the whole world was being an altar boy and getting to dress up for mass.

Then Fr. Michael marched in holding the baby Jesus high over his head, kind of like he scored a touchdown. It was after midnight so the baby Jesus was now born and Fr. Michael carried him to the nativity scene and laid him in the manger full of hay. Sr. Vivian pumped the organ as Sr. Joanita waved her baton and the choir burst out with "Joy to the world, the Lord is come." The choir filled the church with music. What a beautiful sight I looked down upon.

I watched Daddy as he sang along with us, mostly a whisper so he wouldn't cough and have to leave. I thought my heart would burst I loved my family so much. If only Freddy had come home for Christmas.

"Gracie, I sure wish Mama hadn't moved into the pew with April Leigh and Isaac. I wanted to watch and see what else they might be up to."

Sr. Agatha Boiling a Horse

"IN THE VILLAGE, they were boiling a horse." Sr. Agatha, the librarian, was reading to us from some old book she found, not as old as the Bible but almost. I sat freezing on an old wooden bench beside the table I shared with Gracie and Mags in the library at St. Joseph's. Sr. Agatha kept the steam radiators turned low. "The air gets full of steam, the humidity goes up and that will ruin a library. Our job is to keep these books dry. That way they will last forever." And I think they did.

I thought she liked to torture us. It was almost March but winter was still hanging on and the wind blew cold under the windowsills and whistled around the doors.

"Gracie, my legs are turning blue. These skirts don't amount to much in winter. The boys get to wear overalls and don't have to go through what us girls do in the winter. I wish I could wear my jeans to school."

I heard Gracie's petticoats rustling as she tried to block the breeze. Out of desperation I raised my hand, waving it till Sr. Agatha finally called on me.

"Can we boil a horse and make our own glue?" I asked. "That would sure warm us all up."

"June Ellen, why would you ask such a question?" Sr. Agatha said.

"I was just using my imagination like you told us. I'm imagining chasing Old Blue, who used to live in our pasture, and then trying to get him in our bathtub, which sits in our backyard. We could build a fire under the bathtub, which sits way up on claw feet, so there's plenty of room. Every time we went to Hancock's feed store to buy oats, Daddy said Blue's ready for the glue factory."

Sr. Agatha's jaw clenched and her lips disappeared. Her forehead knit itself together like the raggedy wool scarf April Leigh knit me for Christmas, full of ridges and hard nubs that scratched like the dickens.

I just kept on, imagining out loud. "We would just have to figure out a way to keep him in there till it gets hot enough to boil him down to glue. Sister Agatha, wouldn't a horse just jump out of the tub when it got too hot? I'm pretty sure Old Blue would. How'd they do it in that village?"

"June Ellen, do you really want to boil a horse alive?" Sr. Agatha shrieked.

Excitement rippled through the whole class now. Nobody minded the cold benches on our behinds.

"No, Sister Agatha, I wouldn't do that. I was just imagining how we could as a class project make our own glue. How much glue would a horse like Old Blue make? Enough for the whole school?"

Everybody was laughing now. "Enough for all the school kids in Paris, Arkansas? We might have glue forever."

Sr. Agatha's eyebrows met in a straight line and her two eyes became one deadeye, the evil eye. She said, "Dismissed. Return to your classroom now."

I looked at Gracie. "Sister's getting a little hot under those robes. Don't you think?"

After school I found Mama in the kitchen stirring a pot of something on the stove. She was stirring so fast it splattered all over. She was in quite a tizzy or in all of a dither, as Sr. Agatha liked to say.

"What's going on, Mama? Is Daddy sick?"

"No, your daddy's not sick. I don't know what's going on, June Ellen. Clucker and some of the other hens are out of sorts today. I'm heating up some chicken mash with sugar water. Clucker hasn't laid an egg for three days now and she's always been my best layer. I'm going to try this and see if it helps."

"Mama, if we still had old Blue, do you think we could make glue and sell it? Then you wouldn't have to work at Fr. Michael's and Daddy wouldn't have to work so hard in his coal mine."

"June Ellen, where do you get these ideas? Sometimes I wonder what they're teaching you at St. Joseph's."

"Mama, Sr. Agatha was reading to us about boiling a horse and it just got me to thinking is all."

"You have such a wild imagination, I know it doesn't take much to get you started." Then Mama started laughing. "I can just guess what those sisters must think. One thing Sr. Sarah always said, you keep them on their toes."

"Mama, why are those chickens squawking like that?"

"They've been raising a ruckus all day. Go out there and see if you can figure it out. I keep checking to see if some raccoon or hawk's been hanging around, but I'll swan I don't see anything."

"Okay, Mama. I'll take Rex and we'll go spy on the hen house."

"Change your clothes and your shoes first."

I put on my jeans and my old tennis shoes and my worn-out, hand-me-down blouse from April Leigh. None of the buttons matched anymore, Mama had replaced so many. The wind had died down and the sun warmed up enough I was ready to go out and scout.

"Come on, Rex, let's go spy and see if we can catch a raccoon or something." Rex was always ready for an adventure after school, 'cause he'd been resting all day. We took off for the hen house and they were all running around, truly just like chickens with their heads cut off. Clucker, Mama's favorite, was huddled with a few others in the corner of the pen.

"What's wrong with you, Clucker? Mama's making you something special." She answered in chicken talk without much enthusiasm, unusual for Clucker, who was quite a loudmouth, spoiled by Mama, Daddy always said.

"Rex, you stand guard out here and I'll check out the nesting boxes inside." Mama won't let Rex go inside the hen house, even though I told her he would only do what I said.

I walked into the chicken coop and it was empty, no predators or chickens. I looked inside each nesting box for eggs and there were none and nobody setting either. I looked inside Clucker's box hoping she would have laid an egg for Mama's sake and there in Clucker's box was the biggest rat snake I'd ever seen. And inside its mouth was a huge egg.

I jumped back quick. I'm not afraid of much and often admire snakes when I see them. I wished I could slither around like them all quiet and almost invisible. Most girls were scared of snakes. But not me. Lots of boys liked to catch them and then try to scare the daylights out of girls. I'd even caught a few myself. But this big old snake with that big old egg in its mouth took me by surprise.

"Mama, Mama, come here quick. Come see what's in Clucker's nest." I yelled as loud as I could and that snake never moved.

Mama came running, her apron flying. "What'd you find, June Ellen. You stay away if that raccoon's back."

"No, Mama. There's no raccoon, this time. It's a big old rat snake with one of Clucker's eggs in his mouth."

Mama just stood there dumbfounded, with her mouth open. Then she started laughing. "June Ellen, that's the funniest thing I've ever seen.

That egg is so big, that snake can't swallow it and he can't get his head back out of that hole in the wall and he sure can't spit it out. He's caught between a rock and a hard place for sure. You're a good spy to catch him in the act."

Then Mama reached into that snake's mouth with her hand and snatched that egg right out of his mouth. That snake backed up out of that hole and took off like a racer. I'd never seen a snake disappear so fast.

Mama said just as matter of fact as anything, "I don't think he'll be back, but I'm going to cover up that hole for sure. Poor Clucker."

"Mama, you're as brave as Dale Evans. I've never seen anybody reach inside a snake's mouth before."

"A body does what a body has to do, sometimes, June Ellen. No way was I going to let that snake have any more of my eggs."

"You're as brave as Daddy, Mama."

"Thank you, June Ellen. That's a real compliment."

"Can we still eat that egg, Mama, or is it poison?"

"It's a special egg now, June Ellen, and I think you and I are going to have it right now."

Mama went in and fried that egg sunny side up and brought it outside. I didn't even have to go inside and sit down at the table. We each got a bite and Rex too. That's how happy Mama was, I'd never seen her so happy and she just kept chuckling and grinning.

"June Ellen, I can't wait to tell your daddy. He's going to be so surprised. It'll be a good laugh for him too, after being down in that mine all day."

"Mama, you sure are funny today."

"Problems don't seem so bad if you keep yourself cheerful, June Ellen. Tonight's bingo and I'm feeling awful lucky."

[20]

The Toad Man

"LET'S GO, JUNE ELLEN, it's too durn stuffy in this house, no air moving at all. The only thing that's going to cool me down is a cold beer and Herman's fans blowing on me."

If Daddy got too warm, he'd get to coughing. Last week we were freezing, but this week, March came in like a lamb. Old Herman bought the fresh air blowers when they tore the old coal shacks down at the old Comet #2 mine. He screwed them into the wall across from the bar, Daddy's favorite place to sit. It was barely March, but when Daddy came in, Herman always turned one on for him, no matter the season.

Mama let me go with him because she knew I'd take care of him, which meant he'd come home by supper. Dr. John told Daddy he needed to go to the Veteran's Hospital in Little Rock to get an X-ray. They had new machines that could look inside and see Daddy's lungs. Daddy didn't want to go but Mama told him he had to.

Before Daddy got so sick, he and Uncle Albert often stayed at Herman's till he closed at midnight. Then they would drive around the back roads, weaving in and out of old homesteads, visiting old fishing holes. Sometimes they just sat on the top of Horseshoe Mountain and wished upon the stars and stared at the moon if there was one. Daddy liked to explore like me. He just couldn't do it like he used to.

I knew all this because I got to go with them once. All H-E-double toothpicks broke loose at our house that time. But I got to see the most beautiful sunrise I'd ever seen. We'd sat on Horseshoe Mountain, the highest rockiest bluff, and watched the sun peek up over the Arkansas River valley making the river look like the golden path to heaven. The sky lay behind like a beautiful stained-glass window all rose and orange and peach colored. I knew then that I believed in God and angels, and that's who I prayed to when I saw Mama's face when Uncle Albert had turned into our driveway. We hadn't gone on a long drive at night since.

At Herman's, I learned to suck the foam off Daddy's glass of beer. He said it got stuck in his throat and made him cough. I knew I had to do it and I got pretty good at it. Anyway, Daddy and I hung out at the beer joint with the Toad Man and Sheriff Tobe Riley. Riley was one of the most important men in our town. He wore a holster with a pistol all the time. He took the shells out and let me play with his pistol right there at the bar.

The Toad Man was also well known in these parts. He always came to the beer joint with a gunnysack full of bullfrogs. He'd been out frog gigging all night and he smelled like backwater mud. He sold frog legs a nickel apiece, only you had to buy two because they were still attached to the back of the frog. That's why they called him the Toad Man.

Daddy told me his name used to be Oscar Blinz. "Oscar used to be part of the night crew at the Dixie mine. He was one of the brushers. They brush up when everyone leaves and that extends the entry for the next day's shift. Well, Oscar got too close to where they were setting off short shots of dynamite.

"They do that in the evenings to put cracks in the coal veins so the guys coming in the next day can go at it with their picks and shovels. Oscar was pretty badly hurt by the explosion. They got him out of the mine and took him to the Paris hospital and Dr. John saved his life, but his face was blue afterwards from embedded coal dust from the blast.

"He changed after that, June Ellen. He wouldn't go back down in any mine. He camped in the woods along the river. Said he couldn't stand to be shut up inside anything with four walls again, not even his own home. That's how come his wife took off with all his kids. You be nice to him, June Ellen."

I'd never noticed how blue his face was because he had whiskers everywhere. Now I looked real close and I could see the blue pock-marked skin under his hairy beard. After that whenever I had a dime, I bought two frog legs. Mama almost always fried them up for me and Daddy.

When the Toad Man got enough money, he'd buy a glass of beer. When he talked, he liked to slam his beer mug on the old wet wooden bar and say, "Damnation."

Daddy said, "The Toad Man spills as much beer as he drinks. It's a good thing he knows how to gig frogs."

I often went out to our old barn when I got home and practiced slamming a jelly glass full of water down on a board stretched across the pig pen and yelling, "Damnation," though we hadn't had a pig since Porky and we had him last Easter and were still eating on him. A jar of pickled pigs feet was about all we had left. The Lahoskys raised one for us now, 'cause Daddy couldn't do it and it was too much for Mama.

It felt good slamming that jelly glass full of water down and yelling damnation. I could see why the Toad Man did it.

[21]

Easter Dress

THAT EASTER MARCH came in like a lamb, but it went out like a lion. Many stores on the square were running low on coal and needed just enough to get them through this last cold spell. Mr. Haney told me and Lizzie all about it yesterday.

Daddy kissed Mama first thing at breakfast this morning. "Cora, I have a good idea to get us some pocket money and pay off a few of these bills."

Mama looked at Daddy with that serious dead-eye look. "Don't forget Dr. John ordered an X-ray of your lungs at the Veteran's Hospital in Little Rock. It's up to you to set up a time."

Daddy smiled and said, "I'll see him after I sell some of that dirty coal laying around. When the big companies were operating, coal had to be sorted and cleaned when it came off those big conveyors unless it was cut in chunks of pure coal and sometimes good coal ended up on the slack pile. I decided to go through the old slack piles left by the old miners as well as our own and clean up the good coal that may have been overlooked."

Mama patted Daddy on the shoulder. "Well, Fred, that sounds like a good plan for you and Albert. I sure could use some pocket money for our own household. You'd be up top too and not breathing dust or setting off gas. Just promise me you'll make that appointment and you'd better be sure someone will buy it before you take a whole day digging and cleaning it."

Daddy said, "Some of that dirty coal is anthracite. It'll burn good enough for this cold snap and folks around the square need some. I've already had a couple of folks ask me, did I have any?"

Mama was studying Daddy real hard. "What about the coal in that rail car you've been working so hard to fill?"

"Albert and I've been working on filling that car full of good anthra-

104

cite coal to send up north to the factories. They pay the best money for that hard coal and that's our ticket to get out of debt. I don't aim to sell it local for less and diminish our supply."

"Can I have some money, Daddy, for the movies and the soda fountain?"

"We'll just have to see about that, June Ellen. I'm sure there'll be a quarter to spare. But you have to work for it."

"You mean I get to work at the coal mine with you and Uncle Albert? I want to be a coal miner." I was dancing around the kitchen and Rex was jumping with me.

"No, you may not, June Ellen. You stay away from that mine. I don't know what you are thinking, Fred, but that is out of the question." Mama's smile turned into one hard line.

Daddy laughed. "No, I sure wasn't thinking that. I thought you'd like to be in charge of sales, June Ellen. Everyone down at the Paris square knows you, and you already stop in and talk to them. After school today, you just pop in each of them stores and see who needs a little coal to get them through this last bit of winter before spring weather finally gets here. Albert and I'll start delivering first thing in the morning."

"Can I help you deliver the coal, Daddy? I could be like the delivery guys who help unload and get the tickets signed and collect the money."

"Well, I think your mama and I can work something out for you to ride with us anyway."

I looked at Mama. "Okay, June Ellen, you're growing up way too fast, but your daddy's right, you're a good talker and I'm sure you could sell anything you set your mind to. I'll let Fr. Michael know, you're taking a day off of school to help your daddy."

Albert drove up in the old truck to pick up Daddy.

Daddy greeted him with a big smile. "Albert, we need to clean up some of that dirty coal buried in those slack heaps and go through some of the old tunnels and cut off the croppings the big mining companies left. We could get enough to fill the truck and probably sell it all by just driving around the square in the morning. This late cold snap has people looking for some coal to get them through. It'd be nice to have some pocket money again."

Albert treated Daddy like he was the boss. "Okay, Fred. A little money in my pocket sounds good. Annie would sure be happy."

Daddy sure was smart. After school I walked around the square and talked to the store owners and other people hungry for some of Daddy and Uncle Albert's coal. Haney's, Murray's Barber Shop, the Green Frog, Schmidt's grocery, Clem Wald's, even the Paris Bank and Hardware. The funeral homes weren't interested. They said they needed it cold for the bodies. The next day, I rode in the truck loaded with coal and took orders for Daddy. I even helped push the wheelbarrow full of coal. The best part was helping him keep track of his customers and counting the money he took in.

After Daddy emptied the truck, he came home happy and smiling. "Here, Cora, you go and buy everybody new Easter clothes. No hand-me-downs, flour sacks, or remodels for my girls. I want all new for you, April Leigh, and June Ellen."

"Fred, don't be silly. That's too much money when we can make do with what we have. How much beer did you drink? None of us mind wearing last year's anyway."

"I do, Mama," I piped up. "I want a new Easter dress. I don't want to wear April Leigh's old one."

"June Ellen worked real hard today, Cora. I think she earned a new dress."

Mama was about to give me her hard-eye look, but when Daddy started laughing, she smiled.

"Cora, I just came from the bank. I haven't had a thing to drink, but I think I'll head to the Green Frog with Albert this evening. My girls deserve a pretty dress, especially their beautiful mama."

Then Daddy grabbed Mama and gave her a big hug. Mama slapped at him, but she was smiling. He picked up the picture of them on their wedding day. "Cora, look how beautiful you are in that hat. I want you to get yourself one of those new fancy ones, with flowers all over."

"Oh, Fred."

Daddy laughed and kissed her on the cheek. "See you girls later."

My mama loved hats. In the picture she wore a big straw hat with a wide brim around it. You can hardly see her face because the brim dipped down real low.

"Mama, how come your face is hid?"

"Hidden, June Ellen." Mama looked at the picture and smiled.

"That was the style then. I wore a long white dress with lots of lace and buttons down the front that I borrowed from my cousin Martha, because we didn't have any money for a wedding dress. But I had some money saved for a new hat, and I knew I could wear that hat lots of other times. I bought a bright pink satin ribbon and wrapped it around the brim then tied it in a bow at the side. That ribbon was the prettiest piece of pink satin I ever saw."

Saturday, Mama took us to Mode O'Day on the Paris square. I tried on all kinds of dresses, but I wanted one with a billowy skirt. I was a tomboy most of the time, but I liked to wear dresses with big flouncy ruffles that go way out when you twirled. I'd go 'round and 'round till I was dizzy. I felt like I was flying.

I found a pink dress with butterfly sleeves and a swing-out skirt with a big white lace ruffle on the bottom. I put it on, and it felt like I was wearing cotton candy. I twirled all over the store till Mama made me sit down.

Miss Friddle, the store clerk, walked over and said, "June Ellen, you need a new petticoat that would make that skirt stick straight out."

Mama answered right back, "No, you have a good slip at home, and you need no help with that frilly dress."

Miss Friddle brought one over anyway. She placed it on the floor, and it stood up all by itself. It was all ruffles and white lace with wires that ran through them.

She looked at me and said, "June Ellen, this is what cowgirls wear when they go square dancing."

I had to have it. I ran over and grabbed it while Mama was trying on another navy-blue dress in her fitting room. It seemed like that's all she wore, navy blue. I went into my own fitting room and put the cowgirl petticoat on under the pink dress with the swingy skirt.

"Wow." I looked in the mirror and thought I looked like Shirley Temple if I only had some of those great sausage curls. I bet April Leigh could help me with those. I walked out and twirled around the store. It was like wearing a merry-go-round. I twirled and twirled.

April Leigh was watching me, and I knew I needed her on my side. April Leigh had on a brown-and-white-checked skirt and blouse with a fat red belt around the waist. She looked pretty and fashionable. I decided to tell her.

"April Leigh, that outfit looks great on you. You remind me of a graham cracker with peanut butter and marshmallows spread all over it."

"Yuck, June Ellen. Where do you get those silly, stupid ideas of yours?"

"I was just trying to tell you how good you looked. Do you like my dress with this square-dancing petticoat?"

"You look like a pink marshmallow. I'd like to put you on a stick and hold you to the fire till you're toasty brown."

I ran over to kick her, but Mama walked out of her fitting room just then. She was beautiful. She had on a navy-blue dress with red roses and bright green leaves that were like vines trailing all around.

"Oh, Mama. You're so pretty. Wait till Daddy sees you in your new dress."

I could tell even April Leigh was taken aback. Her mouth hung open. "Mama, you look like you just walked out of the Sears & Roebuck catalog."

Miss Friddle walked over. "Well, Cora, that dress was made for you. Try this hat on with it. It's made of lightweight sisal straw with a full bouquet of spring flowers around the brim, the latest fashion that only Mode O'Day carries on the whole Paris square."

I'd never seen Mama look like that before. She looked like she had a basket of flowers on her head. I could hardly talk so I just ran and threw my arms around her and hugged her tight. That day, I walked out of Mode O'Day with a new dress and a cowgirl petticoat. I never forgot that Easter dress or that cowgirl petticoat.

[22]

April Leigh's Birthday

DADDY DROPPED ME OFF at Hancock's Department and Feed Store. "June Ellen, I'm going to the barbershop for a while. Go on in there and find something for April Leigh for her birthday. Remember she's in high school now, so, no paper dolls or coloring books."

"I know, Daddy. She's not an explorer like me anymore." Daddy laughed and handed me two quarters. We had sold the whole truckload of coal from the slack piles, and Daddy and I were both still rattling change in our pockets.

"Thanks, Daddy. I have a whole dollar to get April Leigh something."

I stood at the jewelry counter looking at the flashy rings, with pearls and diamonds and emeralds and rubies. They were expensive. Some even cost five dollars. I looked at the charm bracelets and all the charms. April Leigh wanted one of those, but I only had enough money for one charm and what good was a charm without a bracelet?

My eyes kept returning to the round silver locket that opened with two pictures inside. I imagined my school picture in the silver framed oval. I really wanted that for myself, not April Leigh. For one more dollar and thirty-nine cents I could buy it and keep a lock of my own hair in it or a lock of hair from my boyfriend when he went off to war like Freddy did, though I didn't want to think much about that.

I wanted to be like Dale Evans and Roy Rogers. They each had their own horse and a jeep. Dale Evans got to drive her jeep all over the mountains and the ranch anytime she wanted to. That's how they caught all the bad guys. I could put their picture in it or, even better, I could put Trigger's picture in it.

I wasn't sure what I'd put in it, for April Leigh, maybe a picture of the Blessed Virgin Mary. She could grasp the locket and pray to her. She'd be like that little girl in Guadalupe that Mary appeared to.

Maybe the Blessed Virgin Mary would appear to me in Paris, Arkansas. Then Daddy wouldn't have to go to work in the coal mine.

But I didn't have an extra dollar and thirty-nine cents, so I walked over to the cosmetics counter and looked at all the lipstick. Evening in Paris lipstick cost ninety cents. April Leigh loved crimson rose, but Mama said no lipstick. And the Naylon fingernail polish, all those colors, pink popcorn, roman candle, and congo red. Wow. I could buy April Leigh some fingernail polish for seventy-two cents and have enough left over for a Dr Pepper and peanuts. Maybe she'd let me use it, or I'd just sneak it.

April Leigh had told Mama just this morning, "I am just weary of sharing a room with June Ellen. She's always in my stuff. I have to watch her all the time."

Mama told her, "Well, April Leigh, if you want to, you can just move out on the back porch. It might get cold in the winter, and you know those bugs in the hot summer. They sure do find a way to get in."

"Can *I*, Mama? Can I move out on the back porch? I don't mind the bugs or the cold." I pleaded.

"No, June Ellen, you may not."

April Leigh did her disgusted look, rolled her eyes, and walked off.

Ima Jean walked up. "Can I help you, young lady?" Ima Jean wore big black rubber-soled shoes so she could sneak up on you. She told Mama she could work all day in them and not have sore tired feet. They sure were ugly though. Her hair was pulled back in a bun so tight her eyes were slanted. I wondered if it hurt. She wore little glasses on a chain around her neck. I noticed she always took them off when she waited on men. I thought it looked funny to have glasses dangling on your bosom instead of on your face.

I also noticed it made the men look at Ima Jean's chest instead of her face. Ima Jean had a big bosom, which she kept shoved up high, and it bounced and wiggled when she walked or talked. Her adam's apple (and she had a big one) kept bobbing in between them, and those glasses just bounced and bounced all over.

"I need a present for my sister, April Leigh. It's April so it's her birthday and she's turning fifteen. She wants grown-up stuff and Mama says she can't have it."

"Well, it sounds to me like some nice jewelry might be just the thing. June Ellen, don't put your dirty fingers on the counter. I'm the one who has to keep that glass clean."

"I'll just look around by myself if you don't mind, Ima Jean."

"Don't you touch anything unless you're buying it. You kids get everything dirty in here and then leave without buying anything."

I put my hands on my hips and gave Ima Jean my dead-eye look. I liked to touch everything, get a feel for it before I buy it. Finally, Ima Jean went to the other end of the counter. I walked over to the hair stuff and thought about some barrettes. They had all different kinds, silver or gold with roses or bluebirds, even daisies. They even had some with hearts.

Ima Jean came back. "Don't you have to go home soon? You've been in here an awful long time."

"No, I don't have to get home soon. My daddy is over at the barbershop and he told me to take my time; he was going to be visiting a while."

Ima Jean knew she'd lost this time, so she just snorted and walked away. I was mad now. I wanted that locket so I could clasp it to my breast like Scarlett and get strong and brave and have courage. That's what I wanted, and I had to spend my money on April Leigh and I didn't want to. I made a face in the mirror at the cosmetics counter, and then stuck out my tongue. Life just isn't fair sometimes.

Ima Jean looked down at me again. "Well, young lady, have you made up your mind?"

Her face pinched up like a prune when she talked. When April Leigh or I made a face, Mama told us, "Your face is going to freeze like that." I wanted to tell Ima Jean, your face is going to freeze, but I didn't.

Instead, I said, "No, thank you, ma'am. I haven't."

Mr. Haney from Haney's Rexall walked in just then, and Ima Jean took off her glasses and went to help him, jiggling her glasses all the way over, and sure enough Mr. Haney watched her glasses the whole time.

I looked one more time at the beautiful silver locket with the painted flowers on the front wishing I could just open it once; I pretended I was at Tara with Rhett Butler, clutching the locket to my grieved heart. I knew it would give me strength and courage. Just then I heard a horn honk and sure enough it was Daddy with Uncle Albert.

I grabbed some barrettes, a package of six. Shiny gold ones with white daisies, silver ones with blue birds on a tree limb, and my favorite, red ones with zebras. I'd give two sets to April Leigh and keep the red ones with zebras for me. I went to the cash register at the front of the store. I sure wasn't going to give my money to Ima Jean.

When we got home, April Leigh was draped across the porch swing with her best friend Mary Alice. She wouldn't let me hang out with them and Mama said I couldn't. I had to resort to spying, which was easy, 'cause our bedroom window opened right out onto the porch. I crouched down underneath the window.

"Mary Alice, I'm thinking of cutting my hair into one of those bobs like Patti Page in *Billboard* magazine. But Daddy doesn't want me to. What do you think?"

"April Leigh, you have the most beautiful long blonde hair at Paris High. Everybody says so. Boys like it long."

"That's what Isaac told me. I'm going to be fifteen and I'm still not allowed to go on a date by myself. I have to wait till I'm sixteen. It's not fair. I feel like I'm the only girl at Paris High not allowed to date. I'm going to work on Mama about that one."

"My mama doesn't let me go out with boys either. But that's okay with me. What do you want for your birthday, April Leigh?"

"Well, I used to love Hank Williams, but now I love Frankie Lane. I sent off to one of those movie magazines and they sent me a postcard of him. I have to hide it from June Ellen though, and that's not easy in this house. I'd love to have my own record player, so I could listen to Frankie any time I wanted."

"Do you think you'll get one for your birthday?"

"I saw a Silvertone table phonograph in the Sears & Roebuck catalog, but it costs twenty-six dollars and ninety-five cents. I hate being poor. I'm going to Little Rock when I graduate and marry one of those rich guys. That's where Daddy says they all live."

"Fr. Michael said it's a sin to listen to rock 'n' roll anyway," Mary Alice said.

"I don't think it's a sin if you're in high school. At least I can turn the radio on and listen to whoever I want. If Mama's not around anyway."

"I'm so glad your mama's letting you spend tomorrow night with me, April Leigh. I can't wait to see those horror movies."

"Your brother Jimbo's great, letting us go with him."

"Because he's letting us tag along?" Mary Alice asked. "Well, don't be too impressed—he only gets to take the car if we're with him and he's trying to impress his new girlfriend. So, we're actually helping him out."

"Well, I still think he's pretty swell. I miss my big brother Freddy. We don't know where he is and it's hard on all of us. Jimbo reminds me of Freddy, so it's pretty great for me to go to the drive-in with him. But don't say anything to June Ellen 'cause she'll want to come. It's our secret. I find that the older you get, the more you have to keep secrets. I don't know why that is, but it's true."

April Leigh was having her own adventures and I hated being left out. I kept the gold barrettes with daisies, too.

[23]

Happy Mother's Day

TODAY WAS RELIGION CLASS with Sr. Annunciata and the sixth graders. Sr. Annunciata passed out Holy Cards of the Assumption; that was when the Blessed Virgin Mary ascended into heaven without dying first. Stars surrounded her head like a halo, and she was wearing the same sky-blue robes she always wore, just like the nuns—only their robes were black.

I wished they'd wear the sky-blue ones sometimes just for a change. I wondered if Sr. Annunciata wished she could wear a different color. I started to raise my hand to ask but caught myself because I knew Sr. Annunciata wouldn't like the question.

Sr. Annunciata told us she was named for the Annunciation; that was when the angel came to Mary and announced to her she was going to have baby Jesus. She told us in religion class she chose that name for herself because when she saw a picture of Mary after the angels announced this to her, she wanted to be just like the Blessed Virgin.

"The angel was so divine, with beautiful wings outlined in gold leaf, and Mary had a halo made of gold with silver light that streamed right into my heart and told me. And, girls, you will know too, when Jesus tells you."

I told Gracie, "I haven't yet found a Holy Card, or a picture in the Bible that told me any such thing."

"Now class," Sr. Annunciata said, "Sunday is Mother's Day and for class today you are going to make a Mother's Day card for your mother. First, I'm going to pass around some construction paper in these pretty pastel colors, pink, blue, and green. Pick your mother's favorite color."

I didn't know my mother's favorite color and she never said, but I loved green so I picked it.

"Take your construction paper and fold it in half, make a crease, and you have a card."

I did like she said and ran my thumb down the edge and sure enough I could open it like a card.

"Look, Gracie, it's just like a card."

"Shhhh, June Ellen. You're going to get us in trouble."

That was what she always said when I talked to her, and we did sometimes, but I didn't let that stop me.

"June Ellen," Sr. Annunciata said, "you're so fidgety today, why don't you get up and go to the supply closet and get the jars of paste and pass them out."

I often got to help. I heard Sr. Annunciata tell Mama once, "If I can keep her busy, it helps keep the class in a calmer state."

I jumped up quick. I liked to move around and not just sit still for so long. "I'd be happy to help, Sister Annunciata." I knew my manners.

"Give a jar of paste to each pupil in rows one and three. Then each of you share with the person across from you in rows two and four. Paste your Holy Card in the center on the front of your card." Sr. Annunciata walked around helping those who needed it to get their cards centered right. Not me, I pasted my Holy Card right in the center.

"Open up your cards and on the right side. I want each of you to write a letter to your mother and tell her all the ways she's like the Blessed Virgin Mary. The Blessed Virgin was a good and holy woman. She took such good care of the baby Jesus. Think how your mother is like her as all our mothers try to be."

I told Gracie, "She didn't always take such good care of him. She let him run around with that guy Judas and look how he died. Mama wouldn't let me wander around in the desert all alone for forty days. I just now get to go to the square by myself for a few hours in the daytime only."

"June Ellen, do you really want to go to your eternal damnation? It sure sounds like it."

Gracie got real serious sometimes and acted all holy like.

I looked hard at the Holy Card trying to see Mama in there. The Blessed Virgin Mary wore a sky-blue robe with a beautiful white front outlined in gold, and there was a gold crown on her head with silver stars on each point. Her eyes were a soft, warm brown and her hands were long and slender, open with the palms up streaming light, kind of like Superman.

Mama's hands were more on the thick side, kind of red and spotted looking. They were either wet from washing dishes or wiping the table down with a washrag or covered with dough or flour. Or full of something, fresh-picked beans, a pail of water from the pump on the back porch, her sewing or her mending. No, Mama's hands weren't that kind of white and pure looking. Mama's hands were working hands.

On the Blessed Virgin Mary's chest her heart lay open, with tongues of flame whipping out in all directions, and in the very center was a special little flame on a little torch called the Holy Ghost. The Blessed Virgin's feet lifted off the ground as she started to ascend into heaven.

"Now, class, take a piece of paper out of your Big Chief tablets and write your letter there first. That way you won't make mistakes on your card and tear holes in it when you try to erase."

Dear Mama, Happy Mother's Day. You are pretty just like The Blessed Virgin Mary.

I looked hard at the picture again. The Blessed Virgin Mary's face was pearly white, clear with pink cheeks, and thin. Mama's face was round like a clock; her skin kind of sagged in places. April Leigh said Mama had a double chin and she had some faint black hairs coming out of a mole there. The Blessed Virgin Mary had warm brown holy eyes. Mama's eyes were a hard dark brown.

I crossed out, *you are pretty like The Blessed Virgin Mary,* then I thought Mama was pretty when she got all dressed up for bingo or church, just different. Her eyes were like chocolate milk when she smiled. I felt like she was drinking me up when she was happy to see me. Her eyes crinkled and shot out their own kind of white light when she and Daddy were having fun.

Dear Mama, Happy Mother's Day. You are pretty just like The Blessed Virgin Mary.

In every picture I ever saw of the Blessed Virgin Mary she looked happy. Sr. Annunciata called it beatific. That means beautiful, holy, and heavenly happy all at the same time, or else she looked sad holding Jesus in her arms.

Mama always had a mad look on her face. Mad at me, mad at Daddy at the beer joint, mad at the stove 'cause it wouldn't get hot quick enough. She also had a pinched, hurry-up look. "Hurry up and get ready, June Ellen. Hurry up and eat. Got to get the washing done, got to get the biscuits in, got to get the peas shelled, got to get the mending done." Gosh, Mama sure hurried a lot.

She did laugh when she played bingo, except when Aunt Annie won, and then she got all mad again. She was really happy when she won, and she never missed bingo because the money was for St. Joseph's building fund.

Dear Mama, Happy Mother's Day. You are pretty just like The Blessed Virgin Mary. You are a really good Bingo player. The Blessed Virgin Mary would like that because you do it for the church.

"Now, class, some of you seem to be having a hard time with this. Think of all the things your mother does for you. Who do you think did the washing and the cleaning for Jesus?"

Thank you for washing my clothes and letting me wear my jeans to Haney's for a soda pop. The Blessed Virgin Mary kept Jesus' clothes clean too. She always let him wear his sandals, and I like it when you let me wear my tennis shoes. As you know I don't like wearing my white Easter sandals with those white anklets with the pink ruffles around the top. You don't make me wear them except to church and church stuff. I don't like sandals like Jesus did.

I remember when Daddy gave you that new navy blue purse with a gold clasp, right after you bought your navy blue Easter dress. Your face lit up just like Mary's on the front of your card. That's my very favorite look on your face.

Sr. Annunciata went on, "And who fixes your dinner?"

Mama cooked all the time for us. I wondered about the Blessed Virgin Mary. They never talked about Mary cooking for Jesus in the Bible. It seemed like Jesus and the apostles took care of the food and Jesus changed the water into wine. Boy, would Daddy be happy if Mama could do that. But she probably wouldn't. The apostles caught the fish and bought the loaves of bread. Jesus multiplied them. I only remembered one picture in my Bible history of them sitting down to eat and that was at the Last Supper. Maybe Mary cooked that with the help of Mary Magdalene. They must have stayed in the kitchen.

And thank you for cooking for us. I especially like your homemade bread and jam and your biscuits. My favorite dinner is your fried chicken with mashed potatoes and gravy. And my other favorite is your macaroni and cheese. I don't think The Blessed Virgin Mary helped out with the food very much, but I bet she understands and appreciates that you do so much of it all by yourself. I sure do.

I love you Mama. June Ellen.

"Okay, class, time to finish up and get your words written on the card. If you run out of room just turn it over and finish on the back."

Boy, was I glad to hear that. I ended up finding a lot that Mama had in common with the Blessed Virgin Mary.

And when I gave it to her right before church on Sunday, she got tears in her eyes. She tried to wipe them away before anyone saw them. She got one of those smiles just like the Blessed Virgin Mary, beatific. She let me wear my jeans for Sunday dinner and she cooked all my favorite foods. Her hands looked really beautiful all covered with the batter she dipped each piece of chicken in. Her eyes were shooting out streams of light all day just like in the picture. She told Aunt Annie her favorite color was green.

[24]

Jeremy's Store

DADDY FINALLY WENT and got his X-ray in Little Rock. At that time, X-ray machines were a new thing, invented during the war, I guess to take care of all those soldiers getting shot.

"June Ellen, they take a picture with a machine like a camera only it shows your insides. It didn't hurt at all. My lungs were black, just like coal dust. It was the darndest thing to see what's inside you like that. I have to be more careful down in the mine is all." Dr. John had told him not to go back down in that mine, to stay on top and run it from there. Of course, Daddy refused to do that.

School had finally let out and three whole months of summer vacation stretched out in front of me. Daddy had decided to get some help breaking out coal. Mama helped him make that decision because he wasn't supposed to be down there working so much. We drove over to Jeremy's Mercantile. Daddy was looking to hire some of the men hanging around Jeremy's to work for him. Everybody knew Daddy leased and ran the Shoal Creek mine and that it belonged to me, too. Many of the folks around these parts still felt the effects of the Depression and the big coal companies leaving these parts. Men often waited at the store to see if Daddy or any of the other scrappers were hiring.

Daddy and Jeremy helped each other out. Jeremy allowed Daddy and his miners to run up tickets for supplies or food they needed, and Daddy signed for all the tickets because Jeremy knew Daddy would pay when he sold his coal. Daddy did so much business there, it kept Jeremy's going.

"This store's important, June Ellen, for the folks 'round here, lots of squatters, and people down on their luck," Daddy said.

The store came close to being a shack with a porch made from warped planks resting on old tar buckets. A few nails still held the porch to the shack, one of which would tear a hole in your pants if you leaned up against the wall just right. Many of us wore patches to prove it.

"Jeremy sells the bare necessities for living with some sweetness thrown in," Daddy always said. "And Mrs. Bonnett, who runs the milking farm where Freddy used to work, provides Jeremy with all the milk and butter he sells. It's not the freshest, but fresh enough for poor folk."

In the store on the left resided a pot-bellied stove that in winter glowed red-hot. Across the back of the store stood the meat counter with mostly bologna and pickle loaf and hard cheese. Hi Ho Sunshine crackers and Sunshine Krispy saltines lay stacked on top.

Daddy said, "That's what fills the miners' buckets most of the time."

Barrels full of beans, flour, sugar, and pickles filled up the space next to the counter with just enough room to squeeze between them. Board shelves lined the walls full of everything else.

A row of gallon pickle jars filled with candy sat on one shelf, a short row with only eight jars; not like Haney's Rexall with rows and rows of fancy cut-glass jars of all different kinds of candy. But Jeremy did carry one of my favorites, red-hot cinnamon jawbreakers—they lasted forever and burnt your mouth the whole time. On the end of the shelf sat the Planter's peanut jar full of packages of roasted, salted peanuts.

A leaky icebox propped up one wall. Inside were Grapette and Orangette sodas, Royal Crown, Dr Pepper, and Coca-Cola. Sometimes, after payday, Daddy treated every kid in the store to a jawbreaker. Since we leased the coal mine, the kids and most of their parents thought we were rich. I didn't let on any different. We dressed more like them than we did rich people.

Daddy liked to hang out and talk to the drifters, find out what was going on in other parts of the world, like Fort Smith and Little Rock, or as far away as Texas and Oklahoma.

Jeremy told Daddy, "Things aren't quite picking up for all these men back from the war who need to work."

I always got a Royal Crown Cola and a Moon Pie. I liked to sit on the front porch and talk to the other kids. They were good at filling me in on things, especially if we all were sucking on jawbreakers. They knew a lot about the world, and some of the boys were hobos riding the rails with their dads. Boy, did I want to do that. They said girls couldn't be hobos. Somehow I knew they were right, but I didn't want to admit it.

Daddy wanted to know all about these men and their kids. He tried to help them out, especially if he hired them to work in the coal mine.

Mama told him more than once, "Fred, you're going to put us in the poorhouse yet."

Daddy and Uncle Albert were working on a big vein of coal and needed some help to get enough to fill a railroad car so they could get paid. Daddy hired a man called Hoyt and his brother Alton. Daddy liked to hire family. "June Ellen, family will always stick together in a coal mine and take care of each other.

Hoyt and Alton wore the most faded-out blue overalls I had ever laid my eyes on. They looked like they'd been wash boarded till the color scrubbed right off, but they were clean. Daddy told Hoyt and Alton to be at the mine come daylight Monday.

"You need a lunch pail, a miner's cap, gloves, and a carbide lamp with carbide to run it. Jeremy here will fix you up with whatever you don't have. I'll sign for you till you start getting a regular paycheck. Make sure you bring a lunch or you won't last. You'll also need a pick, a shovel, a sledgehammer, a wedge, and a coal-breaking bar. I have extra if you need it, till you can get your own."

Most of the men Daddy hired couldn't afford to buy their own tools. Daddy worked out a deal with Jeremy to provide the men their equipment, and Daddy would sign for it till the workers paid it off.

I watched Daddy sign each man's tickets. Sometimes Daddy let them charge groceries, too, mostly beans, lard, onions, coffee, taters, flour, salt, and sugar. He made sure Mr. Conley threw in a chunk of bologna and a box of crackers.

"Mining is hard work, Jeremy; they got to have lunch. I can't stand to see kids go hungry, and if those boys are going to work for me, they need all the strength they can get. I'm not paying them to be worked out before they start."

Alton said, "Thank you, Mr. Thackeray, you won't be sorry you helped us out like this. We'll always give twice what you give us. My family will eat some decent meals for the first time in a long time."

Daddy smiled and shook each man's hand. It was times like this I loved my daddy and wished I could be just like him. It's hard being a girl sometimes, even though I mostly didn't let it get in my way. Not being allowed to go and be a part of Daddy's coal mine just hurt.

"You know, Jeremy, I'm good for all these tickets. We're getting a few tons of coal a week now, and I should be getting a payload soon."

"You're an honest man, Fred. You always pay up in the end." He looked at Daddy and then dropped his gaze. "I need to tell you that Tildie's mother's real sick over in Ozark. She's going over there to take care of her. Be there, you know, till the end."

"Sorry to hear that. But I guess it's what families do, Jeremy."

"She wants me to go with her."

"What about your store? Who's going to run it? What're you going to live on in Ozark?"

"Well, her brother Wyley has a little store, a lot like mine, only in a real building made of brick. He likes his moonshine if you know what I mean, and he's tired of running the store. He's decided to head out to California and try his luck, and he offered it to me for moving over there and taking over the care of his mother." He gave Daddy a look again. "I'm considering it, Fred. It's a good deal for me, a move up, if you know what I mean."

Daddy got real quiet for a long time. "What about this store? What's going to happen to these people? You can't leave them out here with nothing."

Nobody moved or made a sound in that old shack of a store. I quit gnawing on my jawbreaker and felt the burning on my tongue. The burning felt real but nothing else did.

"There's a new guy in town. A Mr. Mackey. He's rented the old Doc Watson's house on Hospital Hill, that big two-story Victorian just up from Dr. John's. From Tulsa, I think he said. He runs little stores like this in Booneville, Morison's Bluff, Greenwood, all over. Everywhere there's a coal mine and a town to go with it, he keeps up a little store to help the miners. And he's bought a few of the mines too."

Daddy got real serious looking. His black bushy eyebrows came together in the middle and he had dark furrows across his forehead. He was chewing on a sassafras stick that he spit out in little pieces.

"Sounds like a company store kind of guy to me, Jeremy. The kind that owns your soul and you can't never buy it back."

"Now, Fred, you know me better than that. I told Wyley I was going to take my time finding a new owner, make sure I found the right guy. Then I'd give him whatever I got for my store. It won't be much, but it will give him a stake for getting to California."

Daddy tried to look stern, but his eyes gave him away. They always stayed warm, almost watery, but not teary, just soft and brown. When he tried to look stern, mostly he looked worn out and sad.

I could hardly stand it. I stood up tall beside him. I gave Jeremy my own hard-eye look.

"What do I owe you, Jeremy?"

"Don't worry about that yet. I'll see what I can do. Heck, you're what supports this store, you and your coal mine up there. Without you, there'd be no store. I told Mr. Mackey that. Anybody who buys my store is going to know that and I won't leave you here without a store, Fred. I promise you that. Till it's sold, I'm here."

"If he buys your store, Jeremy, and my tickets with it, he'll come after Shoal Creek next. You know that, don't you?"

"This is hard times for a lot of us, Fred. I'll see what I can do. I'm sorry."

Daddy didn't stay much longer. "Let's go, June Ellen. Something's turned my stomach sour."

Daddy stomped out and I stomped with him.

[25]

April Leigh Has a Date

I STAYED PRETTY ANGRY at April Leigh that summer. She only thought about herself, not Daddy or our coal mine. She was in our room, primping, combing her hair over and over trying to make it flip up like Lauren Bacall on the cover of *Screen Stars*. She sat there, staring at that movie star then looking at herself in that old, cracked mirror on the vanity.

I left and slammed out the front door. Daddy was working late at the mine, breaking out coal. He wanted to pay Jeremy for those tickets real bad, so nobody could take Shoal Creek. I sat on the porch swing dragging my feet. My red tennis shoes had holes in the top from me just sitting and swinging. I'd push off big, trying to reach the ceiling, and then I'd drag my feet all the way back. The toes of my red tennis shoes had faded to two perfect white circles. Mama was in the living room mending Daddy's overalls.

I jumped off the porch swing and yelled for Rex, "Come on, Rex, let's go on an adventure."

Rex crawled out from under the porch and wagged his tail, jumping all around. He was the finest bird dog ever, although Daddy didn't hunt anymore. It was too hard for him to breathe and carry a rifle and walk through the woods. Rex became my partner and an explorer like me. He had picked up on it real quick. He loved adventures with me as much as he ever loved hunting. He told me himself.

I decided to be like Annie Oakley that afternoon. She had the best Wild West adventures. "Let's go get my lariat, Rex, and practice."

Rex came with me, but he refused to let me rope him. I was stuck with the scarecrow in the corn patch or a fence post. Mama told me to leave the scarecrow alone 'cause I roped his head off once.

"It's hard being a cowgirl in this family, Rex."

I cut through the hedge and started walking back toward the barn when I heard an old car rumbling down the road. It backfired and stopped in front of our house.

"Rex, somebody's at our house. Be quiet and come here. We have to sneak up and see who it is." Rex liked to bark at people so I had to keep reminding him that spying meant being real quiet. We crept back under the bushes; I crawled on all fours like Rex.

It was Delbert Jenkins, the junk man. "What's he doing here, Rex?"

Then Isaac Jenkins, April Leigh's boyfriend, slid out of the car door with his head hanging down and his hands in his pockets.

"Boy, I'll be back to pick you up when it's dark." Delbert tried to roar off, but that old Ford hiccupped its way up the road.

Isaac watched his uncle drive off then reached in his back pocket and pulled out a black Ace comb with missing teeth and combed his hair backwards. His stiff black hair wanted to stand straight up, but he kept at it; he used his own spit trying to make it sweep up and back.

"What are you doing, Isaac? Your hair's standing straight up like corn stubble."

Isaac jumped. "June Ellen, you like to scared me to death. What are you sneaking around for?"

"I'm not sneaking around. Me and Rex are on an adventure. We're spying on you to see if you're friend or enemy."

"June Ellen, how would you like to make a dime by going to get me a spoonful of your mama's lard?"

"What for?"

"I need it to slick back my hair. Come on, I'll give you a dime and a nickel if you don't tell no one and an extra large scoop of chocolate in your ice-cream soda at Haney's."

I shrugged. "Okay. Come on, Rex."

I walked around to the back porch and slid my hand down the side of the screen door to a gap where it did not quite meet the splintered wood frame and gently opened it. I slipped into the back porch knowing I would never get to the lard if Mama heard me.

Rex slunk right along with me. The kitchen door stood wide open to catch any breeze that might come along. I tiptoed into the kitchen and spied the can of Honey Dew Brand Pure Lard on the top shelf of Mama's pine hutch.

I needed to climb up there and get it without arousing any suspicion. Our old metal step stool was folded up, leaning against the icebox. I knew it was going to squeak when I opened it up, but I had to have it. I continued on my tiptoes and crossed over the cracked linoleum and picked up the step stool, then crossed back over to the pine hutch. I set it down as gently as I could and pulled the hinged steps from under the stool. The rusty hinges creaked and groaned and hardly wanted to move, but I kept at it till they finally let go with a squeal. I held my breath till I was sure Mama didn't hear me.

I climbed up the step stool and grabbed the lard can and opened it. "Rex, it's almost empty. There's only enough here for biscuits on Sunday after church."

Then I spied the grease can full of cold bacon grease sitting on the back of the cookstove right beside me. I climbed down the step stool and looked into that grease flecked with bacon.

"Rex, I think this is worth a dime, don't you? I don't want Mama mad at me for using up the last of her lard, and I don't want to give up biscuits Sunday morning with Mama's cream gravy."

Rex agreed. He loved biscuits and gravy and he always got his own plate with grits.

I found one of Mama's jelly glasses and filled it with big white globs of that grease. I picked out the bacon scraps as best I could and put the step stool back. Rex and I crept back around to the front yard.

"Here you go, Isaac. Here's your ten cents' worth."

Dusk was settling in on us and shadows were looming and Isaac couldn't see the lard very well and he had more on his mind I guessed than the lard.

He stuck his hand in and grabbed a fistful of that bacon grease and slathered it all over his hair. He combed his fingers through his hair, slicked it all straight back, and pulled it into a little knot at the back.

"How do you like my ducktail, June Ellen?"

"I think you need a little more to keep your ducktail wagging."

"Okay." He stuck his hand back in and got another big glop and stuck it on top and smushed it down on his ducktail.

Rex jumped all over Isaac and tried to lick his hands. He loved bacon grease.

"June Ellen, what's wrong with your dog? Tell him to get off me."

"Where's my dime and extra nickel for my silence?"

Isaac reached in his pocket and pulled out some change. He handed me a greasy nickel and a dime. I rubbed it in the grass and walked off.

"Come on, Rex, let's go out back to the barn. And don't forget about my ice cream, Isaac."

I walked off and went around the house in plain sight making sure Isaac saw me. Then Rex and I waited. I heard him knock on the door, then the screen door opened and April Leigh walked out. I waited and the swing started to squeak.

Rex and I snuck around the corner of the house, and I slunk down to all fours again like Rex. We crawled behind the hydrangea bushes, which were all leafed out and about to bloom. Thick green leaves grew on sturdy stems that were almost as tall as me. The hydrangea bushes lined the rock foundation of the porch, and Rex and I hunkered down to watch and listen.

I heard the porch swing creaking back and forth, creak, creak. Then Isaac leaned close to April Leigh. "Your eyes are sure bright, April Leigh. They are like stars in the sky."

"That's sweet, Isaac."

Then I saw Isaac's arm inch toward her shoulders. April Leigh shrugged and shifted away from him. Isaac quickly dropped his arm behind the swing. But his shoulder touched hers. I swear I felt the tremors go down both their arms. April Leigh moved a little closer but didn't touch him.

"April Leigh, I'm going to be the captain of the Paris High Eagles football team this fall. I'll buck hay all summer and build my muscles as strong as Tarzan in that movie we just saw."

"Oh, Isaac, that's great."

"How would you like to be a cheerleader or homecoming queen?"

"Oh, Isaac, I'd like that a lot."

April Leigh moved closer to him. I saw her thigh touch his and his whole body jumped, and she shivered like it was cold out, instead of a warm spring evening.

Isaac slowly lifted his arm up from the back of the swing and gently let it float down to April Leigh's shoulder. His back was stiff, and his head went straight up from his neck like Frankenstein's. It took forever for him to get his arm to her shoulder.

April Leigh started to lay her head on his shoulder then Isaac turned toward her with his lips all pursed up. Then she turned toward him with her lips puckered.

"Rex, they're going to kiss," I whispered. I couldn't help myself. But they paid no attention.

April Leigh started to sniff. "What's that smell?"

"It's nothing. Just a skunk walking by," Isaac said.

He rubbed her shoulder and April Leigh touched his neck slowly and gently. Isaac was breathing hard, and April Leigh ran her fingers over his ducktail.

She yelled, "Yuck, what's this?"

She had bacon grease all over her hand. A big glob of it dripped from her fingers. April Leigh screamed. "Oh my gosh. What's on your hair? It smells like spoiled bacon."

I laughed so hard I rolled out from under the hydrangea bushes. April Leigh leapt up and just about tore off the screen door getting in the house. Just then Delbert Jenkins drove up and tooted his horn. Rex ran around the corner, jumped up on Isaac, and licked him all over hunting for bacon grease. He was a happy dog.

[26]

The Red Cowgirl Hat

"JUNE ELLEN, go get Rex and let's you and me go down to the Green Frog to cool ourselves off. I need to talk with your uncle Albert about some mine business. He'll be by in a few minutes."

"Did you tell him about Mr. Mackey?"

"Don't you worry about Mr. Mackey, June Ellen. Your uncle and I are figuring that one out."

"Maybe Freddy'll come home soon and help us, Daddy."

"He just might. You never know. I reckon he's got his hands full where he's at right now. He's doing some mighty important work on that ship. Uncle Sam needs him worse than we do. I think I'm ready for a cold beer."

"Daddy, does Mama know we're going?"

"She knows I got mine business to go over with your uncle. As long as I take you and don't leave you here alone, she'll let us be."

"Okay, Daddy. I can always use a Dr. Pepper and some peanuts."

I went with Daddy to the Green Frog. We both needed some time away from the women. Daddy needed a cold beer to soothe his throat, after his coughing fits. April Leigh still refused to talk to me, and Mama fussed at me and Rex all the time. Daddy talked to the other miners who were there and asked how much money everybody was getting for their coal.

"Gabe, what are they paying the Purity mine for a short ton?"

"We're getting almost five dollars, 4.90, to be exact."

"Last week, 4.90. This week I got 4.86," Shorty said. "How about you, Fred?"

"Pretty much the same as you. I was hoping it'd top five dollars by the time we got our next load."

"What we're getting now doesn't pay like that good hard anthracite we mined before the war ate it all up," Shorty said.

Daddy and Uncle Albert went off to a corner table by themselves.

I listened for a few moments; mostly they talked about Jeremy maybe selling his store and all the tickets Daddy had to pay off.

Uncle Albert told Daddy, "With that big vein we hit last week, you can pay those off. All we need is a little time."

"Let's go, Rex. I think it's time to take a walk around the square and see what's going on. Daddy and Uncle Albert are gonna figure something out, I'm sure of it."

Rex jumped up eager to go. He was just as curious about people as I am.

I stopped to look in the window of Hancock's Department and Feed Store. They sold mining clothes as well as cowboy clothes. They had a whole row of cowboy and cowgirl hats on a stand in front of the window. My eyes got swept up by a red cowgirl hat, a bright red straw hat with a beautiful white band that ran all the way around the crown.

The white band showed a cowgirl sitting on a fence rail watching a cowboy twirling his lariat. She wore a Dale Evans's cowgirl skirt, brown and yellow with red and yellow fringe around the bottom, and a yellow cowgirl shirt with snap buttons. That's how you knew it was a cowgirl shirt.

She had on golden brown cowgirl boots with black-and-white stitching of horses rearing up on. I wanted that red cowboy hat and those cowgirl boots, but I wanted to wear my own jeans with leather chaps and spurs, like the boys.

And I didn't want to just sit there either; I wanted my own lariat to practice twirling.

I pressed my nose against the glass so hard I breathed fog and steamed up the window until I couldn't breathe.

I let up a little and on the plate glass was a perfect impression of a pug nose with two holes. I moved over and did it again, then again and again. They started to look like smashed hearts with two eyes. I kept going till I had a line of pug-nose hearts all the way to the door. Rex followed me wagging his tail. He appreciated all those pug hearts, I could tell.

Then I heard Gracie yelling at me. "June Ellen, June Ellen, what are you doing? Hey, Rex. How are you, boy?" Rex got really happy seeing Gracie and jumped up to greet her.

"Oh, June Ellen, that's gross. Your nose is full of germs and so is the window. Ima Jean's going to kill you when she sees that."

"Let's go in. She won't even know it's me. Don't you think it looks like a line of hearts with eyes?"

Gracie couldn't help herself and started laughing.

"Rex, wait here. Ima Jean won't let you come in."

We walked in and I went right to the red cowgirl hat. Ima Jean walked right over when she saw me.

"Drats," I said to Gracie. "There are no other customers around so she has to bother me."

"It's her job, June Ellen."

"She knows I don't hardly have any money. And she hates to wait on me, because I like to try out everything."

Ima Jean's bosom pushed up over her low-cut blouse, like usual. April Leigh told me Ima Jean was still looking for a husband and thought she could attract one that way.

Today I thought her bosom looked like bread dough risen twice. I imagined poking them and watching them deflate like Mama does her bread dough. But I didn't want to get that close.

"I'd like to try on that cowgirl hat, Ima Jean. The red one with the cowgirl sitting and watching that cowboy twirl his lariat."

"Do you have any money, June Ellen? I don't want you wasting my time today. I have other people who I need to help."

"Of course, I do." I stuck my hand in my pocket and jingled the silver dime and nickel I got from Isaac. It didn't really jingle but I could imagine it anyway.

Ima Jean had no choice. She had to let me try it on.

"Is your hair clean, June Ellen? Mr. Hancock doesn't want anybody trying on his hats that don't have clean hair. Come here and let me smell your hair."

No way was I going to let Ima Jean smell me.

"Let's go, Gracie. Daddy's at the Green Frog. He'll bring me back here and make Ima Jean let me try on that cowgirl hat."

Ima Jean smirked as I walked away.

I marched out the door with Gracie and looked at my row of pug hearts. I smiled. "I hope Ima Jean gets to clean this window."

Gracie laughed. "Bye, June Ellen. I have to be home by supper."

Rex and I walked back to the Green Frog. Rex was welcome there. Daddy and Uncle Albert were back at the bar laughing and having a beer with the other miners. I guess their business was done.

"Daddy, I need you to go with me to Hancock's to try on a red cowgirl hat with a cowgirl sitting on a rail fence with her horse right beside her. Ima Jean wanted to smell my hair first and I wouldn't let her."

"Not today, June Ellen. It's supper time and we had better get home. I don't want Uncle Albert to get in trouble again."

"Well, Fred, I think you got that backwards." Uncle Albert laughed.

I knew it was no use changing his mind. "Let's go home, Rex."

I grumbled my way out of the Green Frog with Rex, and we climbed in the back of the truck so we could plot together and figure out how to get that red cowgirl hat.

We got to our house and Mama was standing on the front porch waiting on us. "Uh-oh," I said to Rex. We both hunkered down.

But Mama was laughing and jumping up and down. "Oh, Fred, you won't believe it."

Daddy hardly got the truck door shut when Mama ran and grabbed him so hard that I thought Daddy might crack in two.

"Our boy, Freddy, Jr., is coming home. And he's all of one piece. The Greyhound bus will drop him off Tuesday."

Rex started barking and jumping, and I shouted hurrah all the way up to the sky. Daddy and Mama did a jig, till Daddy ran out of breath, and was about to start coughing, then Uncle Albert took over till everybody was out of breath, even me and Rex. Then we collapsed on the tailgate and laughed till tears started flowing down our cheeks. Then everything and everyone got real quiet. It was a solemn moment, I thought.

[27]

Freddy Home from the War

HE STOOD AT the bus station with a big cigar hanging out of his mouth. My brother Freddy was home from the war. He wore a dark-blue navy uniform with the white collar and a white sailor's hat like Popeye.

I rode with Daddy and Uncle Albert in his Ford coupe to pick up Freddy from the war he had gone to fight so he didn't have to go work in a coal mine with Daddy.

Mama and April Leigh had stayed at the house to get dinner ready. In his letters home, all Freddy talked about was Mama's cooking and how much he missed it.

Mama said, "I'm going to cook all of Freddy's favorite foods, fried chicken, creamed potatoes, milk gravy, home-grown string beans, dilly beans, and biscuits with my own fresh-churned butter and molasses."

We were all looking forward to that dinner.

I ran and grabbed Freddy around the legs, and he hoisted me up on his shoulders. "You've sure grown, June Ellen, your feet are practically at my knees."

"I'm almost as tall as you, Freddy."

He started laughing. "I'm home for good now, Snapper."

He hugged Daddy and then Uncle Albert. We were a sight there on Main Street.

"Daddy, and Uncle Albert, I've never been so excited to see the Paris square before. I never thought I'd want to eat another bowl of beans at the Bunny Hop Inn, but just the thought of it makes my mouth water. I can't wait to taste Mama's fried chicken."

"Freddy, you're home, son. God bless us today. Your mama has cooked up a feast for you."

Uncle Albert clapped Freddy on the shoulder. "Yes, our boy has come home safe and sound with two legs and two arms from that war."

Uncle Albert grabbed Freddy's army-green duffel bag and threw it in the back seat. Then Freddy and I climbed in.

Freddy said right off, "Daddy, Uncle Albert, I'm finished with this damn war, and I'm ready to go back to the coal mines. After my feet darn near rotted off from being wet all the time in that boat, I think I could stand being underground again in the belly of the earth."

"Son, last time you went down in a coal mine, I ended up digging you out. I believe that was when you ran off and joined up to see the world."

"I know, Daddy. I saw the world all right, and it's not near as pretty as you think. I watched bombs explode around me and on top of me. I've watched boats blown right out of the ocean. I prayed to be underground in a coal mine."

Daddy touched Freddy on his arm, gently.

"I got tired, Daddy, real tired, of being out in the open, a sitting duck on a ship in the middle of the ocean with no land in sight."

Daddy said, "I remember coming home after the First World War. I remember the first time I went underground into that old Bear Creek mine, we dug out by hand. It was cool, damp, and quiet. No bullets here and no nerve gas was my first thought. I know differently now, Freddy. There's other kinds of gas and other kinds of killers."

Daddy had a coughing fit just then from just thinking about it, I guess. He covered his mouth with his handkerchief until it quit.

"I know, Daddy," Freddy said. "I just want to go under the ground and slide through the red Arkansas clay. I want to lie on that trolley going down those tracks under the earth. I want to be surrounded by huge black coal veins. Striking it, hammering it, till my own pores are black with rock and dust."

I watched Freddy and didn't say a word.

"Daddy, the only way I know to get my feet back on the ground is to get under the ground."

"Your mama's going to have a fit, Freddy, after your last time in a coal mine."

Freddy shut his mouth and just stared out the window.

Daddy sighed. "All right." He looked at Uncle Albert.

"You'll be a big help to us, son. Jeremy's talking about selling out his store. I'm trying to get a big enough payload to buy back all my tickets before he sells out to some company man."

"Daddy, that store owes you everything. If Jeremy does that to you, he's just another scoundrel. That doesn't sound like Jeremy to me."

"His wife's mother has taken sick and her brother offered him a better store in Ozark, if he'd move there and take over the store so his wife can take care of her mother. People do things sometimes because they have to, just to make ends meet."

"I'll help you, Daddy. We'll cut and ship enough coal to pay off everything. They can't take your lease because you have a few tickets owed."

"I hope you're right, son, but I'm afraid it's more than a few tickets. But in the meantime, it's good to see you home and that's enough today to make me happy. How about you, June Ellen?"

"Freddy, you're our good luck. I knew you'd take care of our coal mine if you were here, and here you are."

"Albert, take Freddy by the Mercantile in the morning and get him some pit clothes. Your dinner bucket's still on the back porch, and we'll round you up some tools at Shoal Creek in the morning."

"Daddy, can we drive by Hancock's Department and Feed Store? It's almost my birthday, and I want to show Freddy my red cowgirl hat in the window."

"Not today, June Ellen. We don't want to be late for your mama's dinner."

"That's right, June Ellen. You don't want to miss your aunt Annie's chocolate cake or strawberry rhubarb pie," Uncle Albert added.

"Freddy, don't you want to see it?"

"I can't do everything my first day home, June Ellen. Eating is the only thing on my mind, right now, and hugging Mama and April Leigh and Aunt Annie."

I sighed just like Daddy.

"Damnation," I muttered. Nobody heard me, so I tried it again, this time a little louder, "Damnation."

"All right, June Ellen, that's enough. You sound like the Toad Man," Daddy said.

Freddy laughed and hugged me. "June Ellen, you're all grown up."

I smiled 'cause I knew he was right. I was really happy Freddy was home, and dinner was sounding pretty good.

Mama cried and hugged Freddy all at the same time. April Leigh grabbed him around the neck and jumped on his back like she did when she was a little girl, before she went to high school. Aunt Annie laughed and clapped her hands till finally Freddy was free to give her a big hug.

"Eat, Freddy, eat." Mama and Aunt Annie both started loading up the table. First with a big platter of fried chicken, then mashed potatoes and gravy. Freddy sat down and just looked at all that good food.

Daddy bowed his head and started praying. "Bless us, O Lord, and these thy gifts, for which we are about to receive. Thank you, O Lord, for bringing our dear Freddy home. From thy bounty and our hearts to our home. Amen."

"Thank you, Daddy. And, Mama, your cooking fills my heart to over-flowing, and my stomach. I haven't seen food that looked like this since I left almost a year ago." He grabbed a chicken leg and tore into that crispy crust. About that time Mama pulled a pan of hot biscuits out of the oven. He grabbed a biscuit and ate it in one bite. "I'm in heaven now. Mama, you're my angel."

"Your daddy's right, Freddy. We're blessed to have you home. Food comes from the heart and my heart is singing right now with you sitting here, all of a piece, eating like a pig, which I will let you get away with this time." Mama laughed.

Aunt Annie put her famous strawberry rhubarb pie and chocolate cake right in front of him. "You too, Aunt Annie, you're my other angel." Aunt Annie looked like she had just won another blue ribbon. Mama didn't care, she was happy.

[28]

Freddy Sees Lizzie Again

FREDDY WENT RIGHT BACK to work with Daddy. Mama decided a coal mine was better than a battleship. She told Aunt Annie, "I feel better with Freddy down there with Fred. He can take over some of the heavy work and keep Fred from breathing that much coal dust. I never thought I'd say that, but Fred's coughing fits worry me."

I hardly saw Freddy. He worked from before daylight to dark. He came home and ate what Mama put in front of him then went to bed. Friday morning, though, he woke me up before he left. "June Ellen, do you still meet Lizzie at Haney's for sodas on Saturdays?"

"Sometimes, if she has cheerleading practice or comes to town to shop."

"Tomorrow's payday and Daddy's letting us off at noon. How about I treat you to a chocolate ice-cream soda? Is that still your favorite or have you changed on me? Seems like so much has changed since I've been gone, even you. April Leigh's more like a young woman. I don't hardly know what to say to her."

"High school's made her different and it changed how she looks too. I'm not gonna change like that, Freddy."

"Sometimes, you just can't stop those kinds of changes. I sure found that out in the navy."

"Okay, Freddy. You can come with me to Haney's tomorrow and buy me whatever I want."

"Ha, June Ellen. I don't know about that, but you can count on me for an ice-cream soda."

"And will you go with me to Hancock's? I just gotta show you the red cowgirl hat I want for my birthday."

"You drive a hard bargain, June Ellen, but, okay, I'll go with you to Hancock's. I'm off to the coal mine, then tonight I'm going out for a while."

136

After lunch the next day, Freddy came running in and gave Mama a big hug. "June Ellen, I have to wash up and change, then you and I will be on our way."

"Where's Daddy? Is Daddy okay? He sure coughed a lot last night."

Mama smiled real big. "Yes, June Ellen, your daddy's fine. He stopped off at the bank to talk to Mr. Blackstone. Uncle Albert's with him. I imagine they'll stop off at the Green Frog. That soothes his throat, he tells me." Mama smiled when she said it. "It's okay, he's earned it this week. He can finally get some rest this weekend. That always slows down his spells."

When we got to Haney's, I grabbed a stool at the soda fountain. Isaac, April Leigh's boyfriend, still worked there and he had gotten over being mad at me, and he was so embarrassed, he never told anyone he had put bacon grease in his hair. Rex still liked him a lot and that helped him when he came to visit April Leigh. Rex stopped barking at him.

"I want a chocolate ice-cream soda and maybe a Dr Pepper with peanuts." I didn't say anything about the extra scoop of chocolate since I never got him any lard. I looked around for Freddy to see if he said no, but Freddy was pacing in front of the window looking up and down the street. "Freddy, cheerleading practice isn't over for fifteen minutes." I told Isaac, "He's looking for Lizziebelle."

Freddy gave me that look, but he didn't say anything. He looked nervous and kept slicking back his hair. He took his own Ace comb out of his back pocket and combed his hair back. This time Isaac and I both laughed.

Freddy finally came over to the soda fountain and sat down. "Freddy, do you think you'll get enough coal to pay off Daddy's tickets?"

"There's plenty of coal down there, June Ellen. We just need some time. Daddy gets used up too quick, so I have to step in and do his job while he rests. Hoyt and Alton are good strong workers now that they're working regular and eating steady. Uncle Albert says they're doing twice what they used to. If we keep this up, it won't be long till we have another load. We just need Jeremy to hold off selling."

"I'm so happy you're back, Freddy. Now Jeremy will surely wait for Daddy to pay off his tickets." Just then the door opened and Lizzie walked in.

"Hi, Lizzie, Freddy's home and he came to see you." Freddy turned bright red and looked like he was going to bolt out the door.

"Hello, Freddy." Lizzie stood there and looked at him with her dark eyes.

"Hi, Lizzie. How are you?"

Isaac brought me my ice-cream soda and I decided to just concentrate on that for a while.

"I'm good, real good. I'm glad you made it home safe." And she smiled, then Freddy's eyes went all soft and his shoulders loosened up.

"Can I get you a Coca-Cola or something to drink?"

"Okay, I'll have a Coke."

"Two Cokes, Isaac."

"I'm ready for my Dr Pepper and you forgot my peanuts, Isaac." I knew Freddy wasn't paying any attention to me.

"Lizzie, do you think you'd ever go out with me again? I know I took off pretty quick last time. It's just that . . ."

"It's okay, Freddy. I know what happened. Thank you for the note and June Ellen did keep me informed and I do think you owe me."

Freddy looked quite relieved. "Yes, I sure do. How about tomorrow after church? Maybe we can start over, go to a movie or something."

"My parents don't mind movies, like some, but they prefer I don't go on Sundays. How about a walk along Shoal Creek this time?"

"I'm working at the Shoal Creek mine again."

"You know that mine's right below our farm."

"I remember from the last time we were at your farm," Freddy said.

"June Ellen, how about you come with us again? Then my parents won't say no."

I couldn't believe my luck. Maybe after all this time I would finally get to see our mine. "Oh, yes, Lizzie. I would love to come. I'll bring Rex for a long walk and Daddy'll be so happy."

Freddy was looking a little stunned, but didn't say no. He knew when he was licked. Besides he couldn't take his eyes off Lizzie. I don't even know if he heard the plans Lizzie and I just made.

"I'd like to see your farm, Lizzie," I said. "And Freddy could show us where the mine is. I'd like to see what a mine looks like, wouldn't you?"

I could feel his hard, suspicious eyes burning a hole in my back.

"I mean from outside, where your farm overlooks it and Shoal Creek." My head was spinning with the effort of figuring how to get in that mine.

Freddy looked at me and at Lizzie. "No, I don't think going up to the mine is a good idea. We don't have any business going there tomorrow."

"It'll be great fun, June Ellen, just to walk the creek. Maybe another time," Lizzie said.

"Well, I guess, I'll see you after church," Freddy said.

"Make it around two o'clock. It's our turn to feed Reverend Spicer. I'll bring some ham sandwiches and sodas. And, of course, some Moon Pies. How does that sound, June Ellen?"

"Sounds really good to me, Lizzie." With Freddy looking at Lizzie like that, I knew I had a chance to at least see the slope going into the mine.

Freddy was in a good mood and didn't lay into me on the way home. He was whistling and I told myself he was trying to figure out some things too. Freddy didn't take me to Hancock's, but I didn't care so much. Rex and I had to get ready for our adventure to Shoal Creek mine.

[29]

Down in the Coal Mine

I COULD HARDLY LOOK at Mama when she had that hard-eye look. I just wanted to tell her everything. I just kept fiddling with the cuffs on my cowgirl jeans. They were lined with red flannel cloth with pictures of cowgirls who wore jeans just like mine and twirled their lariats. I wore my lucky tennis shoes again, the ones I used for adventures. They were all I had for going exploring.

I wanted to shout, "I'm going down in our coal mine." I knew better, though.

I had a plan all drawn up to get into the Shoal Creek mine and saw immediately how easy it would be. Freddy only had eyes for Lizzie.

Freddy took us down an old logging road to the bridge over the creek. He parked on the other side of the bridge under a big sycamore tree. The logging road took a sharp left before the bridge and that was where it became the supply road for the mine.

Freddy said, "Let's follow the creek down to that big pool with the sandy beach. It's a great place for a picnic. I'll bring the picnic basket and the drinks."

"Yes, Freddy, that's a beautiful place for a picnic. Come on, June Ellen, you can wade around in that big pool."

"No thanks, I think I'll go up the creek the other way so Rex can get a good walk in, then I'll join you."

Freddy smiled and looked relieved. "Good idea, June Ellen. Take Rex for a walk first. Don't be gone too long and don't get lost."

"Oh, Freddy. I've been here a hundred times, all you have to do is follow the creek."

"You're right, June Ellen. I'm not used to you being all grown up."

As soon as Freddy and Lizzie took off, Rex and I ran across the bridge and started up the supply road. It was uphill, but a well-worn smooth road made walking easy and we made good time. I rounded a corner at the top and there it was, the Shoal Creek mine. There was a large door, with a big arch that opened into the side of the mountain, with railroad tracks running down inside.

The tracks held two coal cars hooked together. On the other side of the cars sat the washhouse with dirty mining clothes hanging there. Next to it was the blacksmith shop. I'd seen all that before and I wanted to get down into that mine before Freddy missed me.

The slope looked like it had been tunneled out of the earth. Some would call it ugly with the slag heaps and coal dust covering all the bushes and leaves on the trees, but I thought it was just beautiful.

I walked slowly down the slope with Rex. A chill went through me and the hairs on my arms stood up. "This is an exciting day, Rex." Rex sensed it too. I could tell by the way his bird-dog nose went to work.

A cave of dark opened before me, black walls, and a dark roof. I pulled a candle out of my pocket. I'd brought five matches and I struck one on the train track and lit the candle. I wrapped my hand around the candle and then used my other hand to shield the flame to keep it from blowing out. I'd searched all over our house for a carbide lamp, but they were locked up.

I remember Daddy told Freddy when he started his first day at the mine, "Son, this lamp is the most important piece of equipment for every coal miner. This is your sunshine and your canary. When you are kicking out coal and release methane gas trapped there for over one thousand years, you can't smell it. You watch that flame and it will get brighter and brighter, and you'll know to get out of there."

I swallowed hard. All I had was a candle. "Rex, help me watch this candle."

I turned into a big tunnel with a railroad track that ran down the center. My arms tingled with excitement, and my legs itched to jump in an empty coal car, release the brake, and take off down into my daddy's coal mine. Rex hung behind me in the growing dark. I thrust the candle down low to light up the tracks, but I didn't like bending down all the time. I liked to look where I was headed even if it was too black to see. I held the candle in front of my eyes lighting up midnight on a moonless night an inch at a time.

I stepped gingerly between the railroad ties, bumping each one with my toe to keep me going the right way. I realized as I walked what color coal black is. It was no color at all. My heart raced; I trembled, thrilled to be on this train track going down underground into the belly of a real coal mine.

My candle flickered, throwing shadows of light around the tunnel, reminding me I was under the earth where there was no light except for what I carried. "Have you ever had such a grand adventure, Rex?" Rex hung his head low and sniffed the ground for something familiar, I expect.

Then the track ended. I bent down in the candlelight to look where my foot was going. I took one more step and the tunnel floor stopped. There was nothing there to stand on, just open space. I held my candle down low, close to the ground, careful to keep it shielded, and saw I was at the end of a rock ledge.

I sat on the edge and Rex bumped up right next to me, all hunkered down. I pushed my feet down feeling for the bottom. I stretched and stretched my right leg; glad for the two inches I grew this summer till something solid met my foot. I held my breath and eased myself down careful to keep the candle lit. I landed on solid rock.

In the shadowy light I saw several tunnels leading off the one I was standing in. I looked back for Rex, my candle held out at arm's length. His body, a dark shadow crouched by the tracks. He growled low in his throat, and then whined to me, "I don't want to jump down there."

"Come on, Rex, come on, boy. Just a little bit further. Look at these tunnels, like a honeycomb. Don't you want to see where Daddy and Freddy work? This is our chance."

Rex slunk to the edge. I grabbed some fur on his back in one hand and pulled him down. He yelped. "Good boy, Rex." I patted his head. "Follow me."

I turned into the first tunnel I came to, which forked into two more. I crept slowly into the right fork. The ceiling, solid rock, was only about four feet high, and my hair touched it when I walked. Creepy. I hunkered down like Rex. Several cave-like holes about three feet up from the floor emerged from the shadow of the candle. The candle flame flared and startled me, but I felt air on my sweaty skin. An airway I figured, like Freddy talked about, not methane gas.

"Rex, smell that fresh air; we're okay here."

Then the candle flared up again and this time blew out.

Coal-black darkness deeper than any night I ever experienced took hold. I wished I'd brought a jar to cover my candle with. I felt in my pocket for the matches I took from the cookstove. I struck one against the track and it sputtered then fizzled out. The brief sputter only made the dark blacker.

"Be careful," I scolded myself.

My fingers touched the matches. Only three left. I carefully pulled one from my pocket and struck it against the rock wall. This time I carefully shielded the lit match in the cup of my hand, the way I watched Freddy and his buddies light their cigarettes. I touched the match to the wick and it spurted to life, feeble but warm in my hand. It flared up bright but held this time.

I scouted the cave-like holes in the black rock wall. They must be what Freddy climbed into to get to the coal. A step dug into the wall of an opening became visible, and I jumped on it and leaped through the opening and tumbled hard down to solid, flat rock. My candle flew out of my hand and the flame went out.

I'd never seen black like this. It wasn't like night or coal-black shoe polish or coal blacking for stoves. It was dense, terror crept up on me.

"Hail Mary full of grace," I prayed to the Virgin Mary. Then I thought of Annie Oakley when the robbers cornered her in the abandoned silver mine. She didn't give up.

I reached my hand out and felt around the cave. Wax coated my fingers and I followed the wax trail till I found the candle. I gripped it hard not wanting to ever let it go. I pulled myself up and searched my pockets for a match. "Only two left, Rex." I struck the match, touched the wick, and light filled the cave. Only one match left, but I had light again for now.

Rex refused to jump up into the small opening. He hunkered down with his head between his paws. He didn't say a word.

"Okay, Rex, wait there; I just want to see what a wall of coal looks like. I swear I'll be right back. Cross my heart, hope to die, stick a needle in my eye."

Rex believed me.

In front of me, the wall of coal stretched farther than my light. Up close, it glittered in the candlelight, reflected a silvery sheen like the scales on a bream in sunlight. I touched it with the tips of my fingers, sliding down an open seam; the coal was hard with a softness when I rubbed it. Soot covered my fingers. I held them to the candlelight and they were black. I held the candle as close to the wall as I could. I feared I might set it on fire if I got too close.

Big cracks and dents showed where the pickaxe had broken out chunks of coal. I stuck my hand inside the hole feeling around its jagged edges, rough and sharp. The ceiling, gray, black rock, hung low like a tomb; slate Freddy called it, held up by huge pieces of timber.

I kicked my feet at the soft mounds underfoot and stirred up coal dust like black flour, laying thick on the floor. I coughed and sputtered as I breathed it in. It was like dust on the road when a car goes by on a hot dry day. I felt it settle all over me, in my hair, on my clothes. In the candlelight a cloud of black dust surrounded me. Every time I tried to take a breath, I choked and coughed. I couldn't even catch my own breath.

Daddy coughed like this I thought. This was what filled up his lungs and took away his breath.

I touched my finger to the fine black powder and imagined it going into my lungs and living there forever. I tasted it. I had to. Fine grit got in between my teeth and burnt my tongue. I spit and spit to get it out. My throat was dry and swollen. I wiped my mouth with the back of my hand, and I felt the black coal dust spread over my face.

I reached down to the floor with my candle and saw the shine in a piece of coal. I picked it up, overcome by that shine in this place where there was only black dark. I touched the surface, rubbed my thumb along it, smooth anthracite, cleanest-burning coal in the country. I wanted a reminder of my daddy's coal mine. I felt proud because it belonged to him, which meant it belonged to me too. But the coal mine and the coal dust frightened me.

I remembered some words from the poem Sr. Agatha read us in the library when a miner got trapped down in a coal mine and died. It was about listening to coal for a tale of leaves and ferns and frond-forests. 'Cause that was what coal used to be. And this poet, Owen, said when coal burned, you could hear the moans of the boys who died there writhing for air.

I bent down and scooped up a handful, feeling the coal dust leak through my fingers. I thought about the miners hurt and killed by it, but mostly I thought about Daddy lying in bed at night coughing and hacking up black snot; his lungs full of what I held in my hand.

This was what feeds us and kills us, I thought. I threw it to the ground, which stirred up more and I coughed and coughed, spitting my own black snot.

"Let's get out of here, Rex."

I thought of Freddy and Lizzie up on top sitting on a blanket drinking their Coca-Colas. I also knew they might be wondering where I took off to. I wanted more than anything to be back up on top of the Shoal Creek mine, not down inside this hard black cave of fossils, coal, and slate.

I sprang up from the hard rock floor determined to find my way back. I called out, "Rex, where are you? I'm ready to get out of here. I'm ready for a cold root beer." I heard a whining sound and carefully made my way toward it. "I'm coming, Rex."

The dark scared him, but he was loyal and fierce and stuck it out with me. I scrambled over the cave opening and again hit the ground hard. I forgot about the step. Total darkness took over, the candle flame snuffed out again, but I gripped the candle tight until my fingerprints marked the candle. I wasn't going to drop it again.

"I'm okay, Rex, don't worry."

Another whine, louder this time, greeted me. I dragged myself up slower this time. I felt bruised all over, and my elbow stung where I scraped it. I reached into my pocket again for the last match. I prayed to all the saints again, then I struck the match against the hard rock wall, shielding it from any wind and it spurted to life. I touched it to the wick, careful to keep anything from blowing it out, and I could see faintly in front of me again. I peered into the dark for the right tunnel.

"Rex, where are you?" I cried out.

He answered me.

I smelled like coal. I could feel the dust in the pores of my skin. I was afraid to think what my cowgirl jeans looked like and my blue checked blouse. I wished I had miner's clothes to wear.

"Oh bother, Jesus, Mary, Joseph, please just get me out of here." I trudged down the tunnel.

"Rex, you back me up when I tell Freddy I fell chasing you chasing a rabbit. Oh, he probably won't even notice with Lizzie there."

A whimper told me I was getting closer.

"Rex, you're here. I'm almost back." Rex whined and started barking, loud. The bark echoed through the honeycomb of tunnels and caves.

"Quiet, Rex, we don't want a cave in, and we sure don't want Freddy to hear you." I walked toward the sound of Rex barking. The tunnel opened up into another tunnel and there was Rex waiting. I'd arrived at the fork.

Rex jumped up on me with lots of licking and slobber and I have to admit, it felt real good.

"Rex, keep licking until all that coal dust is gone. I'm going to share my Moon Pie with you, I promise. Just get me to the slope and I'll take over from there."

The ceiling was much lower here and I walked hunched over. My candle flame created more shadows than light, but I could see other tunnels, dark holes opening off this wider tunnel.

"Okay, Rex, it's your turn. I want you to be Lassie and find our way back to the slope. You scout for me now."

Rex sniffed the floor of the tunnel, smelled the air, and took off down the first opening on the left. Rex used his nose to hunt, and I trusted his sense of smell and took off after him.

"Rex, you're the best hunting dog ever. Wait for me," I yelled, cupping my hands around the candle.

I'd used up all the matches and swore to keep it lit till I saw daylight. Rex bounded back to me, circled my legs, and I almost tripped over him. We made our way down the tunnel, and the shadows from the candlelight loomed in front of us like monsters.

I told Rex, "Keep going, don't get scared, it's our own shadows."

Rex skidded and stopped, hunkered down, and growled. The ledge appeared in front of us and Rex could go no further.

I walked to the stone ledge and felt the edges, smooth and worn. I knew the tracks were there that would guide us up the slope. Rex hugged my legs with his body. I had to get Rex up there and keep my candle lit. I put the candle in my mouth and clenched the very end between my teeth, while I tried not to gag. The flame warmed my cheek but didn't burn it.

My feet touched the ledge wall and I slowly bent down and grabbed Rex. I placed one arm under his chest and the other arm under his belly, while I held my head as high as I could. I didn't want to burn his fur. I heaved with all my might till his front paws touched the floor of the slope. Then he took over, pushed his legs against my body, and leapt to the slope.

I took the candle out of my mouth, my throat constricted like it wanted to puke. The candle was still lit and that was the most important thing. I wanted a drink of water, but there was none.

I just had to use my arms to pull myself up to the tunnel floor. I put the candle back in my mouth; it was shorter this time, but still just warm on my cheek.

I choked back my heaving throat and I thought of Nancy Drew in *The Haunted Bridge*, pulling herself out of the cold river water onto a haunted bridge. With all my might I pulled myself up till I could throw one leg over, then scrambled my whole body to the top of the ledge. I jerked the candle out of my mouth. My bite marks had about cut it in half. I gagged a couple of time then lay there panting like Rex, the lit candle safe in my hand, my fingernails like claws dug into it. We were back at the slope, still pitch black.

"Okay, Rex, lead me up this slope. We have no matches left. Remember there is a Moon Pie waiting and a root beer." Rex leapt up and bounded down the tunnel. "Wait," I yelled softly. "We have to go slow so our candle stays lit."

Rex heard me and slowed down, whining for me to hurry. I walked fast, shading the candle, eager to see real sunlight again. It was easy having the tracks to follow.

We passed several doorways framed with big post-oak timber, bigger around than my daddy's arms. I rubbed each one for good luck as we passed. It just seemed like the right thing to do. Rex barked at the next doorway and darted through it, like a fox going through a briar patch.

I scampered to keep up and protect the candlelight; I had to trust Rex. He had never let me down, and I didn't think he'd let me down this time either. I just kept my mind on Moon Pies and root beer while I prayed Hail Mary over and over.

First, I noticed the dark changing in the mine, it was still black dark, but there was a light to it I couldn't explain. Then I smelled sweet air, different than the dank air of the coal mine. Rex ran faster now and was way out of my sight but it didn't matter; I knew now I was on my way up the slope and out of the mine.

I burst out of the mine opening into the bright sunshine and started gulping air. I snuffed out the candle and stuck it in my pocket.

"Rex, we made it; we did it, you and me. We're the bravest two people I know, well, the bravest girl and the bravest dog," I said as I threw my arms around him.

"Ouch," I cried as my skinned elbow stung rubbing against his fur. "You are better than Lassie. Let's go find Freddy and Lizzie."

Then I noticed my clothes. "Oh, Sweet Jesus." My cowgirl jeans were mostly black now, and the cuffs held coal dust, so much I could barely make out the pictures. Each step I took, black clouds surrounded my feet.

Then I saw my blue-checked shirt. "I ruined it, Rex. I ruined my good shirt. Look at the black snot down the front and the ripped sleeves. It's like a black shroud over me. What am I going to do, Rex?"

I walked down from the mine to the creek where our picnic blanket lay on the ground. Lizzie paced back and forth. "June Ellen, where have you been? Freddy is off looking for you." Then she saw me and my clothes.

She looked hard at me and Rex. "You had better come up with a good story."

"I know, Lizzie, but I had to see our mine. I'm really thirsty and hungry. So is Rex." My hunger and thirst took away most of my fear.

"The soda is in the creek staying cold and the Moon Pie is in the basket. Help yourself as I'm sure you will."

I bounded down to the creek, saw the fishing line tied around my Grapette soda, and pulled it in like I was catching a fish. The opener was lying on the bank right where Freddy left it. I grabbed it, opened my soda, and took a long cold drink.

Rex lapped water from the creek like he'd been in the desert. And really I guess he was. I scrambled up to a nice sitting rock, let myself down gently, and slowly unwrapped my Moon Pie. Rex heard the paper rustling and rushed up to where I was sitting. That Rex never forgets a promise.

Together we devoured that Moon Pie, which made my stomach hurt a little. That piece of coal lay heavy in my pocket and I felt torn about our coal mine.

Lizzie took off to find Freddy. I hopped down from my rock perch and walked back to the picnic basket. I decided to enjoy a ham sandwich and think about my troubles later.

Pretty soon there was a commotion in the woods coming down from the mine slope. I heard Lizzie yelling, "Freddy, Freddy, she's back. June Ellen's back."

I had just bit into my ham sandwich when Freddy came running out of the woods, with Lizzie trailing behind. Freddy ran up to me and grabbed me by the arms pinning them to my sides. He picked me up and held me in the air, like he was going to shake the living tar out of me. The sandwich fell right out of my hand, and Rex grabbed it in midair and took off to the bushes.

"Where in the Sam Hill have you been, June Ellen? I ought to turn you over my knee right now."

Those are fighting words to me. "Put me down, put me down, you crap-covered rat." I tried hard to kick him, but he held me out too far. Then his eyes grew wide and I saw flames shooting out. He set me down. He looked at his hands covered with coal dust from my shirt.

"You didn't . . . you went down into that stinking coal mine. June Ellen, you could've hurt yourself real bad down there." Freddy was spitting nails. "No miner ever goes down into a mine alone because of the danger . . ."

Then Freddy stopped, his face grew pale. He walked around clenching his fists. He shook his head like he was trying to clear it. "I saw a lot of good men die on that ship, some were brave and some were just plain foolish. June Ellen, going down there alone was just plain foolish. You could have died down there."

I'd never seen Freddy get so riled up. "I didn't go that far, Freddy. I just walked down the slope to get a feel for it. I wanted to see where you and Daddy worked. It was real dark and Rex took off, so l had to chase him down and that is when I fell and got covered in coal dust."

I figured Rex had deserted me and took my sandwich; I sure didn't need to protect him anymore.

Freddy was stomping around and cursing by now. I cannot repeat what he said. It's not allowed to even say those swear words under my breath. I had learned that sometimes it was best to just keep quiet and that was what I did. Freddy scared me, staying mad like that for so long. I stood there and waited for him to finish. I about lost my appetite. War sure does change a person, I thought. Thank goodness, Lizzie stepped up.

"Freddy," Lizzie said, as she touched his shoulder gently, she let her fingers rest there for just a moment, then she slowly slid them off and squeezed his arm as she let go. Freddy got real quiet and looked at her and she looked back right into his eyes. He calmed down some and I was spellbound by the sight.

"I'm sorry, Lizzie. I saw things in that war and I know what can happen." He gave me a hard look. "Sometimes June Ellen just scares me. She's too much like me, I guess." Then he ran his fingers through his hair.

"I'm okay, Freddy," and I ran and hugged him tight. He looked daggers at me and grabbed me around my shoulders, then hugged me tight. Now he was covered in soot.

I said, "That coal dust is something, it sticks to everything. I can sure see how it gets in your lungs and just stays there."

"June Ellen, you are not out of trouble with me yet."

Lizzie said, "Let's eat. No sense in letting these Moon Pies and ham sandwiches I made special go to waste."

By this time, my mouth was dying to bite into another ham sandwich. We ate up everything. Adventure and curiosity made a person real hungry.

Freddy said, "I hope you have a good story for the shape your clothes are in, June Ellen. You can't hide coal dust."

I'd forgotten and now I looked at myself. My excitement and hunger made me forget for a time about going home.

"If you think *I'm* mad, you just wait."

Lizzie jumped in again. "Hey, let's go to my house. My parents are gone visiting all afternoon. We'll wash up your clothes, June Ellen, and I do believe I can sew the rip in your blouse, so you can hardly tell."

"Those clothes won't dry in time for us to get home for dinner," Freddy said.

"June Ellen, I will give you some of mine to wear home. Tell your mama and daddy you fell in the creek and got all wet and muddy, and I offered to wash and dry them for you."

"Lizzie, you're as clever as Nancy Drew," I said.

"That's a great compliment coming from you, June Ellen. Let's get to my house and get your clothes taken care of."

"Freddy, we have to do this again, since we didn't get to enjoy this pool and Shoal Creek. Next Sunday we could just start over. Don't you think that's a good idea, Lizzie?"

"Hold on, June Ellen. I think Lizzie and I will do this again, but I don't think you'll be along. What do you think, Lizzie, next weekend when I'm not working, just you and me? Maybe dinner and a movie? I think I owe you for June Ellen ruining our afternoon."

"I think I can work something out with my parents, Freddy, and, June Ellen, I'll just have to see you at Haney's."

"I'm sorry, Freddy. I just had to see where you and Daddy worked." My throat still hurt from swallowing that coal dust. "Now I know why he coughs all night till he can't talk. Freddy, you have to pay off Daddy's tickets."

"June Ellen, I'm working on that with Uncle Albert. You're right about Daddy, he can't keep going down in that mine when he's this sick."

I wanted to help Daddy keep our mine going, too. But I knew better than to say anything.

[30]

Jeremy Sells the Store

SUMMER WAS IN FULL SWING when a new, different whooping cough vaccine became available. Mama told me and April Leigh at breakfast, "You both have to go get a shot at Dr. John's for whooping cough. There's a new vaccine, and if you don't get this shot, you could die like the Fisher baby. Whooping cough makes you cough till you're blue in the face."

I told Mama, "I'm not a coward, but I can't tolerate someone sticking a needle in me. Cross my heart, hope to die, stick a needle in my eye. That's one oath, Mama, that I don't ever want to go back on."

Mama said, "When we were kids, June Ellen, your aunt Annie and I, they used a Victrola needle to give us our whooping cough vaccine. It was an epidemic and they ran out of needles. But my mama, your grandmother, made sure all her kids got that vaccine. She watched too many babies die from whooping cough."

I told April Leigh, "I hate shots the worst, especially a big shot like the one for whooping cough. That Mr. Mackey, now there's a big shot. He wants to steal our mine, the Shoal Creek, one of the last working coal mines in Logan County. But why does a rich man get to be called a big shot?"

April Leigh tried to get all huffy and walk away but she stopped. I saw the frown on her face go soft. "June Ellen, I just don't know anymore. Everybody's talking about it. Daddy needs to stay out of that mine to save what is left of his lungs.

"But Daddy's doing everything he can to hold on to it. Mr. Mackey's not sick and he has lots of coal mines."

Daddy walked into the kitchen and looked at both of us. He tried to grin. "You girls don't need to worry so much. I got a good crew and we're working on it. Mr. Mackey is like those men in the big outfits. He never goes down in his own mine if he can help it. He pays other people to do all the dirty work, takes it out of their hide. Leroy Phillips, Frank Zimmer,

LB Elsken, all worked for fellows like Mackey, got coal dust in their lungs like me and had to quit."

That's when Jeremy showed up at the house to talk to Daddy. They went out on the back porch and me and Rex sat on the stoop. Daddy never said a word, so we stayed right there and listened.

"Fred, Mr. Mackey bought the store and all your tickets with it. There was nothing I could do. I had too many debts and he handed me a wad of cash like none of us have seen in a long time. Enough to take over Tildie's brother's store in Ozark and give him a stake to move on."

"You tell me straight up, Jeremy, what's he want with my old mine? There's barely enough coal for scrappers like me left. There's nothing there for people like him."

"It's kind of like you tried to tell me, Fred. I'm not the smartest guy, you know. I don't catch on quite as quick as some. It turns out he's part of a bigger outfit that's mining differently. Mining's changed a lot since the war. You know that. They've got these new-fangled machines that eat up the mountaintop. They get the coal that's way back under these old hills. There's no way you can get to what he says he's going after. I'm awful sorry, Fred."

Jeremy shuffled his feet and tried to look Daddy straight in the eye, but he couldn't do it. Daddy never took his eyes off Jeremy, though.

"I told him about your coal mine, Fred, and how we worked together. He asked to look at your tickets and I let him. I told him you found a good vein and could finally pay up. He wanted to know how to get hold of you. Go talk to him, Fred. See what kind of guy he is. Maybe you can work something out with him."

"I wished you hadn't done that, Jeremy. I like to keep our business private."

"I know, Fred. I feel bad about the way things turned out."

Jeremy didn't look at Daddy. His eyes pretty much stayed on the floor. His hands shook a little, hoping for a handshake, I guess. He and Daddy always shook hands when they finished their business. Then he turned and walked out. I thought he looked sad but didn't want anyone to see it, 'cause that was how I got when I couldn't bear my own sadness.

Daddy said, "I'm going back to the mine. We've got to get that load out and pay off those tickets. It's the only way we'll keep that mine now." He took off for the Shoal Creek mine where Uncle Albert and Freddy were already working. No one said a word, not even Mama.

Later that day, Aunt Annie came over to talk to Mama.

Rex and I pretended to be asleep on the back porch on Daddy's cot. That way we could spy and hear everything.

I listened while Mama told Aunt Annie about what happened with Jeremy. "Mr. Mackey owns all Fred's tickets now, I'm afraid."

Aunt Annie shook her head. "I swear, Cora, I don't know what this town is coming to. First, the Depression, then the war, now the coal's about gone, and what's left, this Mr. Mackey shows up to steal."

"Oh, Annie, Fred says if he can't pay the tickets, Mr. Mackey will just take the lease to the mine. What's he want with that old worked-out mine anyway?"

Aunt Annie was quiet for a minute then she said to Mama, "Well, I did do some checking with Ima Jean at Hancock's before I rushed over here. She knows all the scuttlebutt on everybody around here. Ima Jean said Mr. Mackey and his wife rented the old Watson house and that his wife's a real looker.

"Albert thinks there's still enough coal where they're working now to pay off their tickets. He told me the vein that he and Fred are working on runs for over one hundred feet. Course Albert always exaggerates when he's talking about that mine. Albert thinks Jeremy told Mr. Mackey about what they're working on, and that's what got him going after it."

"Fred's not getting any better, Annie. There's a part of me that wants him to be rid of that mine."

I lay real still, I could hardly breathe hearing Mama say that.

"I know, Cora. Albert can always work with his brother at the body shop. Of course, he wants to work with Fred. They've been miners their whole lives and they always took care of each other."

"And you know, Annie, I don't want Freddy down there at all. I just don't know what Fred'll do if Mr. Mackey takes his mine."

I held on tight to Rex, so tight he yelped.

"June Ellen, are you lying out there awake?"

"Yes, Mama. I just woke up. Is Mr. Mackey taking our mine?"

"I don't know, June Ellen. We just have to wait and see. Your daddy and Uncle Albert are doing everything they can to keep it."

"Freddy'll make sure they keep our mine, Mama. I know he will." But I didn't know anymore. Everything was moving too fast. "I think Rex and I need to go for a walk."

"That's a good idea. Don't you worry, June Ellen. Your daddy will get it all sorted out."

"Mama, do you want Mr. Mackey to take our mine, so Daddy will get better?"

Mama looked straight at me. "I don't know what's best anymore, June Ellen. I just try to let God handle it."

"Bye, Mama." Sometimes I wondered about God.

"Be back by supper time. I'm expecting your daddy and Freddy'll be home late tonight."

"Rex, I know why they call them big shots, 'cause they hurt you like a needle sticking in your heart. I think it's time for an adventure. I know what Nancy Drew would do. She'd go spy on Mr. Mackey and see what terrible thing he's up to, then get the sheriff to help her. Sunday, after church Mr. Mackey's sure to be home and we'll go to the old Watson house and spy on him."

That evening Freddy drove up to our house in Uncle Albert's truck. He jumped out and yelled, "Mama, Daddy had a coughing fit and I took him to the hospital. Dr. John is seeing to him now. I think you'd better come. It was a bad one."

Before anybody could say anything, Rex and I both jumped in the back. We weren't going to get left at home, and Mama was too over-wrought to notice. By the time we got to the hospital, she didn't care.

Freddy said, "Mr. Mackey showed up at the Shoal Creek mine today with all of Daddy's tickets and all his workers' tickets that Daddy signed for. That big shot Mr. Mackey gave Daddy two weeks to get him his money. Mackey said our mine was all worked out and he was just helping us out. Why would a man like that want to help us out? He's the only one with any money 'round here."

"There he is, Mama. That's Mr. Mackey driving that big black Oldsmobile. He lives up here now on Hospital Hill."

We stood outside the truck and I looked at the man coming toward us. He pulled over and looked at Mama. He was big and pasty looking.

"How do you do, Mrs. Thackeray? I'm Mr. Mackey, but you probably already know that."

"Yes, I know who you are."

"I'm sorry about your husband being so sick and all. Coal mining seems to have done him in. I hope he gets better."

Mama pulled her lips in tight, trying to mind her manners. "Well, I'm sure he'll get those tickets paid off, Mr. Mackey. We'd be thankful for some time to do just that."

Mr. Mackey gave Mama a sly kind of smile. "We'll see about that, Mrs. Thackeray. I don't know how much time your husband has left. To pay off those tickets anyway."

"Mr. Mackey, my husband is a just and honorable man. He works hard to do right by folks. I pray that others [Mama paused right there for a long second] do the same. Good day, Mr. Mackey. I need to go see my husband."

Mr. Mackey got in his car, tipped his hat, and drove off.

"Mama, you sure told that Mr. Mackey. You shut him right up," Freddy said.

"Mama, you remind me of Dale Evans, standing up to bad men, like him."

"I need to see your daddy."

I whispered to Rex, "We'll take care of Mr. Mackey later."

"Let's go in, Mama," Freddy said. "Dr. John'll be looking for us. Don't worry about those tickets."

We sat in the waiting room for Dr. John to tell us we could go up and see Daddy. I wanted to run right up there, but Mama wouldn't let me, and Freddy just kept talking.

"That Mackey's a real scoundrel, Mama. But Daddy stood right up to him. He told him, 'I'll pay my debts, Mr. Mackey. I always do. You can ask anybody. Now, get out of my way and I'll get these cars loaded and get you what's owed.'

"Then Mackey came right back at him. 'I'm going to do you a favor and pay all your debts. You'll be free and clear of this worked-out coal pit. You can take anything you want with you. I don't need your junk. You got two weeks to get a good enough load to give you a stake to get something else going.'"

"Daddy didn't back down one bit. He told him, 'I'll pay my debt when I get this payload to the station.'

"That Mackey got kind of mean. 'Two weeks, then I'm taking the lease. There's not enough coal in those cars to pay off your debt. I don't know what that Jeremy fellow was thinking letting you run up this kind of bill.'"

Mama looked like she wanted to spit nails. She kept wringing her hands.

Freddy looked like he wanted to cry. "Then, Mama, he handed Daddy a bill for over six hundred dollars. Daddy kind of lost his temper then. You'd be real proud of him, June Ellen. He got right close to him and told him he'd never give up the Shoal Creek mine. He was yelling by then, stomping his feet and telling Mackey what was what and really got his self worked up. That Mackey fellow backed up a few yards, for sure."

Freddy's voice got real low.

"That's when Daddy started coughing and he couldn't stop. Pretty soon he had no breath left and he just collapsed. I've never seen Daddy collapse before, Mama. I grabbed him and tried to get him to stand up. Uncle Albert rushed over and we carried him to the truck. Mr. Mackey tried to help, but I wouldn't let him touch him. I left Uncle Albert at the mine with Mr. Mackey."

Now I was spitting nails. I hollered at Freddy, "Mr. Mackey can't have our coal mine. You and Uncle Albert have to take care of it till Daddy's better."

Mama grabbed me by the arm and yanked me down beside her. "June Ellen, don't you say another word and stop that yelling, right now. Do you hear me?"

She was pinching my arm, she held it so tight. I had to answer so she'd let go. "Yes, ma'am," I said.

"Behave or go to the house."

Dr. John walked in right then. "He's breathing better, Cora, but he needs to get some more oxygen in his lungs. I'm keeping him in the oxygen tent a few more hours. But he's ready to get out of here."

"Thank you, Dr. John. I don't know what we'd do without you."

"Cora, he can't keep breathing that dust. See if you can't talk some sense into him."

"Dr. John, I'm gonna go see my daddy, right now." I didn't look at Mama, but I could feel her eyes boring into my head.

Dr. John laughed. "Well, June Ellen, I think that's a right smart idea. You always did perk him up."

"Dr. John, June Ellen and April Leigh need a whooping cough shot with that new vaccine."

"Bring them in first thing in the morning. That's a smart thing to get, June Ellen. I'm sure you'll oblige your mama on this one. Won't you?"

Dr. John knew my history with shots. I was caught good. "Yes, sir."

Then I took off running up the stairs to the second floor. Mama and Freddy let me go. I had to see Daddy right away. I had to help him save our mine. I saw him lying on a cot over in the corner with the oxygen tent over his body. His skin was white, the palest I'd ever seen on a living body. I could see his ribs moving up and down.

"Daddy, you sure are skinny." He turned to look at me and tried to laugh, but his chest just shuddered.

"Don't worry, Daddy. Uncle Albert and Freddy'll get that payload to pay off that big shot, Mr. Mackey."

Daddy turned away from me.

"Don't give up, Daddy."

He looked back at me. He spoke in a whisper, fighting to get each word out. "I'm not done for yet, June Ellen."

But he sure looked all done in.

I ran out of the room and down the stairs straight to the truck where Rex was waiting. "Rex, come on. Let's get out of here. It's time for a long walk."

Spy on Mr. Mackey

DADDY CAME HOME from the hospital and went right to bed. He didn't get up for church on Sunday, either.

"Let him sleep, June Ellen. The more he sleeps, the better he can breathe." After church, Mama made us oatmeal and sausage and Daddy got up to drink his coffee. Sunday dinner was at Aunt Annie's and Uncle Albert's today. Aunt Annie only wanted to clean up her kitchen once, so we ate at two o'clock. And that was it for Uncle Albert, though he did get to eat cold chicken and biscuits in the evening.

"Daddy, are you going to Sunday dinner with us?"

"Well, June Ellen, I think I'll stay here with Rex. He might need some company. I'm sure hoping you'll bring me something to eat when you come back home."

His voice still creaked and I could hear the wheezing in his chest. He wasn't all gray like before, but I couldn't see much color either.

Mama made him an egg to go with his sausage. Daddy wouldn't eat oatmeal. Mama buttered up a slice of her homemade bread then layered it with our favorite, strawberry jam. "Eat, Fred, you need to gain some weight. Dr. John said."

"I'm glad you're home, Daddy."

"Me too, June Ellen. I think Rex needs a good walk today, don't you?"

"Yes, Daddy, I do. I think Rex is ready for an adventure. He's been stuck at home all weekend."

Mama gave me one of her looks. "Don't wander off too far. Be back by 1:30, or you won't get Sunday dinner."

"Okay, Mama. Come on, Rex, let's go."

Rex and I took off to Hospital Hill. We walked easy, up to Dr. John's, then over the top of the hill to where the hospital stood. Across the way, we could see the Watson house. It was hidden on the back side by overgrown cedar trees, perfect for a cover to get close. We crept up to the house then onto the veranda and looked through a shiny, silver metal screen without a bit of rust on it into the dining room. The big window was open to the sweet June breeze blowing down from Horseshoe Mountain.

"Quiet, Rex," I whispered, "and don't thump your tail." I hid behind a big green plant with leaves as big as my notebook. It sat in a cement planter that rich people like to put on their porches. Our plants all grow in our yard or garden. We have a front porch; rich people have a veranda. April Leigh told me. Rex crouched behind me, all hidden just like I taught him. He's the best spy dog. I rubbed the piece of coal I had in my pocket for good luck. I remember that shine. I threw away the rabbit's foot; it stopped working when my daddy got sick.

I looked through the window and spotted Mr. Mackey right away. There he was. He sat at the biggest dining-room table I ever saw, but the table was set for only two people. He sat on one end; his wife sat at the other. No one talked. They looked awful lonely. Mrs. Mackey looked forlorn, her eyes sad. She stared at her water glass.

She needs an adventure, I thought.

Mr. Mackey had a big belly so he sat back a ways from the table. His belly fell over his belt and onto the chair. I watched him lean over it to eat. He tried to keep his soup off his shirt, but I could see where he dribbled. He didn't have his hat on, and I could see his shining bald head.

Mrs. Mackey was real slim. She looked like a model in the Sears & Roebuck catalog. She wore a green silk dress with pink buttons on the front that went from the bottom all the way to the top. She sat close to the table and didn't dribble her soup at all.

Mr. Mackey looked at Mrs. Mackey. His eyes searched her face. She glanced once at him with pity, I thought. Then back down at her soup. Her fingers twisted and turned her wedding ring all which ways.

"This is a sorrowful place, Rex," I whispered.

Mrs. Mackey got up and went to the sideboard and picked up the biggest platter of roast beef I'd ever seen. A huge painting of *The Last Supper* hung on the wall right above the roast beef. There were lots of people at that table. Baptists must like *The Last Supper*, too. Carrots and potatoes and onions circled all around the roast, which lay in a bed of dark brown gravy. We never had that much roast beef and vegetables at our house, even when we were all home and Aunt Annie and Uncle Albert came too.

It smelled so good, my mouth watered, and I wasn't even hungry. I was afraid my stomach might growl, but it didn't. Rex moved slightly. I could hear him sniffing through his nose. I leaned down, "Not yet, Rex.

Later, we'll have our own Sunday dinner." Rex lay back down with his head on his paws.

Mrs. Mackey looked real pretty. She had on pink high heels that matched her dress buttons perfectly. She walked over to Mr. Mackey to serve him.

He smiled up at her, raised his hand, and touched her waist gently. She backed up like she got snake bit. She tried to smile at Mr. Mackey, but she just couldn't.

His face fell, all the way down to the floor. He could hardly pick it back up, but he tried. Mama would say he was putting on a good face.

I heard her through the window where I was hiding. "For God's sake, Ernest. Do you have to touch me like that when I'm serving you your roast beef and overdone vegetables covered in this greasy gravy, just the way you and all those other people down here in this godforsaken place like it?"

She slammed the platter down in front of him. Some of the gravy jumped over the side and took a carrot and piece of potato with it. "Serve yourself."

Mr. Mackey threw down his napkin and quick, stood straight up, tall, towering over Mrs. Mackey by a good six inches. He slapped his hand on the table, hard, just missing the spilled gravy.

Mrs. Mackey jumped.

Mr. Mackey's face came back together as he tried to smile at her, but the corners of his mouth kept turning down. He sat back down, real heavy like.

Mrs. Mackey stood frozen like her feet were stuck to the floor.

Mr. Mackey wiped his brow with his handkerchief. "Sit down, Pauline, please. Thank you for this fine Sunday dinner. Let's just eat and be civil to each other."

"I'm sorry, Ernest. I just can't believe what we've become. There's no place for me here."

Their eyes met again, his were sad and pleading. Mrs. Mackey looked just plain weary.

"Don't ever leave me, Pauline."

Mrs. Mackey walked over to him and touched his shoulder for just a brief moment. "Eat, Ernest."

I lowered myself down below the window. "Let's get out of here, Rex," and we both crawled over to the steps. I slowly stood up on my feet but stayed hunkered down beside Rex. I held on to him and we carefully made our way down. When we got to the bottom, Rex took off and I ran as fast as I could to catch up with him. I wanted to be a good spy and get away without them ever knowing I was there. But I was unnerved. That means my nerves left me. I wanted to get away from that sadness more than I wanted to be a good spy.

When I got home, we went to Aunt Annie's house for Sunday dinner, me, Mama, Freddy, and April Leigh. I looked up at her picture of *The Last Supper* and thought about the Mackeys lonely, empty dinner table. We fit around our table just right, no room was wasted. It was loaded with fried chicken, mashed potatoes, gravy, green beans, and corn plus home-made rolls with blueberry jam. I knew that we were richer than Mr. Mackey would ever be, and we were a happy bunch, but I missed Daddy.

[32]

June Ellen Turns Eleven

MY BIRTHDAY FELL on the thirtieth, the last day of June, the month I was named for. Mama woke me up early for my birthday breakfast, before she left to take care of Fr. Michael. April Leigh was still sleeping, and I watched as her face twitched and her lips puckered up.

"Isaac, Isaac," she yelled and puckered up some more. I kicked her till she woke up. She sputtered and threw up her arms. "What, what's happening?"

"Wake up, April Leigh, you're yelling in your sleep. You're dreaming and your lips are all puckered up like a prune face. Who are you kissing, anyway?"

"June Ellen, I'm the homecoming queen and Isaac, the captain of the football team, is just getting ready to crown me. I'm going to kill you."

Mama yelled at us, "Get up, now. Your pancakes are ready."

I jumped out of bed and ran to the kitchen. April Leigh just turned over and went back to sleep. There was fresh-churned butter and maple syrup set out on the table. Daddy was frying bacon, special for me.

It smelled good. So good, I didn't mind Mama getting me up. Daddy made me my special cup of coffee and poured it into my special cup with the pink rose painted on the bottom, half coffee and half rich cream. I poured in the sugar. I was eleven years old now.

"Daddy, the first sip of this coffee is still the best. You made it just like I like it."

"Well, June Ellen, you're eleven years old now, you might just have to make your own coffee."

Mama gave him her look. Daddy just laughed. I was excited for my birthday, but I was mostly happy that Daddy was not so pale looking and he was getting around real good, good enough to make me my birthday bacon and birthday coffee.

"June Ellen, I'm ready to get out on the town a little bit today. How

162

about you and me go see what Hancock's might have for you. Aunt Annie's letting me use the car, because Albert and Freddy need the truck at the mine. Your mama and I can't get you anything just yet, but next week we're hauling out a load of coal."

"Okay, Daddy. I know just what I want, that red straw cowgirl hat."

"June Ellen, mind your manners and remember we can't afford any high-priced cowgirl hat." Mama said, "Look at some summer shorts and nice blouses."

I ignored Mama and so did Daddy. She had to say that.

I ate my pancakes and bacon and drank my coffee. What a great way to start my birthday.

"Come on, Rex. Let's go for a birthday walk. I'm eleven today and we can go wherever we want."

"June Ellen, where did you get an idea like that? Your aunt Annie's coming at eleven. If you're going with your daddy, you'd best stick close to home, until he's ready."

First, we walked to the Lahoskys, right across the road. "Howdy, Mrs. Lahosky. Today's my birthday, I'm eleven and I'm looking for an adventure."

"Well, Miss June Ellen, you're all grown up, I can tell. I have some fresh corn muffins here. How about a birthday muffin with some fresh butter and strawberry jam?"

"Thanks, Mrs. Lahosky. Rex would like one too." She looked at me kind of hard, but smiled and said, "Okay, since it's your birthday. But I don't usually let dogs eat my muffins."

She fixed me one and gave me one for Rex. It was turning into a good adventure, but I remembered, I had to be home by eleven.

I spied the old dusty road to Thelma Hazelwood's next, so Rex and I decided to take it. Thelma wasn't on her porch this morning, and no hound dogs came for us. Since I was eleven, I walked right up to her front porch and knocked real loud. Then the hound dogs started hollering.

I heard Thelma say, "Shut up, you lazy mongrels." And they did. She opened the door and they ran under the porch just like last time.

"Howdy, Miss Hazelwood. Remember me? I'm June Ellen. You're still alive, I see. I think that's good, don't you? Where's your hat, the one you wore to your pretend funeral? It sure was pretty."

"I know who you are, and my hat's put up till the day I die."

"That seems a waste, Miss Hazelwood. Mama got a real pretty hat for Easter and she sure won't save it till she dies. She wears it to church and bingo and even shopping sometimes, so everyone can see it. Don't you want me to admire your hat?"

"My hat is none of your business, and I don't want you looking at it."

"Today's my birthday. I'm eleven years old. That's how come I'm here, by myself, visiting you."

"I ain't got nothing for your birthday, so don't you go thinking I do."

"That's okay, I'm getting a red Dale Evans cowgirl hat. Me and Rex are going to be cowpokes."

"You done wore me out, you go on home, now. Yore mama's fixing to be looking for you."

"Bye, Miss Hazelwood, nice visiting with you." She slammed the door before I could tell her I'd be back.

"Let's go, Rex. Time to go try on my cowgirl hat. I bet Daddy lets me put it on layaway, and Ima Jean has to let me try it on."

Daddy was waiting when I got to the house. He was all dressed up in his best overalls and they were clean. He'd spit shined his shoes too.

"Daddy, did you put some of Freddy's grease in your hair? It looks all shiny."

"Thank you for noticing, June Ellen. I sure did. Do you think Ima Jean'll like it?"

I laughed. "Sure, Daddy. You look awful handsome. And Ima Jean's glasses'll jiggle all the way down the aisle to talk to you."

We both laughed.

By the time we got to Hancock's Department and Feed Store, I could see Ima Jean dusting the counters. The cowboy hats were moved to the back and the front window was filled with bathing suits. I wasn't interested in them.

I ran right to the cowboy hats. "Where's the cowgirl hats today, Ima Jean? I want to try on the red Dale Evans hat and my daddy's here and he's gonna buy it for me when he sells his load of coal next week. You have to let me try it on."

Daddy caught up with me then and said, "June Ellen, mind your manners. What would your mama say?"

Ima Jean, of course, took off her glasses and jiggled over. "Why, Fred, don't you look handsome. You must be feeling better, too."

"Well, I tell you what, Ima Jean. That Dr. John is a miracle worker as far as I'm concerned. He fixed me right up. Just call me Lazarus, I guess."

"It's my birthday, Ima Jean. I'm eleven now, and I've decided to be a cowgirl now that I'm grown up. I want the red Dale Evans cowgirl hat."

Daddy scratched his whiskers and smiled. "Yep, my youngest is all growed up today, and she's decided to be a cowgirl for a living, so I thought I better get her that hat."

"I'm so sorry, Fred. That hat got sold last week. A young girl from Morrison's Bluff bought it with her babysitting money. She loved that hat, and she was determined to have it. June Ellen, go look around for something else while your daddy and I talk a little."

I gave her my meanest dead-eye look. Now that I was eleven I could stare right at her for a long time. I felt like spitting fire, I was so mad. I started to stomp my foot, but Daddy grabbed me by the shoulder.

"Now, June Ellen, don't be that away. It's not Ima Jean's fault that little girl bought that hat. Look around, there's lots of good stuff here. Wouldn't you like a new bathing suit? Then you don't have to wear April Leigh's old one."

"No, Daddy, I don't want a bathing suit. All I wanted was a red cowgirl hat like Dale Evans."

I just wanted to get out of there before I did something to Ima Jean. I knew it wasn't her fault, but she hadn't let me try on that hat. I wanted that cowgirl hat more than I wanted anything, except our mine.

"I just can't look at anything else today, Daddy. I feel like I could just spit fire. I think I need a root beer. It sure is hard being eleven."

"Well, I guess I'll just have to join you, then. Lord knows, I could use a beer. Let's head over to the Green Frog and we'll both drink your troubles away."

That night, Mama made me my favorite birthday dinner. Fried pork chops, mashed potatoes, and gravy made from the pork drippings. She opened a jar of dill pickles and her last jar of green beans. Aunt Annie walked in with her famous devil's food cake with chocolate caramel icing.

Freddy came in from work with a tiny little wrapped package for me. "Here, you go, June Ellen. I got you something."

April Leigh handed me a little bag with something in it, too. She did her evil grin. "I know you'll like to play with these with your little friends."

I wanted to kick her, but I couldn't in front of Mama and Daddy. I was trying hard for Daddy's sake to act happy, but I was just plain heartbroken.

Mama was watching me, so I put on a big grin and pretended to get excited about both my presents. I shook each present trying to figure out what was inside.

I smelled the pork chops and saw the steaming bowl of mashed potatoes when Mama put them on the table. That did make me happy.

"Everybody sit down and eat. Don't let these pork chops get cold. June Ellen, sit here at the head of the table."

"Mama, this is the best birthday dinner I ever ate." I wasn't pretending about that.

"Are you ready for your birthday cake, June Ellen? I made it special for you," Aunt Annie said. She set her red devil's food cake in front of me and stuck eleven candles on top. "Happy birthday, June Ellen, blow out those candles and make a wish. I'm sure it'll come true."

Mama put her hands on her hips and looked hard at Aunt Annie. Aunt Annie was good at ignoring Mama since she'd been practicing her whole life. I closed my eyes and wished hard for that Dale Evans cowgirl hat. I couldn't stop thinking about how good that red cowgirl hat would go with that red devil's food cake.

"Time for presents," Freddy yelled. He handed me his little dinky package. I opened it and there was a little box of super bang caps. I thanked him and I meant it, 'cause I was out and didn't have any money to buy more.

"Here, June Ellen, I didn't have anything to wrap it in. It's the thought that counts." April Leigh handed me the little paper bag.

I untied the string and looked inside. A pack of Old Maid playing cards. I pulled them out and thought they looked a little worn. But I knew better than to say anything. "Thank you, April Leigh. I can't wait to play Old Maid with you, since you're going to be one."

She gave me her version of the dead-eye look, not nearly as practiced as mine.

Mama looked hard at me.

"Thank you for my presents."

I felt just wore out and wished I could just go to bed.

"Wait," Uncle Albert said. "What about my present? Did you think your aunt Annie and I would forget?" He walked out to the porch and brought in a big box. "This is something I've been saving for you from the Shoal Creek mine. Just a little something I found up there that reminded me of you. You know, just in case."

His words trailed off, as nobody wanted to say it.

"In case we lose the Shoal Creek mine, Uncle Albert?" I couldn't help myself. It was that kind of day.

"Now, June Ellen," Mama said.

Freddy jumped up right then. "Don't you worry about that, Snapper. Uncle Albert and I are working on that. And Daddy."

Daddy just sat there, looking all pale.

Uncle Albert laughed. "Hey, let's get back to your happy birthday. That old mine ain't going anywhere this evening. Open this old box up, June Ellen."

The lid was tore off the top of the box, and newspaper was all scrunched up in there. I started taking out the newspaper and saw something red. I snatched all the paper out and there it was, my red Dale Evans cowgirl hat.

"Oh, Uncle Albert."

"I think you better thank your mama and daddy on this one. I'm just the delivery guy."

"Oh, Mama. Thank you, thank you, thank you." I threw my arms around her and hugged her so tight and so long, she had to pry my fingers off. "Try it on, June Ellen. Let's see how that hat fits you."

Next, I ran to Daddy and hugged him, but I was careful, I didn't want to crack him. "Oh, thank you, Daddy."

"I heard you never got to try that hat on, so go ahead, June Ellen."

Freddy grabbed the hat and put it on me. "You look like a real cowgirl, June Ellen. If I saw you running across the pasture, why I'd think, there goes Dale Evans."

April Leigh ran and got her fancy mirror and showed me what I looked like. I did look just like Dale Evans. My hair curled up around the sides, brown and shiny. And my new cowgirl hat sat there, just right.

April Leigh said, "June Ellen, that hat looks like it was made just for you."

"You're the prettiest cowgirl I've ever seen. You look all grown up, too, in that hat." Daddy beamed at me.

"Now, Fred, don't go filling up her head with all that kind of stuff." Then Mama laughed and told me, "You're my pretty little girl, June Ellen. And that hat suits you just fine. I think you are strong and brave like Dale Evans. You're growing up."

"Thank you, Mama."

Daddy laughed. "Well, June Ellen, I guess we pulled one on you for a change, didn't we? Even Ima Jean helped. I think tomorrow you'd better go down there and apologize. Don't you?"

"Yes, Daddy."

"Wait," Aunt Annie yelled. "What's this behind the couch?" She pulled out another big box covered in newspaper.

"Oh, that's my gag gift," Freddy said. "I thought I'd pull another one on you, before I knew what Mama and Daddy got you."

"Oh, Freddy, that's okay. Let me see what you got." I tore off the paper and saw it was a shoebox with a picture of boots on it. I was glad I already had my cowgirl hat 'cause to think I got cowgirl boots and then see it was a joke, I just didn't think I could hold in my disappointment. So instead, I laughed as I opened it, but inside was a beautiful pair of golden-brown cowgirl boots with white stitching in fancy patterns.

My mouth hung open and I couldn't talk. I never got so much in my whole life before, not even at Christmas. I looked at Mama and she had the biggest smile on her face I'd ever seen. Daddy was sitting down now. He looked tired, but he hadn't coughed all evening. He was grinning and he looked real happy.

"Aunt Annie, thank you." I ran and hugged her.

"Now, those boots are from me and your uncle Albert. Freddy helped too, with a little of his paycheck, and April Leigh chipped in some of her babysitting money."

I ran and hugged everybody, even April Leigh.

"June Ellen, I need those Old Maid cards back. I didn't buy them for you. I borrowed them from Mary Alice. They were my decoy to throw you off track."

I handed them back to her. "I thought they looked used. I just wasn't going to say anything. That was a good trick, April Leigh."

I put my boots on with my hat and I was so happy, I grinned at everybody. My heart was full to bursting. I loved my whole family, even April Leigh. If Daddy could just keep our coal mine, that would be the most perfect birthday present ever. But I was pretty happy with my Dale Evans cowgirl hat and my very own, first-ever, brand-new cowgirl boots.

Mama looked at me and smiled. "You are really growing up, June Ellen."

[33]

Clem Wald's Shoe Store and Bar

ON SATURDAY EVENINGS, after payday, if they got one, coal miners tended to gather at Clem Wald's Shoe Store and Bar. I often went with Daddy and Uncle Albert and now Freddy. Daddy had gone to work for most of two days now, and he wanted to go be with the other miners and have a beer.

I was wearing my birthday presents today, my red cowgirl hat, my golden-brown cowgirl boots with fancy stitching on each side, and my Dale Evans six-shooters with a leather holster. I'm the only one in Clem Wald's shoe store and beer joint allowed to wear a gun. It's not real, but I did load them with my Old West Super Bang Rolls caps. Rex sat down on the sidewalk under the plate-glass window to wait for us.

It was just turning toward evening, about the time Clem set the shoes aside and started serving beer. Helter picked up the cash register and set it in the back. Beer sales were cash only, no receipt. Clem took thick glass beer mugs with sturdy handles down from the shelf that ran along the back wall behind the counter. A pair of miner's boots and two boxes of Poll-Parrot shoes for boys shared this shelf. Clem was real careful not to sell both at once, 'cause that was breaking the law. Clem and Helter lined the mugs up on a smooth maple board, varnished to a shine that he laid over his glass counter.

Helter told me, "June Ellen, sometimes miners get rowdy and like to slam their mugs down on the bar. Glass just can't take that."

Helter was short for Helter Skelter. That's what people called him 'cause Helter was always in such a frenzy running from one end of the bar to the other. Daddy said it just took Helter a while to switch from selling shoes to selling beer. "Different rules, you know, June Ellen."

People got tired of Helter and his ramblings, but he liked to explain things to me and since I liked to learn things, he and I got along well, and

I wanted to tell him what a great boss and miner my daddy was, unlike that Mr. Mackey.

"Helter, my daddy goes down in his coal mine just like the guys he hires. He stays right there with his men, setting off the dynamite charges or checking for methane gas. That's how he got much of that dust in his lungs. I'm here to help him with his beer, which is like medicine to a coal miner."

"You're right about that, June Ellen. Your daddy is a fine fellow. Everyone says so. Folks around here are awful sorry about the Shoal Creek mine. Maybe he'll outwit that Mackey feller."

Helter started drawing beer. He filled each glass and topped it off with a head of foam. A miner would grab a full glass and pitch a quarter to Clem at the same time. As fast as Helter filled one, Clem caught a quarter. Every now and then all the action stopped, 'cause someone needed change.

Daylight was the dividing line between the bar and the shoe store. Once it was gone, so were the women, except me. I took care of Daddy. It was still my job to suck the foam off his beer. If the foam got caught in his throat, he'd have a coughing fit. Uncle Albert drove us to Clem's and he drank his own foam, even though I had offered to help him.

About the time we all got settled, Mr. Mackey walked in the door. He looked around like he owned it. He didn't look as pitiful like the last time I saw him. He hooked his thumbs in his pants and marched right up to Helter at the bar.

"Hey, kid, give me a Dad's root beer." He drank only root beer because his religion forbid any taking of alcohol.

Helter was no kid, but he got him a root beer. Mr. Mackey threw him a quarter, acting like the miners. "Don't worry about the change, kid. Keep it. You probably don't make much here."

Mr. Mackey took a big swig, then wiped his mouth like he was drinking a beer with foam. He walked over to where Daddy was standing with Freddy and Uncle Albert.

"Well, if it isn't the Shoal Creek boys. How's that load coming? Your two weeks is about up. It's about time to pay up or hand that lease over. By this time next week, the Shoal Creek mine will have a new name, Mackey Mining Enterprise."

Mr. Mackey looked around the room. Everybody got real quiet. He was making sure everybody heard him. I didn't feel sorry for him anymore.

Daddy just shook his head and walked away. Everybody knew Daddy didn't have the money to pay off all those tickets. I didn't like Jeremy anymore. He sold out to Mr. Mackey and slunk off to Ozark like a dog with his tail between his legs.

Daddy walked up to the bar with my brother Freddy. I sidled up to the bar, between Daddy and Freddy and when Daddy tossed a quarter at Clem, Helter slid him over a beer and I sucked off the foam. Then I wiped my mouth with the back of my hand, like cowboys do. I felt better after I drank the foam.

Mr. Mackey walked over to the aisle by the wall of cowboy boots. He didn't mix with coal miners but watched them slug down their beer. He acted like he was better than them, but I knew better. He tried to stare down Daddy, but Daddy paid him no mind.

The miners were all a pretty skinny lot. They worked off most everything they ate. Mr. Mackey stood with his thumbs hooked over his belt, his big belly hanging down low, and he worked hard to get his thumbs over that belt. He didn't work much of anything off, I could tell.

While Daddy sipped his beer, I spotted Truly Wright, talking to Mr. Mackey.

I slipped behind a shoe rack to spy on them. "You'll never get that coal mine from Fred Thackeray," Truly was saying. "I've known Fred a long time and he's always managed to hang on to one of those played-out mines nobody else wants, so I don't know why you want to bother with it." Truly had spent a few quarters by that time.

Mr. Mackey looked like he'd just as soon spit on Truly. He laughed, took a big swig of his Dad's root beer, and said, "Never you mind why I want it. But it'll be a cold day in hell before Fred Thackeray runs another coal mine. He's just a sick old man who can't hardly take care of his own family."

I watched Daddy's face turn red. Freddy jumped up, but Daddy put his hand on Freddy's shoulder and pushed him back down on the bar stool and held him there.

I stomped over to Mr. Mackey in my Annie Oakley cowgirl boots. I pulled out my Dale Evans six-shooter loaded with caps and pointed it at him. He laughed at me. "See there, Fred Thackeray even lets little girls take up for him."

"Mr. Mackey," I said, "It'll be a cold day in H-E-double toothpicks before you take our Shoal Creek mine." I cocked my Dale Evans six-shooter and fired my super bang caps one after the other.

Mr. Mackey jumped up, grabbed his chest with his hand, and looked at it for blood.

All the coal miners laughed and stomped their feet. If Rex had been inside, he'd be barking and jumping around with them.

Then Mr. Mackey came at me, but Helter grabbed me up and stuck me behind the bar. Daddy stood right up to him. "Something you want to say to me, Mr. Mackey?"

Mr. Mackey turned and stalked out of the bar. Clem gave me an ice-cold Dr. Pepper and a package of peanuts on the house. Everyone was laughing and patting me on the back, except Daddy.

"June Ellen," Daddy tried to look angry, but I saw the hint of a smile and his color was better also. "Put your guns in your holster and keep them there. Enjoy your Dr. Pepper and peanuts, 'cause it's probably the last ones you'll see for a while. Then we'll go home and tell your mama what you done. She'll be fit to be tied." But Daddy looked real proud and he stood up straighter, too.

I sat on Clem Wald's special stool behind the bar and enjoyed every last sip of that Dr. Pepper and every crunch of salty peanut. I meant to make them last.

Holy Ghost and Father Michael

WHEN APRIL LEIGH turned fifteen, she spent almost all of her free time with her best friend, Mary Alice. This morning they walked to the square to shop, without me, again. I knew they'd end up at Haney's to watch Isaac work. But this morning I didn't much care.

Uncle Albert picked up Daddy and Freddy and headed to the coal mine. Daddy had been going pretty steady all week. Some mornings Daddy could hardly get up and some nights he could hardly get down, for his coughing. I was glad Freddy was home to get the coal we needed to pay off the tickets. I hadn't given up hope yet.

I heard Freddy tell Mama, Daddy had to sit down and rest more. "He still coughs an awful lot, Mama. He can't get up and down like he used to. But he still checks for gas each morning. That is the one thing he won't stop or let anyone else do."

"June Ellen, eat some biscuits and don't wander off too far." Mama was leaving with Aunt Annie to the First Baptist Church of Free Will for the rummage sale.

She didn't make me go with her and I was happy about that. I had my own problems to take care of today and was relieved everyone was gone and I was on my own. Last night I went with Mama to the Stations of the Cross to pray for the coal mine and Daddy. Mama made me go. "June Ellen, after what you did to Mr. Mackey yesterday, I think you might need to pray for some forgiveness and it won't hurt you to pray for your daddy."

I told Mama I just had to stand up for Daddy, like she did at the hospital. Mama laughed and said, "You're strong-willed, June Ellen, and right now I think that's a good thing. You're going to need that kind of gumption." I knew what Mama meant.

The night before, when I was at the Stations of the Cross with Mama, the Holy Ghost had flown right down from the Tenth Station of the Cross and hovered right over me. He had a cloven tongue with flames and white wings like a dove.

I got so hot I sweated like Jesus in the Garden of Gethsemane. I'm not one to be afraid of ghosts, but that Holy Ghost gave me a fright. I still felt on fire from those flames and I sensed that he wanted me to do something. Mama wouldn't let me talk in church and when I tried to tell her about the Holy Ghost, she made me be quiet, so I never said anything. I couldn't eat and I hardly slept. I made a plan to go back today and find the Holy Ghost.

Mama said, "June Ellen, do you feel okay? You don't look right and your face is flushed."

"I'm fine, Mama."

She felt my forehead. "Well, your aunt Annie's waiting on me. I have to go. I'll be back before lunchtime."

I made a plan to go to St. Joseph's and ask Fr. Michael to help me find the Holy Ghost. I changed into my jeans and shirt and took off for Fr. Michael's house. I knocked and knocked on his door, but he wasn't home. The message on Fr. Michael's door said he was visiting the sick, the elderly, and the infirm. I thought to myself, I bet he went to Mrs. Loretta's. Her husband was poorly, and she made fresh cinnamon rolls every Saturday morning and so people looked for a reason to visit. That was where he was when I needed him, eating Mrs. Loretta's cinnamon rolls.

My stomach growled in response, and I had to admit my mouth watered. But Mrs. Loretta lived all the way out by the Catholic cemetery. It was too far to walk. I told myself, I don't want that busybody knowing my business anyway. I walked over to the church and stared at the stained-glass window where the Holy Ghost with a cloven tongue of flames and white wings floated over the head of St. Peter.

"June Ellen, June Ellen, what are you doing at church on Saturday?"

I looked up and Gracie came rushing toward me, her arms wrapped around two full sacks of yarn. "Hey, Gracie, what are you doing here?"

"Mother picked up all this yarn and construction paper in Fort Smith when she took Granny to the doctor. She's staying with us for a while. I'm supposed to drop it off at the Sister's house, and then go straight home. She bought me new paper dolls. Come over and I'll show you; there's even a cowgirl outfit."

I gave Gracie my hard-eyed look. "I'm on urgent business for Daddy. I need to find the Holy Ghost."

"The Holy Ghost, June Ellen? Your daddy sent you to find the Holy Ghost?"

"No, Daddy didn't send me. You know the Holy Trinity, Father, Son, and Holy Ghost. Fr. Michael talks about it all the time."

"What does that have to do with your daddy? June Ellen, you sound crazy like a loony bird. Did you get into your daddy's moonshine?"

"The Holy Ghost came after me last night when I went to the Stations of the Cross with Mama."

Gracie stood there with her mouth wide open. "Really, June Ellen? You saw the Holy Ghost?"

"I'm telling the truth, Gracie. You have to believe me. Maybe you'll see him too. But you can't tell anyone. I'm desperate to find help for Daddy, and I think the Holy Ghost was trying to help. Gracie, you're my best friend and you always help me. You're a little thickheaded sometimes and right now, I don't have time to explain everything to you. I just need to know if you'll help me find the Holy Ghost."

"I'm not thickheaded, June Ellen. It's called common sense. Something you seem a little short on."

"Daddy needs help. Jeremy's store is closing, and Daddy has to pay all his bills right now or Mr. Mackey is taking over his coal mine."

"What's the Holy Ghost got to do with it, June Ellen? Fr. Michael told us that the Holy Ghost burns all the evil inside you. You want the Holy Ghost to burn up Mr. Mackey?"

"No, silly. I want him to . . . I want him to . . . I don't know what I want him to do. I was standing with Mama at the Tenth Station of the Cross. Jesus knows he's been betrayed by Judas just like Daddy's been betrayed by Jeremy."

"You think Jeremy is like Judas, June Ellen, just because he sold his store?"

"Just listen to me, Gracie. Jesus was all sweaty and his head was hanging low and the Holy Ghost was there, a dove with a tongue of bright red flames right above him. It was so hot, I sweated like a pot of water got thrown on me. Then the Holy Ghost looked right at me and I started to run, but that tongue of flame came over me and just about burned me up. He scorched a red spot on my forehead, it's about gone now, but I can still feel it. I just stood there watching those wings of his fluttering. The Holy Ghost had red eyes like fire, then he looked right at me and said, 'June Ellen, your daddy's in big trouble.' I jumped back and ran over to where Mama was."

"What'd your mama say? Did she see him?"

"No, Mama didn't see him, she was way behind me. When I tried to tell her, she about had a conniption about me talking in church like that during the Stations of the Cross. She made me be quiet the whole time. After we left church, she looked so peaceful, I decided to figure it out for myself."

"June Ellen, that's the craziest thing I ever heard. Why didn't the Holy Ghost just tell you what to do? Do you think he'll tell you now?"

"That's why I need to talk to Fr. Michael. I woke up this morning in a sweat. April Leigh was gone, and I was just hot all over, like the Holy Ghost was a tongue of flame breathing fire into me all night."

"Oh, June Ellen. Were you scared?"

"Do you remember in catechism class when Fr. Michael told us how the Holy Ghost works? You don't see him and you don't hear him, but he's always hovering around at the ready. I thought Fr. Michael could conjure up the Holy Ghost for me and get him to tell me how to help Daddy. Now that I've told you, do you still want to run home and play with paper dolls?"

Gracie juggled her sacks of yarn and construction paper around. "First, I have to take these to the Sister's house then go home for lunch. Then let's go back to the church and see what the Holy Ghost is up to. I'll get all the change from Mama's pocketbook and we'll light all the candles and see if that'll get him to fly down."

"Okay, good idea. Meet me back here at one-thirty sharp and, thanks, Gracie, for going on this adventure with me. It's a little risky and we might be in some peril. But just think about Nancy Drew."

She gave me a dubious look. "I don't think she ever went scouting for the Holy Ghost."

"They had lots of ghosts to deal with, and if they can do it, we can do it. We're just as brave."

I felt better knowing Gracie wanted to help. I decided I'd go home and get Rex and eat something in case the Holy Ghost took a while. I wanted to make sure I didn't cut him short.

I left Fr. Michael a note. Since he almost always came home for lunch, he left a stub of a pencil dangling on a piece of string by his note. I wrote across the bottom.

Looking for the Holy Ghost. Can you help me find him? Meet me at the church, 1:30. In the name of Jesus, Mary and Joseph, yours truly, June Ellen.

That's how Sr. Annunciata signed the notes she sent home with me, so I decided to use it too.

I ran home and was out of breath when I got there. The door hung open, but the house seemed empty. I bumped against the swing as it swung back and forth, with its familiar squeak. Only today without Rex, it felt eerie.

I walked in the open door. "I'm home. Rex. Mama, where are you?"

No one answered. Sweat popped out all over me. It did that when I got nervous or didn't know the answer to a question I really needed to know the answer to. I kept yelling for Mama while I ran all the way through the house and out the back door. No one answered me. Not even Rex.

Rex never left unless he was with me or with Daddy on a walk. Who left the door open? I walked back into the kitchen and saw some bread and butter and Mama's blue-ribbon jam, all laid out on the table.

Beside it lay a note.

June Ellen, Eat this for lunch. Milk in icebox, drink one glass only. Stay home. Mama said. Signed April Leigh.

It was not signed in the name of Jesus so I didn't have to do what it said if I didn't want to.

Besides, it made my hackles rise, like the porcupine Rex chased last week. Why did I have to stay home? Nobody else was there. I yelled out the back door, "Rex, Rex, where are you boy? Come here, boy, come here."

He didn't come.

I wandered back into the kitchen and I told myself I might as well eat something. Everything looked the same, smelled the same. Mama's bread and butter tasted the same, yet I sensed the Holy Ghost all around me.

My face burned hot; my skin broke out in sweat, all prickly. I dashed through the back door to cool off.

I gazed up and I saw him. The Holy Ghost perched in the top of the post oak, a white dove with the sun glinting off its silver wings that shot off sparks all over the yard. Of course the Holy Ghost picked the top of the post oak. Big, thick sturdy branches and knotholes. Perfect for the tongue of flame to hide in. The big shiny green leaves shaped like a fat cross would shield and protect those white wings.

Could the Holy Ghost catch that tree on fire? I yelled up into the tree, "Be careful, you might burn down the tree if your tongue of flame touches anything." I'd better ask Fr. Michael if the Holy Ghost could do that. I bet he had a dial like the volume button on the radio. He could turn the flame up or down.

Just then the Holy Ghost flew out of the post oak headed straight for me. I couldn't help it, I ducked and hit the ground and he flew back up into the post oak. I looked up again and a mourning dove, more gray than white, perched at the crown of the tree. His yellow eyes pierced mine till they watered. But there was no tongue of flame or fiery wings.

I yelled at the dove, "Are you looking for me? Are you the Holy Ghost? H-E-double toothpicks, I need you to answer some questions for me."

I knew I shouldn't swear at the Holy Ghost. I hoped he'd understand that it didn't count if you didn't say the words themselves. The gray dove flew off across the pasture toward the downtown square.

I picked myself up off the ground. It was time to go back to St. Joseph's. I drank down a glass of milk and part of another one, just to show April Leigh, and headed out the door; only this time I slammed it shut. "What a strange Holy Ghost kind of day."

I got to St. Joseph's in a record fifteen minutes. Out of breath I saw Fr. Michael puzzling over my note in front of the rectory across from the church. I ran over even though I had a stitch in my side and could hardly breathe.

"June Ellen, what is this missive about?"

I knew missive was Catholic for some writing on a piece of paper.

"Fr. Michael," I panted, "I need the Holy Ghost to tell me how to help Daddy. Mr. Mackey is taking his coal mine 'cause Daddy can't pay his bills at Jeremy's. Daddy won't have any work and we won't have any money and Mama will have to work here at the rectory taking care of you all the time."

"June Ellen, I think you better stop and catch your breath."

"Okay, Father Michael, but Mama needs to stay home and take care of us, especially Daddy. I can take care of myself. Daddy coughs a lot and gets real tired sometimes, but it's okay cause Uncle Albert and Freddy are taking care of things at the coal mine."

"Slow down, June Ellen. I don't see what the Holy Ghost has to do with your daddy's coal mine."

I told Fr. Michael about how the Holy Ghost had appeared to me.

"You said in Catechism class the Holy Ghost is ready to help anytime, he's always right there waiting. And he was waiting for me."

"Are you sure about that, June Ellen? I've noticed how your imagination takes hold of you sometimes."

"Yes, I'm sure. I went with Mama and right there at the tenth station—the Holy Ghost flew down from the stained-glass window and about burnt me up. He was a cloven tongue of fire just like the Holy Card you showed us. Then he flew right back up to the stained-glass window right over Saint Peter's head."

I could tell Fr. Michael was stumped by the Holy Ghost, just like me. He scratched his beard and squinted his eyes when he looked out his window like he was looking for him.

"I don't know what to say, June Ellen. I'm getting hot just hearing about your encounter with the Holy Ghost. My collar's too tight all of a sudden. How about a cool drink of water? I might get one for myself also."

Fr. Michael tried to loosen his collar, instead he opened his suit coat and undid the top button. "Come on in here and have a seat in my office and let's see what we can figure out about this Holy Ghost."

"Thank you, Father. I sure could use a drink." I gulped the water down so fast I choked and it went up my nose and burned. Fr. Michael gave me his handkerchief and brought me another glass of water. I drank it real slow.

Fr. Michael opened up a drawer in his desk and took out a Holy Card of the Holy Ghost. "Is this what you saw, June Ellen?"

In the center was the Blessed Virgin Mary surrounded by all the apostles. Above Mary's head a pure white dove sat in the center of a golden halo with golden rays of light shooting out in every direction. He was dropping fiery tongues of flame on each of their heads. Nobody seemed to care that tongues of flame were falling on their heads.

I asked, "Don't they burn up when the fire hits them? Their hair's gonna catch fire."

Fr. Michael was known by the parish as a patient man. He stood there with his hands on his hips watching me.

"Well, June Ellen, that's a good question. No, they don't burn up. Look closely at the picture. Do they look frightened to you?"

"No, Fr. Michael, they don't look scared. I just wonder if they know what's about to hit them." I hoped I wasn't being sacrilegious. Fr. Michael could get real stern.

He went on, "That flame is the spirit of Jesus coming down to earth. Once it hits you, it's like cool water from a well flowing over you and it fills your soul. It may seem hot at first, but you won't get burned. You are filled with the gifts of the Holy Ghost."

"Is that what happened to me? But I got mighty hot, I felt like I was burning up. Sweat was pouring off me. It didn't feel like a cool drink of water."

"June Ellen, sounds to me like your gift was the fire of courage, to do what you need to."

"That's why I need your help, Father Michael. I have to ask the Holy Ghost what to do."

"God is all knowing, right, June Ellen?"

"If the Holy Ghost is like God, all knowing, then he needs to tell me what to do about old Mr. Mackey. Let's go to the church, Father Michael. Gracie is meeting me there. We're going to light all the candles and see if the Holy Ghost'll come back down and talk to me. But we're going to pay for the candles. Gracie's bringing all the change from her mama's pocketbook. After she asks her. With you standing there, the Holy Ghost, who's like a holy-know-it-all, will surely appear and tell me what to do."

"I don't think it works that way, June Ellen. Let's go check on Gracie and have her come over here with us. Between the three of us, I bet we can sleuth something out. You know what a sleuth is?"

"Nancy Drew's a sleuth, and sometimes Dale Evans is, too, and I take after both of them. I work a lot like Nancy Drew."

"I thought so."

I walked out the front door and yelled at Gracie, who was standing at the front door of St. Joseph's.

"Gracie, come over here. Fr. Michael's gonna tell us about how to get the Holy Ghost to help."

Gracie came over to Fr. Michael's study and this time he gave us Dr Peppers instead of water. I was hoping for peanuts but decided I'd better not ask.

"Okay, girls, I'm going to explain to you how the Holy Ghost works. June Ellen, I think you already know the answer to your own question, but we might need to solve this like a mystery."

Fr. Michael decided to preach a little. I decided to let him while I drank my Dr Pepper.

"God's spirit is the Holy Ghost, the white dove with the tongue of flame that you saw, June Ellen. The Holy Ghost can endow us with seven gifts, but especially in your case, June Ellen, courage and wisdom." Fr. Michael sat down but kept preaching.

"June Ellen, I believe the Holy Ghost gave you a vision. I really do. The Holy Ghost has touched you. He has given you the fire of courage and the light of wisdom to help you solve this mystery about your daddy."

"Father Michael, I went to spy on Mr. Mackey and see what he's up to. All I saw him do was eat. It was real sad. The Holy Ghost wants me to solve this mystery. I can feel it."

Fr. Michael said, "Before you take off, let's look at the rest of the evidence. There might be some more clues we need to address. How much coal is left in your daddy's mine, June Ellen?"

"Freddy says it's about worked out. They're just a bunch of scrappers, scrapping out what's left. But Daddy and Uncle Albert said they got a payload coming soon."

"Okay, June Ellen. Your daddy's coal mine's about worked out and your daddy has lots of tickets with Jeremy to settle up on. That payload may not go very far. Is that right?"

"I guess, Father Michael. Does the Holy Ghost perform miracles? Looks like we need one."

Fr. Michael looked serious. "This is a tough time for coal miners everywhere, not just your family. What about your daddy? Is he feeling okay working down in that coal mine? What about that coal dust in his lungs?"

"Daddy's real sick sometimes. He coughs more and more and Dr. John can't get all the dust out of his lungs."

"Let's look at all the facts or clues we've gathered and see if we can put them together. Can you girls name them for me?"

Gracie stuttered, "The mine's about worked out and June Ellen's daddy's real sick and he owes a lot of money."

Fr. Michael said, "Maybe the Holy Ghost is trying to tell you something, June Ellen. You're smart. He gifted you wisdom. Did you ever stop to think about how much better your daddy might get if he didn't have to go down in that dust every day? He might find his breath again and go fishing and hunting and take you and Rex with him."

"It's Daddy's coal mine, and Uncle Albert's and Freddy's. It belongs to me too. Mr. Mackey can't have it." I was on my feet now, ready to go find the Holy Ghost by myself. I didn't care if I sinned yelling at Fr. Michael.

"Hold on a minute, young lady. What if your daddy got better if Mr. Mackey takes that mine? God with the help of the Holy Ghost works in strange ways. It'll take a lot of courage on your part to help your family get through this."

"Is that what the Holy Ghost wants me to do? He won't help me get rid of Mr. Mackey?" My eyes got all teary. I tried to hide it. "I don't want Daddy to lose his mine. It's all we have. We don't even have a car." I looked away from him. "Let's go, Gracie. Fr. Michael can't help us find the Holy Ghost."

Gracie just sat there. She wasn't one to walk out on Fr. Michael.

I was so angry; I didn't care. But I didn't really move either. The Dr Pepper was warm and I didn't want it anymore. I wanted to go home and take a walk with Rex and wait for Daddy and Freddy to come home from the coal mine and Freddy would tell me stories about being in the mine and Mamma would fix us supper and we'd all laugh.

Father Michael stood up again. "June Ellen, I know this is hard for you. Change is always hard. But think about your daddy and what he needs right now. Look in your heart, child, and ask your heart what your daddy needs most right now, not you or Freddy or Uncle Albert but your daddy. I do believe that's what the Holy Ghost was trying to tell you."

"Can I go, Father Michael? The Holy Ghost has worn me out."

"That's enough for now. You have a lot to think on. Use the courage he's given you, June Ellen."

I said good-bye to Gracie and walked home slow. I'd forgotten nobody was home at lunch. I was plum tuckered out, as Mama would say. I didn't know what to think anymore.

April Leigh was there on the porch when I rounded the last curve. She saw me and of course started griping at me. "June Ellen, where have you been? Daddy's in the hospital again and Mama said for you to stay home. And now I have to stay home with you. You're such a brat."

"Where's Rex? I don't have to listen to you. I can take care of myself. Is Daddy okay? Is he coming home soon?"

I couldn't hold it in any longer. The tears came and I ran in the front door and slammed it in April Leigh's face. I went in my room and slammed that door. I just wanted to go to sleep. I hated April Leigh and I hated Fr. Michael.

I didn't think much of the Holy Ghost either.

[35]

June Ellen's Dream

ANGELS WERE FLYING all around me and their wings were like a rainbow when the sun came out at the end of a thunderstorm. The colors danced and shimmered, like a Christmas tree full of angel ornaments only they weren't attached. They flew in precision like little toy soldiers marching. Only it wasn't a tree, it was me, and they were pestering me.

Rex and I walked down to Shoal Creek. The angels fluttered over us and caressed us with their wings, only I didn't feel anything. They hovered over Rex too. He seemed so at ease with them. Unlike me. I'm spooked. The creek opened up before us and we raced to our old getting-in place. Then Rex and I were both picked up by hundreds of butterflies. We both just hung there in the air, suspended above our house and the Lahoskys' farm. I felt trussed like a chicken, my arms and legs didn't move.

Rex took off walking through a field of daisies, surrounded by butterflies. They floated down to touch the buttery yellow center of each daisy and covered themselves with golden pollen. The air became a golden cloud and the butterflies returned and filled their nose tubes with nectar, so rich it dripped as they flew.

Rex and I headed for cover in the barn; we were coated and sticky when we rushed inside. The butterfly angels made me feel light and airy, but I hated sticky stuff.

I walked to the stall where I found that old dried-up dead body. It was gone, but in its place I saw Mama's quilt, the one she won at the church picnic. It was a log cabin pattern, dark-blue pieces of fabric at angles like roofs, and light-blue gingham like a square little cabin.

The Ladies Altar Society pieced and quilted it last winter for the raffle. Mama won the quilt and gave it to Daddy to keep him warm when his breath wouldn't hardly come back and he had to stay at the hospital till it did.

Daddy said, "This quilt feels like all of you right here with me."

The quilt was rolled up and kind of long and lumpy and dirty around the edges. I had to save the quilt; Mama was going to be angry. The butterflies hovered around me again, and gently touched my hair, my skin, and my face. I tried to stay still, awed by their rainbow colors and the shimmering light that shot off in all directions. Then they came at me like gnats and swarmed my face. I panicked and tried to beat them away. Then I saw the edge of Mama's quilt and got calm.

I went over to the patchwork quilt to take a better look and leaned down to pick it up and the angels came back. They clustered around my face, my hands, my hair, my arms, and my legs. I swatted at them, even knocked some to the ground.

"Go away," I yelled.

Rex barked and started up a good howl. The angel butterflies turned to attack him and stuck their nose tubes into his eyes and nose, for water I guessed. He scratched his face with his paws. I shooed them away, but they were so thick I couldn't get to him.

But I had to get the quilt back to Daddy. He needed it to get well. I grabbed a corner and start tugging and pulling, then my hands and legs were held down. The quilt wound around me like a cocoon.

My eyes flew open. I was scared and sweaty and I was all wound up in the covers.

"Rex, Rex, where are you?" I squirmed and wiggled trying to get loose from the quilt.

"June Ellen." April Leigh yelled, "Wake up," as she kicked me. "You took all the covers and wadded them up all around you." She pulled the quilt off me and all the angels went with it.

"April Leigh, Daddy's dying. Look, the angels are going to take him."

"Wake up, June Ellen, you're dreaming."

Then I saw my room and realized I was in my own room and I was awake. I'd never been so glad to see April Leigh; I threw my arms around her, and she pushed me off the bed. I didn't care.

"Where's Daddy?"

"He's having his coffee with Mama. He had a bad fit yesterday at the mine. Dr. John made him stay in the oxygen tent all night, but he got up this morning and caught a ride home. Mama said to stay in our room."

"Is Daddy going to die?"

"Dr. John told Daddy to stay out of that mine and not go back down there again. Mama stood up to Daddy and she was fierce. I heard her tell him he has to give it up or he'll die. June Ellen, I don't want Daddy to be a coal miner anymore."

April Leigh looked straight at me, daring me to start a fight. But I didn't want to fight with April Leigh. Between the Holy Ghost and the Shoal Creek mine, I was wore out.

"Thanks, April Leigh, for telling me. I don't want Daddy to breathe any more coal dust, but I just hate to lose our coal mine. It's a part of me, a part of us, our family."

April Leigh came and sat by me. "You're growing up, June Ellen. It's hard for me too, to let go of so much, so fast. Sometimes, we just have to move on."

I sat close to April Leigh for the first time in a long while. It felt good. I sighed and said, "I know, everything just keeps changing."

"Remember, June Ellen, sometimes change can be good, like high school and wearing makeup."

I rolled my eyes—I couldn't help it. "Where's Rex?"

"Outside, on the front porch. He sat on the hospital stoop all day waiting on Daddy. Mama brought him home last night. You slept through it all."

I ran out the door to the front porch. I just had to see Rex. "Rex, you're home. I should've known you were protecting Daddy. What are we going to do, Rex, if we don't have a coal mine?"

Rex didn't say a word, he just lay there with his paws covering his face, all hang dog. I squatted down beside him. He got up and hunkered beside me; we both wanted to howl, but we didn't.

[36]

The Shoal Creek Mine

REX AND I went for our last visit to the Shoal Creek mine. We had come back for one more look and Daddy came with us. When Daddy left the hospital, he stayed home every day. Somehow, he knew I needed another look. He did too, I think. He told me how good he felt not to go back down there.

"June Ellen, I feel better already and I don't miss checking for gas, then having to set it off, one bit. Maybe my hearing'll come back, but I doubt it. If it did, I wouldn't tell your mama." He laughed, then started coughing. "Just gonna take some time to get all this coal dust out of my lungs."

We both knew you couldn't get it out, once it was down there. But we pretended different, together.

"Daddy, let's walk the track to where it ends at the big ledge. I know you brought your carbide lantern."

"What big ledge would that be?"

"The one at the end of the tracks, where it drops down a couple of feet. There's a whole different path down there with all those openings you made. Don't you remember?"

"How do you know what's at the end of those tracks?"

I thought fast. "Freddy told me all about it."

Daddy started laughing and then coughing—he pulled out his handkerchief and held it to his mouth. If he coughed blood, he had to go back to the hospital.

I always held my breath when he coughed. If he couldn't catch his breath, neither could I. When he breathed, I let out a long, slow breath and watched it go right into his mouth and down into his lungs. I imagined I was his walking oxygen tent. April Leigh said that was impossible, but when it was cold I could see my breath. I watched Daddy real close and I saw my breath go right in.

"I'm okay, June Ellen. Now, back to that ledge. Did you think your mama wouldn't figure out why Lizziebelle offered to launder your clothes and bring them back the next day all ironed and mended? Lizziebelle is a good seamstress, but it's hard to cover up a rip in a blouse even with tiny even stitches. I didn't say anything when you came home with Freddy, but I could see the coal dust rubbed hard into your fingers. I'm sure they scrubbed you down, but your ears weren't quite clean either."

"Oh, Daddy, Rex and I just had to see what the Shoal Creek coal mine looked like; it was ours. I wanted to be a miner just like you and Freddy and Uncle Albert. You wouldn't let me because I was a girl."

"Well, what'd you think of our coal mine?"

"It was dark. Darker than you or Freddy could ever tell me and all I had was a candle and some matches. Rex didn't like any part of it. I was scared at first, but then it felt holy, like a tomb. I thought about Jesus coming out of his tomb when they rolled that rock back. I was glad when I could see light again. I remember the coal dust, the grit and the scritch of it. I felt like Jonah in the belly of a whale; it was an oily darkness, no way for light to get in."

"Sounds like you did a lot of praying down there, June Ellen. I sure understand that. I felt like Jonah myself sometimes. I did my best praying down in that belly."

"That coal had a shine to it like a light deep inside."

"Yes, it does, June Ellen. You were pretty brave to go down there by yourself and you are one smart young lady to see the light in a piece of coal. What you see is the light of thousands of years of plants smashed together to make a lump of coal. All that sunshine they took in lies buried in there, somewhere."

"I ate some coal dust and coughed, just like you. So I'd know what the coal dust did to your lungs. I'm glad you don't have to go down there anymore, but I'm sad we don't own our own coal mine."

"We're all going to miss it, June Ellen, but not the hard work and having to breathe that suffocating dust that steals your breath." Rex went over and stuck his head up for a good scratching. Daddy obliged.

I looked down at the railroad tracks; they already had weeds growing over them and rust forming on the sides of the rails. The washhouse looked abandoned. A pair of overalls still hung there mostly torn and shredded, like rags nobody wanted. Next to the washhouse the blacksmith shop stood empty, just an oily smell left. The slagheap loomed over us a like a dark ghost.

I saw the shine in a piece of coal lying there and bent down and stuck it in the pocket of my jeans.

Daddy stooped down to light his carbide lamp. "Okay, June Ellen, let's you and me take a walk down these old tracks to that ledge."

Rex whined around my legs. "Rex wants to stay here."

"Okay, we'll let him."

We stood in the arch carved out of the side of this big old mountain. The air blew cool on my skin as the light slipped away behind us. The dark smelled like old oil ground to dirt. I opened my mouth and took a deep breath of air and felt the coal dust coat my tongue. I tasted the shine in that dust and the dark of the black grit.

Daddy wrapped his hand around mine. It was bonier than it used to be but still strong. I held it tight, and for the last time, we walked down the slope of our coal mine.

From the day I was born, I was determined to grab hold of whatever and not let go. The Shoal Creek mine was a part of me forever. It was in my blood and my bones. I knew Daddy had felt it. This had been a way of life in our family for over three generations. Coal mining connected us to the earth and to all the other miners and their families.

Above ground, Paris, Arkansas, wasn't so grand anymore, but underneath I sensed the grand mystery of the dark beauty around me. Coal, which fed us and about killed us, still felt holy and sacred, a tale of leaves and ferns and forests.

This coal mine had been our center like the hub of a wheel, and we were the spokes fanning out in all directions, held together by the great circle of family and community. Our center was empty, a big hole. Aristotle said that nature abhors a vacuum, an empty space. And nature requires every hole or space be filled.

I waited to see what would fill our center.

Acknowledgements

I honor my ancestors who sent this story of June Ellen to me. My mother, Anna Marie, her sisters, Dorothy, Bernice, Juanita, Josephine, Ethelreda, Betty Jane, and Mary Ellen. My grandfather, Frank Furstenberg, who ran and worked the coal mines till his death from Black Lung, my grandmother, Dora Furstenberg, and and my uncle, Adrian Furstenberg, who worked the mines starting at the young age of 16, till he joined the U. S Navy.

I honor Hens Teeth, my first writing group who witnessed the birth of June Ellen. They were the best midwives. Mendy Knott, Jan Van Schuyver, Susan Raymond, Ann Teague, and Pat Hennon.

I honor the many writing groups from Night Bird Books who listened over and over to all the revisions and never stopped loving June Ellen, and Lisa Sharp (1963–2024), who made this space possible.

I honor my partner, Joanne Olszewski for her unwavering support, her enthusiastic coaxing and on-going encouragement which never stops.

My book designer, Liz Lester, who made this book a work of art.

Special thanks and gratitude to Bob Thomas, Annetta Mullings, Sonja Fletcher and Joyce Friddle for their hard work to preserve the rich history of the Paris-Logan County coal miners and the coal mining industry in their book *Paris, Arkansas and Its People.* This book was very instrumental to my research.

Many thanks to Darlene Becker, Manager of the Paris-Logan County Coal Miners Memorial Museum and to the multitude of others who worked tirelessly to make this museum a reality. For those who wish to know more, I encourage you to visit the Paris-Logan County Coal Miners Memorial Museum. The book, *Paris, Arkansas and Its People* may be purchased there.